By Stephan Talty

Fiction
Black Irish
Hangman

Nonfiction

*Agent Garbo: The Brilliant, Eccentric Secret Agent
    Who Tricked Hitler and Saved D-Day*

*Escape from the Land of Snows: The Young Dalai Lama's
    Harrowing Flight to Freedom and the Making of
    a Spiritual Hero*

*The Illustrious Dead: The Terrifying Story of How Typhus
    Killed Napoleon's Greatest Army*

*Empire of the Blue Water: Captain Morgan's Great Pirate
    Army, the Epic Battle for the Americas, and the
    Catastrophe That Ended the Outlaws' Bloody Reign*

*Mulatto America: At the Crossroads of Black and
    White Culture: A Social History*

Hangman

Hangman

A Novel

STEPHAN TALTY

Ballantine Books
New York

Copyright © 2014 by Talty Creative LLC

All rights reserved.

Published in the United States by Ballantine Books, an imprint of The Random House Publishing Group, a division of Random House LLC, a Penguin Random House Company, New York.

BALLANTINE and the HOUSE colophon are registered trademarks of Random House LLC.

ISBN 978-0-345-53808-6
eBook ISBN 978-0-345-54988-4

Printed in the United States of America on acid-free paper

www.ballantinebooks.com

2 4 6 8 9 7 5 3 1

First Edition

Book design by Virginia Norey

To my brother James, at last

Hangman

1

The white van with NY STATE CORRECTIONS written on the side in royal blue crested the hilltop and a gust of wind pushed it toward the center line. Joe Carlson, a black, thick-bodied guard with a permanent scowl on his face, gripped the wheel tighter and eased his foot off the gas. The Corrections officer in the passenger seat, his name was Brian, looked over.

"Starting to blow, dude," said Brian.

Carlson nodded. He could hear the guy's right foot jittering on the plastic mat of the van, though there was no music; he never played it when transporting prisoners, as music could cover up the sound of them moving around.

Traffic was light today, mostly farm traffic and commuters cutting a corner on the way to Buffalo. Carlson had planned it that way.

"Supposed to be a cold front moving in," Brian said. "Only September and they're talking about a freeze tonight. September!"

Carlson moved the toothpick from the right side of his mouth to the left. "Mm-hmmm," he said.

"Yeah, well, I'm not ready for that shit."

Brian's foot beat a little faster. Tap. Tap. *Tap-tap-tap.* "So, how much further?"

Carlson looked over at Brian. "You nervous or somethin'?" he said.

Brian's face got even whiter and more pinched than usual. "I'm not nervous. I can't ask a question? If I can't ask a question, then maybe the deal's off."

Carlson laughed softly to himself. "About six miles. Take it easy."

"I'm easy, dude," said Brian. He didn't sound it.

Carlson sighed, then glanced up at the rearview mirror. In the second row of seats, he could see the left half of a face: a bald man with a scar on his left temple that seemed to dent the bone beneath. It gave the prisoner's face a funhouse-mirror effect. Carlson looked away and silently reviewed the restraints he'd attached to Marcus Flynn that morning: two thick nylon cords around his waist bolted to the floor with heavy clips. Smith & Wesson Model 380 handcuffs around the wrists, not the ones with the two metal links, but the hinged kind he'd chosen special for the trip. The tactical grade, kick-proof double-lock ankle cuffs with eighteen-inch chain and the ditched jaws now clenched extra tight around Flynn's ankles.

It was the protocol he used only for the most dangerous prisoners. Not the state protocol. His own. Carlson was the transporter of choice for every man and woman leaving Auburn Correctional Facility, and he'd never lost a one.

Houdini would have bust a gut on that rig, Carlson thought. He put his eyes back on the road.

Even after twelve years as a CO, Carlson hadn't known too many serial killers. Two to be exact, the other one being Randy Tucker back at Auburn. Tucker the Motherfucker, people at the prison called him, not really meaning anything by it. Tucker was just an upstate white boy who'd dipped his brain in crystal meth once too often and gone on a tear with his hunting rifle a few hours after he'd gotten let go from the local John Deere franchise. He'd gotten—what, four, five victims?— before sheriff's deputies tracked him to his girlfriend's house.

None of the other COs held it against Tucker. So long as you kept your head down, you could be the Son of Sam and they'd give you a pass. Their prison workers' unofficial motto, after all, was pretty cynical. "Raising your children," it went, "because you chose not to."

Carlson flicked his eyes back to the solitary prisoner for another half-second. Flynn hadn't moved since they'd pulled through the prison gates. Not a millimeter. Was it self-control? Or the result of the dented temple?

This man here was something else entirely, Carlson thought. He didn't know any like Hangman because there *were* none like him.

They passed a sign for the town of Perry.

"Okay," Carlson said to Brian, speaking the way you would to a ten-year-old, calm and deliberate. "It's the next exit. I'm going to drop you off at the AutoZone. If anyone asks any questions later on, the van was low on oil and I sent you in there to get some. I was waiting outside when you came walking out with the oil. Got that? Simple as pecan pie."

"Why can't I come?"

Carlson's mouth opened a little. He said nothing but eased the van off the ramp and down to the service road. The AutoZone was a hundred yards up on the right. He swung through the parking lot, waited for a Toyota minivan to clear the fire lane, and pulled up to the front doors.

"Because you can't."

He popped the locks on the van. Brian grimaced and got out slowly. He looked nervous, like he was being dropped off for the first day of school.

"See you in forty," Carlson said. "If it's an hour, don't go calling me on my cell. Remember what we talked about?"

"Radio silence."

"Yeah. Radio silence."

Brian slammed the door.

"Oh, and *dude?*" Carlson said, leaning over toward the open window. "Buy some oil. Just in case."

Brian nodded, his mouth open. Carlson shook his head slowly as he pulled out of the parking lot. Three minutes later he was back on the highway.

The silence in the van was different now. It was almost like the hum from an electric motor, buzzing, physical. Carlson checked the mirror. Marcus Flynn's left eye, the only one Carlson could see, was locked straight ahead, as if he was still staring at Brian's neck.

An icy tremor zigzagged up Carlson's spine. Those eyes. The last things four young girls saw before they died. It was unnerving was what it was.

Carlson checked his watch. The prisoner was due at Attica by one o'clock. He'd built in some extra time by leaving ninety minutes before his scheduled departure. No one gave a shit. He could take this cracker swimming in the local crick if he chose to.

He drove another three miles, watching the signs. When he saw one for the village of Warsaw, he took the exit, turned left at the end of the ramp, and accelerated up onto a two-lane road that cut between heavily wooded acres.

The country spread out on either side of him, farmland and forest stretching to the horizon. Real backcountry out here, home to your native upstate shitkicker. People didn't know you had shitkickers in New York State, but the woods around here were as thick as anything down South.

Carlson started to count the little country lanes to his left. They were just ten-foot gaps in the trees with two muddy ruts between them. He'd done two trial runs before today and he could tell the lanes apart now. The one he was looking for was the one with the piece of red nylon tape tacked to the tree. The tape he'd nailed into the bark three days ago.

There it was, fluttering in the wind. Carlson slowed and made the turn.

In four and a half minutes, the van emerged from the tree line and out into a clearing.

He eased the van to a stop. They were at the end of the lane, a broad grassy meadow speckled with dandelions ahead of them. Carlson turned the key back in the ignition and the sound of birdsong came wafting in the two inches of open window as the engine noise faded.

He didn't want to turn and look at Flynn. He took the keys out of the ignition slowly, the skin on the back of his neck growing cold and prickly. He swore he could feel the man's eyes on him. But if he looked back, he knew the prisoner would be staring at that empty seat.

Four girls this man murdered, Carlson thought, and now he thinks he can mess with me?

Carlson got out, adjusting his gun belt as he walked around the front. He jerked the slide door of the van open.

Marcus Flynn turned slowly. His eyes were cold as a charcoal briquette the day after a barbecue. Blue, with the memory of fire in them.

Carlson unlocked the ankle cuffs and uncoupled the restraints bolted to the floor, leaving the handcuffs on. Then he pulled the prisoner out of the van. As Flynn's foot cleared the doorsill, Carlson let his supporting hand fall away. Flynn dropped to his knees in the shin-high grass.

"Clumsy bitch," Carlson said. "The fuck's wrong with you?"

Flynn looked up at him, a strange questioning in his eyes. It wasn't just the sudden drop to his knees, Carlson knew, but the wind, the grass, being outside the walls. Flynn was a CU, or control unit inmate, allowed one hour of exercise a day in a chain-link-topped exercise pit, all concrete. If he saw a flower, it was a stray weed growing in a crack in the concrete. Now he was like an animal being reintroduced to the wild; the scents of the pines, the pollen, it must be intoxicating.

Carlson had planned this, too. Keep the man off balance.

He brought his boot up to Flynn's chest, then rested the muddy sole on the prisoner's orange jumpsuit.

"Look what you did, Hangman," he said, smearing mud on the bright orange nylon.

Flynn's eyes, cold as winter.

Carlson leaned down. "You're brain-injured and all," he said, "but you understand *that*, don't you?"

A gust of wind turned the long grass over and shook the tops of the trees. Carlson looked around. The clearing was in the shape of a horseshoe, fringed by thick forest on three sides—he'd never learned the names of trees, he wasn't no nature boy—and open on the fourth, where you could see you were on the top of a tall hill overlooking the valley below.

Carlson braced his shoulders. He reached down and grabbed the prisoner under the left armpit and pulled him up. "I don't have time to mess around with you," he said. "As much as I'd like to."

The prisoner's eyes were staring at his handcuffs. Carlson watched him, a smile on his lips. He felt in control now.

"You think you can slip 'em, Hangman? Well, go for it." He laughed and began marching Flynn toward the open part of the horseshoe, where the breeze was coming from.

Five steps. Ten. The wind was making a roaring sound, like in the mouth of a cave.

Carlson leaned over as he frog-marched Flynn. "Why'd you kill them girls?" he said casually.

Flynn didn't reply. In a little bit, they were standing on the edge of the hill. Eighty feet below them, down a steep cliff covered with scrub and flat rusty-looking rocks, the green carpet of the treetops was cut by a snaking black road. To their left was a gas station, doing some lunch business by the looks of it, with three cars fueling up and another waiting for an open pump.

To their right was a black-shingled roof, angled in the shape of an L. "You see that?" Carlson said.

The prisoner turned his head slowly, looked down at the gas station.

"No, not that," Carlson said, pointing at the shingled roof. "That place there."

Flynn's gaze rotated slowly to follow the guard's finger. When they reached the roof, the sound of an indrawn breath.

"Yeaaah, you know it. The Warsaw Motel."

Flynn's mouth worked, causing the muscles in his cheek to flex as Carlson watched him. This boy never fattened up on that starchy prison food, Carlson thought. Slim as a panther. The arm was strong, and the muscles were taut now. Oh, Flynn knew this place.

"That's what I brought you up here to see, Hang-man."

The prisoner turned toward him. His face was chapped by the wind, the ridges of his forehead red with exposure. The eyes were angry now.

"Where's the girl?" Carlson whispered. "The last one, Sandy Riesen. The one you brought to the motel. The one they never found."

That got to him. Flynn's face contorted now as if he'd tasted raw flesh.

"Did you bury her up here?" Carlson whispered.

He leaned in and kept his mouth next to the prisoner's ear, blocking his view of the gun as he brought it up in his right hand. Then

Carlson pulled back, and let the prisoner see the Smith & Wesson with the sun glinting dully off its nickel plating.

Flynn's eyes grew big. Like a horse looking at a dog that had snapped at him before.

"Tell me," Carlson said. Up here on the hilltop, he could feel a weight in the moment. He had Flynn dead to rights, just the two of them. He could kill the cracker if he chose, say he'd tried to escape and had nearly made it down the hill before Carlson had caught him with a lucky shot.

Justice for those families. His gun hand tingled.

"Last chance, brother," he said, and his voice cracked just a bit. "It's been five years now."

He brought the barrel of the gun up.

"Five."

He spun the barrel.

"Long."

Carlson pulled the hammer back, and the snap of the spring was clear in the cold air.

Flynn's eyes closed.

"Years. Where's the goddamn girl?"

The prisoner turned. The look in his eyes, it wasn't what Carlson had hoped for. He'd expected the man to beg for his life, spittle running down his chin. He'd wanted to crack the man wide open, have him begging for mercy.

But Flynn wasn't crying. His eyes weren't even on the gun. They bored into Carlson's like a hot drill.

"You think I'm playing?" Carlson whispered.

Flynn stared him down.

Oh, no, thought Carlson. Don't tell me that girl, the last one, really is alive. Not after all these years. Christ, what would she even look . . .

The prisoner was leaning forward. He'd whispered something, but the breeze ruffled in Carlson's ears at just that moment and all he heard was the wind.

"What?" Carlson snapped. "What did you say?"

Flynn leaned closer. The guard watched his lips, wanting to read the words if he missed them again.

"The girls . . ."

Carlson shivered at the voice, thin and ghostly, the voice of a man who has nothing to talk to but concrete walls. The guard felt his stomach flutter.

The gun bobbed a little before he got it steady again.

"Yeah. The girls what?"

The sound of the wind rose a bit and Carlson felt his hand sweat on the faceted surface of the gun grip. Flynn whispered:

"The girls are waiting for you."

2

Absalom Kearney worked quickly. Down on her knees in the backyard, she could feel the wind starting to move around the garden. She wanted to get six bags of mulch around her squash plants before lunch. The forecasters said the first frost was going to be a killing one, and the plants were her babies, the first things she'd planted in her first-ever garden.

She took a sheet of *The Buffalo News*—yesterday's paper was fluttering under a rock next to her—and laid it on the top level of mulch, then piled some of the leafy stuff on top. The plants danced in the wind, the tomatoes red with stripes of green.

She'd put one of the speakers up to the back bedroom window and the radio was playing. It was something people used to do during high school parties back in the County, the two-fisted Irish American stronghold she'd grown up in on the south side of Buffalo. She was playing NPR on the local station, *Science Friday*. She wanted to hear voices as she gardened. The host was talking to some UCLA physicist about the Higgs boson. Dark matter and dark energy and hidden dimensions. Their voices drifted out over the backyard, interrupted by the buzzing of bees and the scrape of leaves as they were blown across the wooden fence before falling to the ground.

Abbie usually loved to feel the loamy mulch on her hands, but she'd just had a mani-pedi the day before and didn't want to ruin her sparkling red nails. She breathed in the stuff's rich fragrance as she spread it evenly in the small garden, and smiled as she did so. The big Victorian painted Kelly green was her first place with a yard and she'd surprised herself at how she'd taken to gardening, to anything connected with nature, honestly, as she'd always seen herself as a city girl. But now she wanted to hold on to her first summer here, to have one last crop from her little stakehold.

The fourth bag of mulch was gone. She bunched up the plastic and got up, wiping her forehead with her sleeve and feeling a wave of pleasant tiredness sweep through her. She stopped a moment to watch the wind toss the tops of the hundred-year oaks in the yard next door, Ron and Charles's place. She'd invite them over for dinner when the tomatoes were ready.

Her neighbors. It felt good to say that. She turned and reached for the next bag of mulch.

"Where's that man of yours anyway?"

Abbie looked up. A head had appeared over the battered wooden fence that bordered the side of her yard. Ron.

"He's shopping for his moose-hunting trip," she said, smiling and sitting back on her haunches. "He's Canadian, you know."

Ron rolled his eyes. He was the more sociable half of the couple. Ron was a social worker who dealt with some of the toughest families on the East Side. Charles was a professor at the university, teaching in the English Department, and he had the posture and frostiness of an academic. Abbie had his book on medieval poetry on her bookshelf.

"Nobody's *that* Canadian. He's really going to shoot a moose?"

Abbie laughed. "Next month, if he can find one. If not, he'll drink with his buddies and dream about me."

Ron scoffed. He had reddish hair and a broad, pleasant farm boy's face. "I hope for your sake that he doesn't dream about one of those buddies. Do they have beards?"

Abbie stood up, stretched her back, then walked slowly and laid her arms across the top of the fence. It needed painting. Maybe she could get it in before winter came. "No recruiting people's boyfriends. 'Specially mine. How's Charles?"

Ron made a face. "Fine, I guess. He's giving one of his tours."

Abbie's house lay smack in the center of Buffalo's arts district. Downtown Buffalo was thick with history and she'd found that a surprising number of her neighbors were involved with preserving it. Half of them seemed to be on the landmark commission, and Charles took visitors through the local sites on guided tours: the Albright-Knox Museum, the Frank Lloyd Wright House, the twin spires of the faded but still glorious Buffalo State Asylum for the Insane.

"Which one is it today?"

Ron rolled his eyes. "I think it's the architecture special. Or the tour of the old Erie Canal. You know, the *exciting* one."

"Why doesn't he start a famous murders of Buffalo tour? I could lead that one."

"He's going to be *in* that one if he doesn't get home soon."

Abbie gave him a mock-horrified look. "You need a drink, hon?" she asked.

"I do. I have a foster mom whose fat neck I'm considering strangling. You'd be saving a life."

"Give me ten minutes and I'll—"

The phone in her pocket buzzed.

Ron, hearing it, widened his eyes and wagged his finger back and forth with an alarmed look on his face. "Oh nuh nuh no. We have an oral contract. My need for alcohol is much more pressing than some . . ."

Abbie said, "Hush," brushed her hands off, and reached for the phone. Don't let it be work, she thought. I could use a drink, too. She felt peaceful, the fall glory of her yard filling her with a strange contentment.

The message was from the Buffalo PD's emergency channel.

MARCUS FLYNN ESCAPED. ALL PERSONNEL REPORT HQ.

3

The crowd on the second floor of Buffalo Police Headquarters was as big as Abbie had ever seen it, except for last year's
mass-disaster training day where the city had simulated a terrorist at-
tack. Then there'd been sheriffs, firemen, deputies, everything in uniform above the rank of school crossing guard, socializing before they'd
gone out to tend to the fake victims with blood painted on their faces
and leg wounds provided by the university's theater department. It
had been a carnival of local law enforcement, the mood light. Abbie
had eaten a hot dog and enjoyed herself.

And why not? As one cop had said, "What kind of dipshit is gonna
bomb Buffalo?"

But now there was a dark electricity in the air as Abbie walked
through the room. She felt it in her chest. Usually when there was an
emergency, you could sense a barely repressed excitement, the guilty
little secret of law enforcement. We love the big cases, she thought,
the scary ones, the spectaculars. Anything to put us on the front lines
and take us away from the dreariness of people stealing from the local
Wegmans to feed their kids.

But as she scanned the crowd, she saw something else. Gray, drawn
faces, strangely bloodless. Stiff postures, hands clenched behind backs.

A few men with the corners of their eyes ticking. This is like a funeral, she thought, but where nobody knows yet who died.

Chief Albert Perelli spotted her and nodded. He was dressed in a checked blazer and dark slacks, a white shirt open at the neck. He was talking to a sheriff in a broad-brimmed hat who looked like his face had been carved out of granite.

"See me after," Perelli mouthed, and Abbie nodded back, taking her place at the back of the crowd.

There was a thrum of low conversation as Perelli spoke to the sheriff, his head ducking down to listen. Then he nodded and straightened up, looked over the room. He waved his hand in the air once. There was no platform for him to step on and address the troops, so he stepped up on a sturdy wooden chair.

"Everybody listen up," he said sharply. The voices in the room subsided almost immediately.

"You've all heard the news, I'm sure. Marcus Flynn, aka Hangman, escaped while being transferred from Auburn Correctional to Attica. A Corrections officer was killed by two bullets to the head. His service revolver and his watch are missing. The escape location is about fifty miles east of here and most of you will be headed that way in a few minutes. The collection point is behind 74 Franklin and you'll be going up in vans to the different checkpoints. That's what we're here for. We're building a perimeter out there and we *will* have this . . . this . . ."

Perelli's eyes grew wide as he looked for the right word.

"This *prisoner* in jail by morning."

Abbie noted the respect given to Hangman. "This prisoner," not the usual cop talk of "this freak" or "this scumbag." Perelli's eyes swept from left to right.

"We have a hundred and fifty men and women here. Syracuse will contribute, Rochester, too, and the Wyoming County Sheriff's Department is already manning roadblocks on Route 20A and its feeder roads. Let's hope that by the time you all get halfway up to Warsaw, the prisoner will be back in custody. I'm sure that'll be the case but to make it happen I need you to listen very carefully."

He paused.

"This is not a time for individual heroics, this is a time for what will work most effectively. And that's teamwork and communication. You're going into hunter's country up there. People have guns and they're not shy about using them. I don't want to lose two men in the effort to catch one. Wear your orange vests if you're going into the woods, and only go into the woods if you're told to."

Perelli motioned to a man next to him wearing the sheriff's outfit.

"This is John O'Neill. In case you don't know him, he's with the Erie County Sheriff's Department and he's got the duty roster. Most of you will be stationed on the highways and local roads coming west. The Syracuse PD will be coordinating all recovery operations east of the escape point. Know where you are. We're about"—he swiveled around toward the plain clock on the back wall—"six hours till nightfall and I want Hangman in custody before we get there."

Perelli paused for a moment, and Abbie saw something troubled in his eyes, a look of uncertainty. That was rare for Perelli, an expert smotherer of all forms of worry.

"A few words on Hangman," he said, his voice dropping. "He's a Buffalo native. I'm sure you all know that. This is his home territory, this is the place he's most comfortable with, and if somehow he gets through the perimeter that we're setting up, this is most likely where he'll be headed."

He took a breath.

"Now *nobody* wants that to happen. We've seen, most of us here, what he's done to this city before. I'll tell you something: Buffalo has never been the same since Hangman. A killer like that does something to people, permanently. We all still bear the scars."

Abbie didn't know many people in the Hangman's target demographic—all his victims had been young teenage girls from the North of Buffalo—but she imagined many of the men and women in the room had daughters at home. They'd want to stop Hangman before he got near their schools and cul-de-sacs.

And she didn't blame them one bit. Hangman was a scary one. Even from Miami, where she'd been when the murders went down, she'd felt a chill when reading the headlines from her hometown. Hangman was elusive, implacable, a hunter.

Trap the monster where he is, she thought. Upstate in the woods, where the most he can kill is woodchucks. Everyone was thinking the same thing; she felt their strange, trigger-happy dread: *Keep this animal away from my city.*

Perelli stepped down and made a beeline for his office along the far wall.

4

Abbie tried to follow Perelli, but was blocked by a crush of cops trailing John O'Neill toward the exit. Finally, she smiled and pressed her way forward until she'd reached the wall, then turned her shoulder and made her way to Perelli's door.

Once in, she closed the door behind her and the drone of the office—all those male voices, excited, amped up—was snuffed out. Perelli looked up and shook his head. He'd tossed his jacket on a leather chair.

"You got here quick."

Abbie nodded. "When they say Hangman, you come fast."

Perelli closed his eyes briefly, and nodded. "Let me ask you something," Perelli said. "How much do you know about Flynn?"

Abbie shrugged, sat in the chair facing his desk. "The basics. He was from the County, but lived downtown when the killings began. He was in his late thirties, good employment record, no arrests except for two drunk-and-disorderly the year before the murders began. Went to college in, was it Fredonia?"

"Oswego," Perelli said, watching her.

"Right. He killed four girls . . ."

Perelli was about to speak, but Abbie cut him off.

"He killed three and kidnapped one. The last one was never found. All were from fourteen to sixteen years old, all brunettes, and all from the North. They died by strangulation, apparently hanged, judging by the width of the rope burn, et cetera."

Perelli nodded.

"The last victim was Sandy Riesen, the killer's cousin," Abbie went on. "He was caught in a security video putting her in his car three blocks from her house. They put out a BOLO with the license plate of his car and it was spotted pulling into the parking lot of a hotel."

"Motel," Perelli said, nodding. "Called the Warsaw."

"Right, the Warsaw Motel. When deputies arrived, they approached the room and found Hangman with a self-inflicted gunshot wound to the head. Hangman survived with some brain damage and was convicted on all four cases."

"And Sandy?" Perelli said quietly.

"Was never found."

A nod. "So I'm impressed. You know more than the basics. Well, I want you to know everything."

Abbie narrowed her eyes. "This is a search operation, Chief, pure and simple. Why should we reopen the original case?"

"*Now* it's a search operation."

Abbie raised her eyebrows. "What does that mean?"

"What if it goes two, three days? Hangman goes to ground, we can't find him. Then we're going to have to use everything we have. I'm not saying it's likely, I don't think it is. But if he does get past the first forty-eight hours, then it's something else, something where your talents might come into play."

Abbie's gaze was level, intense. "I have talents now?"

Perelli grunted, not quite laughing. "One or two."

"What do you want me to do?"

"You're insurance," he said. "You'll be my lead on this, in case, by some fucking miracle that I don't even want to imagine, Flynn escapes every law enforcement officer in Western New York and comes calling. You're going to try to figure out where he might be headed, who he wants to see. Look the case over, see if the detectives missed anything the first time around that tells us where he was hiding for those months back in '07."

Abbie watched him. "Where do you think he'd go?"

Perelli watched back. "*If* he gets through, we think he'll be headed right here. Like I said. He has friends and family here, perhaps, who knows, he has unfinished business here as well."

Abbie tilted her head down and eyebrows up. "Meaning what, Chief?"

Perelli shrugged and gave her an exaggerated frown. "Meaning unfinished business, Kearney."

"That's awful cryptic."

Perelli grunted. "You've got a highly developed persecution complex, you know that?"

She laughed. "That's why I'm still alive and gainfully employed."

Perelli made a tossing motion with his left hand. "How the hell should I know where he's headed? The guy's been half a retard for the last five years. You know he took a bullet to the brain. Listen . . ."

The chief held his hands out in a calming motion. "It's not going to come to that. We're going to have more people on the ground than looked for the Lindbergh baby. Just do your thing and let me say I'm holding you in reserve."

Abbie nodded. She didn't want to mention what happened to Lindbergh's baby. At least Perelli was being honest. She was political insurance on an explosive case.

"I have to cover every possibility," he said. "Detective Raymond is looking at everyone Flynn knew who's still in the area, anyone he might go to. I jotted his number inside the case file."

Abbie knew about Raymond, a young black detective from Violent Crimes who'd just been transferred to Homicide. His reputation was solid. Non-political and non-County. The black skin had seen to that.

"Norwood and a couple of uniforms are passing by the Riesen mansion every fifteen minutes, in case Flynn wants to harass his uncle, Sandy's father. And what if the killer wants to go out with a few more victims? Or visit the graves of one of the three girls? So . . ." Perelli pushed a thick file toward her. "What can I do but put my best detective on the case?"

There was an electric charge in the dark eyes beneath the bristling eyebrows. Perelli and Abbie had never really worked past what had happened the year before: the Clan na Gael murders and his insistence, right here at HQ, that she'd been responsible for them. He'd apologized formally in the ceremony awarding her a commendation—and her father's detective badge, which she now wore. But he'd never come to her in the hallways of HQ and spoken the words she felt she'd deserved. Personal words, cop to cop.

Abbie held his gaze. No, she didn't quite trust him. "I never said I was your best detective."

"You didn't need to. Everyone else did."

"You'd rather I be terrible at my job?"

"Absolutely not." He patted a thick file marked "Flynn, Marcus" in candy-colored letters arranged on the edge. "That's why I put you on this. If you're ever going to hit a home run, I want you to do it on this one."

Abbie thought this over. Finding no hidden traps in the offer, she reached for the file. "May I?" she asked.

Perelli gave a small smile, then lifted his hand, spreading the fingers as if to say, *Be my guest.*

Abbie flicked open the file. On top was a photo, a video grab from a security camera. Hangman leading his last victim, Sandy Riesen, to his dented black BMW. She recognized the shot; it had been everywhere five years ago. A grainy, smeared image of a tall, striking, seemingly unconcerned girl following the tall, slit-eyed killer to her death.

Just looking at Hangman's eyes, Abbie felt an icy wave go through her.

"There's someone you should talk to," Perelli said. He picked up his phone and dialed a two-digit number.

"Who's that?"

"Raymond. Since Z is still off duty . . ."

Abbie nodded. Z was at home, on disability. He was putting on weight and happy as ever.

". . . he's going to be with you on this."

The door opened behind her and she smelled a citrus cologne. She looked over and saw a slim detective in a checked sports coat, tan slacks, and chestnut-colored shoes standing next to her. Billy Raymond smiled.

"Detective," he said.

Abbie nodded.

"Abbie's going to go look at the escape scene," Perelli said, "see what we got."

Raymond frowned thoughtfully.

"She's the lead," Perelli said.

Raymond looked over at her. His eyes were cool, evaluating. "Fine with me."

"What about Auburn?" Abbie said, paging quickly through the file. "I may need to talk to people there to get a sense of what Hangman was acting like just before the escape."

Perelli spread his hands wide. "Be my guest. So long as you stay away from the roadblocks and don't get involved on the pursuit side, that's fine. But we don't have jurisdiction up there. You'll have to get what you can get on your good looks."

Abbie closed the file. "The thing is, Chief, I can't tell if you're giving me a real assignment or just cleverly getting me out of the way."

Perelli frowned, glanced at Raymond with a *see-what-I-mean?* look.

"Hangman'll be in custody by tomorrow morning," Raymond said.

Abbie turned slowly to look at him. "Is that right?"

"He'll break into someone's house, maybe carjack an old lady," Raymond said. "But we'll get him. He's got no one to run to."

"Sounds like you've got this," Abbie said. "Maybe I'll go home and harvest my fall vegetables."

"Yeah, I got this."

Abbie leaned forward toward Perelli. "Are you telling me everything?"

Perelli glared, then slowly leaned forward. "Excuse me, Detective Kearney? Say that again."

"Is . . . this . . . everything?"

Raymond coughed. He seemed to want to be out of the room.

Something strange in Perelli's eyes. Something she hadn't seen before. He seemed actually distressed. His voice, when he started to speak, was aggrieved and just a tone lower.

"I'm going to give you a pass on that last comment, because you weren't here when Hangman was active." He pointed to his chest, stabbing the tie with a thick index finger. "*I was.* I was a lieutenant in the 5th District. I interviewed the mother of Sabrina Kent, the second victim." He took a deep breath and blew it out. "I had to tell her that we found her daughter's body on Oakland Place between Delaware and Elmwood, *three days* after she went missing. You know what she was thinking?"

"Who killed her," Raymond said.

"No," Abbie said. "Not that. She wanted to know how long she was alive. Or what Hangman was doing with her daughter's body."

Perelli looked down at his desk. "Both. Was he talking to Sabrina? Did he have her propped up on the seat next to him as he drove around the city? Did he use—" He broke off. His face was past anger and Abbie saw what he would look like as an old man.

"So please, Detective Kearney, don't tell me that I'm not doing my utmost here."

Abbie watched him. Perelli was a good actor, she knew that. But she knew just as well that this wasn't acting. She hadn't been here. It was true. Never say you know what it's like when you don't.

"Okay," she said. She didn't offer an apology. How hard she worked would be her apology.

Perelli picked up the phone. "I feel better already."

Abbie stood and brushed by Raymond. He stepped out of her way, then followed her out. "You headed to Auburn?" he said.

"Yeah."

"Cool. I'll let you know when we pull Hangman in."

Abbie stopped, her eyes wide. "You're very sure of yourself, Raymond."

"Best solve rate in the department," he said. "Three years running."

"Not to be picky, but those weren't homicides."

He didn't smile at that one. "You know, most of the guys'd be falling over themselves to work with you. I figure maybe you have something to learn from *me*."

Abbie laughed. At least he was honest. "You know what one of my professors told me in college, Raymond?"

"What'd he say?"

Abbie stopped. "I was a lot like you back then. And what *she* said, my professor . . . ?"

Raymond grinned.

" . . . was this: 'Abbie, be bold. Be very bold. But not *too* bold.'"

Raymond nodded.

"It's an old French saying," she said. "I found it to be helpful."

Raymond's eyes gleamed. He seemed to lean toward her on the balls of his feet. "Shit, Kearney," he said softly, "ain't no such thing as too bold."

5

The file was as thick as a phone book for a midsize city and Abbie stuffed it into a large liver-colored envelope. She grabbed a Lime Diet Coke from the vending machine on the first floor and walked outside. The wind was swatting newspapers and trash around and there was a line of law enforcement types—in and out of uniform—lined up to the right. The seriousness of any case can be judged by how smartly cops line up for it. The line out back could have been cut with a ruler; it was an informal car pool being directed by a BPD uniformed officer.

The others glanced at her, holding the file, as they all shuffled forward. Everyone else was holding flashlights and backpacks or, in the case of two officers, Remington Versa Max shotguns, the tactical models with the eight-round magazine.

Getting in line, she held the envelope in the crook of her elbow. Her favorite reading. She pulled out the file, opened it, holding down the first page so the wind didn't take it, feeling the jangle of excitement that always came over her when starting a new case.

She began to read, shuffling forward with the line.

The file was chronological. It began with the discovery of the first body. Charlotte Breen, sixteen years old, a junior at Nardin Academy, an alternate on the debate team, a fairly nondescript record. On July 2, 2007, Charlotte had told her mother that she was going to bike over to her friend's house and left at around 4:15 p.m. The North was one of the safest neighborhoods in Buffalo, leafy and rich and heavily patrolled by the Buffalo PD, so her mother had thought nothing of Charlotte biking half a mile. But Charlotte never arrived. By 7 p.m. her parents were driving the neighborhood looking for her. Nothing. Vanished.

At 10:32 a.m. the next day, a mailman doing his rounds a mile away from Charlotte's departure point found her bike leaned up against a telephone pole—leaned, thought Abbie, not tossed carelessly or in a panic on the sidewalk. Charlotte's naked body was found three days later in an open field three miles from the Breen house. No marks to the body. No DNA under the fingernails, only dirt. No signs or notes from the killer.

Abbie looked up. She was halfway to the front of the line. She saw vans pulling up and taking in cops, like helicopters landing quickly for paratroopers before lifting off again.

Abbie flipped forward in the file and found a photo of Charlotte. Dark eyes, metal-framed glasses that didn't complement her face, long brown hair, a tiny suggestion of a mustache that Charlotte either wasn't too worried about or had failed to notice. A V-neck sweater with a thin gold chain at the neck. She looked . . . sensible, thought Abbie. She flicked back to the report. The background on Charlotte showed a B- student who had expressed an interest in becoming a dentist. She had two or three good friends, and no boyfriends or girlfriends or romantic attachments. She'd attended the junior prom with a group of girls; her diary had revealed no stalkers, overattentive teachers, jealous boyfriends.

If her friends said there was no boyfriend, I believe there was no boyfriend. But the bike leaned carefully against the telephone pole, that was odd. Abbie wondered if it had a kickstand, and if so, whether Charlotte had been relaxed enough to take the extra two seconds to use it. That would indicate some degree of trust in the person that took her away. One neighbor had seen Charlotte pedaling down Bryant

Street toward her friend's, but that was the last sighting. The girl had effectively vanished just a mile from her own house.

She flipped to the medical examiner's report for all three girls, clipped together near the back of the file. All the girls had died within three to four days of being kidnapped. Sexual abuse of the bodies negative. The toxicological screens had come back negative for the first girl, positive on the last two for Versed, a fast-acting sedative, basically an injectable chloroform. The ME had found puncture marks in Girl Number Two's left arm and Girl Number Three's right thigh, consistent with injection from a needle. Maybe Hangman had trouble controlling the last two. Maybe the first one had believed whatever story he told her at the beginning—*I just want to take you for a drive*, or *I swear I'll let you go tomorrow*—but the other girls knew better. By then, Charlotte was dead . . .

"Where you going, ma'am?" a voice barked.

Abbie looked up. A uniformed cop, a serious mustache bristling above a metal clipboard, was staring at her intently.

"Um, the prison. Auburn."

He frowned and looked down at his clipboard. "The blue van," he said, ducking his head sideways and pointing back along a line of cars and trucks with smoke curling from their tailpipes. "Leaving in one minute."

"Got it," Abbie said. She ran toward the van, confirmed with the driver through his open window that Auburn was going to be his last stop, then nodded at two burly men, one in a gray, flat-brimmed hat, the other bareheaded and dressed in a dark green shirt, who were squeezed into the middle row. She ducked down and scooched into the last row, and sat by the window. Abbie placed the file next to her and slowly opened the soda she'd brought. She had the row to herself.

"Brought some reading material?" said the deputy in the gray hat, turning in his seat. He was older and he looked like a TV dad from some '50s sitcom.

Abbie smiled. "A must for long rides."

He eyed the file, and his smile tightened. "Anything in there," he said, "we should know about?"

His tone was light, but his gaze sure wasn't.

Abbie looked at him in surprise, then down at the file. "Don't think so. Background mostly. I'm just covering all my bases."

The deputy nodded.

The other man—his face looked lean and shadowed in the light of the van, but Abbie could tell that he was Latino—turned to listen to them. She saw the badge on his arm as he leaned it on the backrest. The outline of the U.S. in yellow stitching on a black background. Border Patrol.

Good Lord, Abbie thought, they're calling in everyone except Sanitation.

"I'm sure Hangman will make a mistake soon," she said to the deputy. "That's how these things usually end."

The Latino agent was looking at her now, and said, "All I know is that my cousin just turned fifteen years old last Tuesday. We had a nice party for her. You ever been to a *quinceañera?*"

Abbie shook her head no.

"Nice," he said. "Live band. Real nice."

He looked out the window, then smiled back at her. "I don't think that boy's gonna make it out of the woods, you know what I'm saying?" His voice was quiet, and his teeth in the darkness were even and white. It was as if he were tasting Hangman's flesh between them.

It feels good to saddle up and go hunting wild animals, thought Abbie. Especially when you have something back home that the animal likes. "I hope we take him alive, and learn something for the victims' families," Abbie said, trying not to be too schoolmarmish. "Like where he buried the last girl."

The Border Patrol agent stared at her. "Uh-huh," he said, turning away.

6

The blue van hummed along the 90 toward Auburn. Abbie felt a slight chill from the window, which was frosted with cold mist, hovering a few inches inside. But the driver had the heat on high and the cold was slowly being pushed out. After ten minutes, the men inside the van stopped shifting and adjusting the armrests and the chatter slowly died away. She took a swig of the Diet Coke and went back to the file.

Hangman's next victim was Sabrina Kent. Fifteen years old. Two and a half months after Charlotte was taken, Sabrina had been shopping at the Galleria Mall and had purchased two T-shirts at Abercrombie & Fitch, her credit card billed at 5:38 p.m. on September 12, a Wednesday. The girl had been observed leaving the store by a security guard, who'd found her cute enough to recall her presence. But as soon as Sabrina had left, he'd turned back and kept his eyes on the clientele; the store had been experiencing a rash of shoplifting. Sabrina walked out to the parking lot toward her father's 2005 Mercedes and was never seen alive again.

She was another North girl. Her family lived just off Delaware Avenue. So the killer hadn't been choosing randomly at the mall. He'd followed Sabrina from the North, looking for a moment of opportunity.

If Abbie hadn't known her Buffalo history, her tour-giving neighbor Charles would have filled her in long ago. At the turn of the twentieth century, Buffalo had been rich, with more millionaires per capita than any city on earth. It was hard to believe now, but before the sky came falling down, her city was supposed to become the next Paris or New York. And Buffalo's North is where the newly rich had built their mansions, huge stone behemoths with Greek columns and flying buttresses and an air of permanence that said they'd outlast the next Ice Age.

This was Hangman hunting grounds.

Abbie found the autopsy photos. Another brunette; it would become a signature. Sabrina's body was pale as milk. There were some scrapes on the right knee, but otherwise her body showed no signs of abuse. Not even defensive wounds on the hands. The medical examiner's opinion was that the girls had been hanged. Ligature marks were visible in several close-up photos, and both the thickness of the burn and angle of the rope suggested it.

Why did he take the girls if he didn't want to rape them? Did it indicate a kind of longing—was Hangman looking for a girlfriend? Were they trophies meant to be kept? If they were trophies, did the fact that he discarded them eventually mean that he was living with someone else and couldn't risk the bodies being discovered?

She checked the file to see if any traces had been found in the girl's hair—leather shavings, carpet fibers, anything that might indicate what the killer had used to transport his trophies. But there was no mention of anything. Sabrina Kent had styling gel in hers, and that was all.

Three months later Hangman found Maggie Myeong. Her father had come to Buffalo in the mid-'80s to study at the university, met a North girl, married her and settled down. The father was a chemist with Dow, the mother was teaching biology at Williamsville North High School out in the suburbs. Maggie was the Asian cliché or the Asian ideal, however you wanted to look at it: studious, a bookworm, "never any trouble since she was three years old and got lost in Delaware Park during the Easter Egg Hunt," or so said her father, Walter.

She'd wanted to work in psychiatry and even volunteered after school at the old Buffalo State Asylum for the Insane over on Elmwood. She was a young woman on her way.

Hangman somehow got her out of her house, where she'd been dropped off after school. How, no one knew. No signs of forced entry, no snapped locks or broken windows. He'd spirited her out like a ghost.

But this killing came with a difference: the first message from the killer. On the palm of Maggie's left hand was carved a symbol: a capital A inside a square.

Abbie turned and stared out the window. Capital A, square box. She took out her pen and drew the symbol on the bottom left corner of the manila folder and stared at it. There was something the tiniest bit familiar about the image, and she traced it again slowly.

Did it have anything to do with the fact that Maggie was Asian? What about the anarchy symbol? No that was an A inside of a circle. Abbie thought back to her Mount Mercy days, reading *The Scarlet Letter*. Hester Prynne had been forced to wear an A, for adultery. Could the killer have been jealous of someone Maggie was seeing? Abbie searched through the interviews but there was no mention of Maggie having a boyfriend.

But something about the image tantalized her memories. I've seen this before, Abbie thought.

Abbie flipped open the file and checked the date of the murder. December 19, 2007. The first two murders had taken place in mid- and late summer but by December, it would have been frigid in Buffalo, with girls wearing their heaviest winter parkas with the hoods pulled up, plus hats and scarves. What if the killer only wanted white girls? He'd picked up Maggie, thinking she was as pale as the other victims, but found she had typical Asian features and skin tone. What if he'd felt compelled to mark his displeasure in the form of the A, as a rebuke. What else could the A stand for?

The BPD had publicly denied there was any racial component to the killings, but Abbie could guess that was simply PR. They didn't want any girl or their family getting complacent. They left the victim profile as wide open as possible, to try and save the next girl.

Abbie looked up and stared out the van's fogged windows. They were out far past the city limits now, into the farm country that ringed Buffalo on three sides. Working barns, silos, a line of towering wind turbines half-hidden behind rolling hills, tractors, and old Dodge pickups sitting in the enormous front yards of rambling frame houses. Route 20A cut through good dairy country.

There was one more girl. The missing one, Sandy. The file on her was as thin as a slice of bread. There'd been a huge search effort to try to find Sandy, beginning when her father called in a missing persons report. Hangman had been caught just hours after kidnapping her, but no trace of her had ever been found apart from a red-and-amber silk scarf she'd been wearing when she left her house, retrieved from Flynn's car. At first, the hope had been that there hadn't been enough time for Flynn to kill her, and that she'd be found alive. But the years had dimmed that possibility, and most cops who'd looked at the case believed she was buried out near the Warsaw Motel.

There was another folder attached: a sub-file on the second man theory, the idea that Hangman had a partner in his crimes. It was mostly phone tips: girlfriends calling in boyfriends who'd been acting suspiciously, neighbors snitching on neighbors, bosses ratting on employees who'd called in sick suspiciously often. None of the tips had been substantiated.

At the end of the file, a handwritten note. "Ex-wife G. Payne suggested p. mot. to SecLD. See folder 3CW attached."

"P. mot." wasn't standard for anything, but Abbie guessed it meant "possible motive." SecLD would be "Second Lead Detective." Abbie looked behind Sandy Riesen's manila folder but the space was empty. She frowned, and paged through the folder to make sure she hadn't missed anything, then sighed and was about to stash the entire case file next to her on the bench seat when she noticed something about the manila folder that held all the papers. Abbie brought it closer to the cabin light that shone dully above her.

There, at the top of the folder, was a thin loop imprinted on the thick paper. Abbie traced the shape. It was the outline of a paper clip, even a little mark where the metal had begun to rust and left a trace behind.

Something had been clipped here. But folder 3CW was gone.

7

The van slowed and pulled up to a checkpoint, thrown up in the middle of one of the tiny two-block mill towns that were strung from Buffalo to Syracuse like faded charms on a bracelet. The roadblock was three white barriers with orange striping across the road, plus men in gray with shotguns and rifles.

Soon they were moving again.

Each murder would have gotten progressively harder to pull off, Abbie thought. Teenage girls would have vanished off the sidewalks of Buffalo, kept inside by their parents, and on those rare occasions they were let out to visit a friend or go to church, they would have had escorts. A father. An uncle or older brother. But, still, as rare in public as a four-leaf clover.

Sandy Riesen was next. The famous missing girl, the last of Hangman's victims—and his own cousin. Her body was never found. Hangman had called her the day of her disappearance from his cell phone, and she'd slipped out of the back door of her family home. Hangman had picked her up a few minutes later on a street corner three blocks away. The reason for their meeting had never been revealed.

With the state of panic the city was in, Sandy's father had immediately noted her disappearance and called her in as a missing person.

The license plate of Flynn's car had been put out as a "Be On the Lookout," and the car was spotted by a driver on 20A three hours later, pulling into the twelve-room Warsaw Motel. When cops arrived, Hangman was sprawled diagonally across the full-size bed, a wound to his right temple pumping out a thin stream of blood onto a pale green polyester comforter. Flynn was alive, gasping out quick breaths, but unable to speak. Nitrocellulose and other traces of gunshot residue—in popular CSI terms, "powder burns"—were found around the entrance hole. It was determined that the right-handed Flynn had shot himself once with an unregistered SIG Sauer.

The girl's black nylon jacket, a size 6 from Banana Republic, was tossed casually on the bed, as if she'd stepped out to buy a soda at the vending machine. Her scarf was in the suspect's BMW, underneath the passenger seat. In the file, there were pictures of the two items of clothing, along with a close-up shot of one of Sandy's school photos. The detail that had been blown up for the picture was a gold signet ring with an S written in a jagged medieval script, on the ring finger of her right hand. The next was an emerald ring, big stone. They were the only two pieces of jewelry Sandy had been wearing when she disappeared. Both were still missing. Along with Sandy.

Abbie stared out into the trees whipping by.

She flipped back through the witness testimonies from the early cases. No one had seen anything until the third murder: a six-year-old boy had spotted a man walking out of the field where Maggie Myeong had been found. She found the original interview transcript. "His face was all red. The man's head was covered in red."

The call went out to the public: Look for a man in a red mask. But it was the killer's method of execution, not his mask, that haunted Buffalo. That's what led locals to give him his name: Hangman.

"Five minutes till Auburn," the driver called to her.

She flipped to the beginning of the file, looking for Detective Raymond's number, then called him on her cell.

"What you got?" he said.

"Nothing yet, but I need a few things."

"Shoot."

"Find out if any cars were ticketed within half a mile of the escape site either early today or late last night. Any reports of cars idling by the road? Any nonlocals in the coffee shops or diners that morning, looking nervous?"

"You think there was a vehicle waiting for Hangman?" Raymond said.

"Maybe."

Raymond whistled. "What else?"

"It's going to sound crazy. But have uniforms check with the costume stores, toy stores, anything that sells outfits. Ask if they carry any kind of Halloween outfit with a red mask and if they sold any in the last week; even red ski masks. Maybe Hangman has an accomplice who got him one before he escaped. Most stores itemize purchases now with a description, so there should be some kind of database. Assuming he picks up where he left off, I don't think Hangman kills without a mask. He's meticulous, ritualized. If there are any sales, see if there's a credit card trail with a name on it."

"That is the definition of a long shot."

"They all are at this point," said Abbie.

"Who are you going to talk to first?"

"The person who knew him best up here. Hangman's shrink."

8

Dr. Andy Lipschitz looked like an unkempt bear, a bear raised in captivity that had forgotten how to hunt. He was tall, six feet at least, with lank brown hair and warm blue eyes behind his rimless glasses, a fuzz of reddish three-day beard. He was wearing a lab coat with a black nameplate that read "Lipschitz" and he smiled at her as he entered his office.

"Detective Kearney," he said, tossing a file down onto his desk. "They told me you were here."

Lipschitz's office in the Auburn Correctional Facility was homey and unusually warm. There were two diplomas on the wall, the second one crooked and cheaply framed, a metal desk meticulously neat, with three stacks of papers, a stuffed red bear hanging from the lamp, and a framed photo of a dark-eyed young woman along with others picturing what Abbie assumed were other members of Lipschitz's family. Abbie had taken her coat off when she entered and she was thinking of taking off her black blazer as well. The entire prison seemed to be fed by some enormous boiler that wouldn't stop pumping up heat.

Abbie stood up and Lipschitz took her hand for a languid shake. "I'm sure you've spoken to a few investigators, but I need ten minutes of your time," she said.

"They haven't asked me much," he growled, sitting in a chair and leaning back. "This is a fox hunt. They're not interested in what was on Marcus's mind."

"I am."

"Any particular reason? Hold on, did I offer you coffee?"

"No, you didn't but I'm fine."

Lipschitz nodded. Abbie thought he came across as an overgrown college student, but there was a sharpness behind all the slovenly bumbling.

"Now why do you need to know about all this?" he asked.

"I'm Plan B," Abbie said, smiling. "For that one-in-a-million chance that Flynn makes it through the perimeter. We might need to know what his thinking is."

"Oh, sure, sure," Lipschitz said, tilting his eyes away and studying her. "But I'm not sure that I know what his thinking is. He still had some impairment."

"Can you tell me about his progress? Where was he?"

Lipschitz's eyebrows shot up, and he steepled his fingers under his chin.

"Well," he said abruptly, like a professor giving his assessment of a paper. "We're talking about brain function? I don't know how much you know about his original injury but it was significant. The bullet came in here." Lipschitz took one of his meaty fingers and pointed it above his left eye. "Impacted but didn't destroy the entorhinal cortex, parts of the temporal lobe, and the parietal lobe. He didn't talk for six months and then he had to relearn basic things. Eating, walking, how to function in the bathroom. But within two years, that all came back. Other things didn't. He still can't taste anything; the receptors were too damaged, putting it crudely. He can't do a crossword puzzle. And his memory is often hit-and-miss."

"Does he remember the killings?"

Lipschitz's eyes grew thoughtful. "Ah, the question of all questions. Yes and no."

"Can you be more specific?"

"The thing is, Marcus Flynn is still my patient. Whether he's inside these walls or running around outside, that hasn't changed."

Abbie nodded. "We're not adversaries here, Doctor. I'd like him to continue to be your patient, so we can learn as much about him as possible. I want to get Flynn back alive."

There was a heaviness in Lipschitz's expression, almost a sadness. He said nothing.

"Were your sessions with him taped?" she continued.

"Yes. But I can't release any tapes or records without a formal request. New York State law. I can tell you there wasn't anything in them about an escape or anything resembling that."

Abbie nodded. "It can't be easy, working in this atmosphere," she said, taking her foot off the gas for a moment. "Did you choose to work in Corrections?"

He smiled. "What you mean, Detective Kearney, is did I fuck up or go to some podunk college so that this was the only job I could get?"

Abbie glanced over his shoulder. "I spotted the diploma. Cornell postgrad. You didn't have to come here."

"Damn right I didn't have to come here."

"So why did you?"

"Because half the week I do private practice in downtown Buffalo. The nice parts. And by the second year of *that*, I wanted to quit psychology once and for all. You get a lot of boyfriend talk, a lot of mother talk. Women—" He shrugged and laughed apologetically. "Some women feel they're entitled to perfect lives and are just devastated when they don't get them. Those are the ones who can afford me, so those are the ones I get."

Abbie smiled. "So you came to where the bad people are."

"Yes. I applied to Auburn specifically. I knew Marcus Flynn was here. I wanted to work with him. This place, I like to think of it as a sanctuary from . . . out there."

What a fascinating thought, Abbie said to herself. Prison as a refuge from the real world. As if dealing with Hangman was better than dealing with some neurotic thirty-year-old lawyer in downtown Buffalo. "And did Flynn meet your expectations?"

Lipschitz frowned thoughtfully. "It's a good question. He's interesting enough. When you're sitting with him, it's almost like you're watching pieces of his life come floating back into view. He had hallucinations, and it took time to separate out the real from the imagined memories, but there were times he'd have a kind of flashback. He was just starting to recover sensory information from the time of the murders. Piecemeal."

Abbie felt her pulse bump up. "On which girl?" she said.

Lipschitz studied her. She had the feeling in the quiet of the room that he was sorting information, putting it in two piles. Some for release. Some not.

"Dr. Lipschitz," Abbie said, leaning back. "I've heard the bloodhound teams in Wyoming County are the best in the state. Do you really want them catching Hangman? Or someone like me? Trust me, in this circumstance at least, I'm nicer."

He didn't answer. Finally, he let out a breath. "The last one," he said.

"Sandy Riesen?"

"Yes."

Abbie felt a tug of excitement. "What exactly did he remember?"

Lipschitz stood. "Excuse me," he said.

Abbie wheeled her chair toward the door and Lipschitz went by her in the tiny office. He walked to a slim black filing cabinet in the corner, took a set of keys out of his pocket, found a small snag-toothed one, slipped it into the small stainless steel lock on the second drawer from the top, then slid it out. He flicked through a few files. Abbie's eyes wandered over his desk, looking at the framed photos, the scattered files.

Finally he took out a manila folder and pushed the drawer shut. He walked back to his chair and pulled two sheets. "Marcus wanted to remember Sandy. Sandy was the one everyone talked about, the one the press focused on, because her body was never found. And, of course, he was related to her. The impression I got was that he was *trying* to remember her."

He handed over the first sheet. "Eighteen months ago, he drew these and hung them on his cell wall."

It was a series of small sketches of human heads. The drawings were roughly the size of apples. Done in a soft pencil, not a drawing pencil but something a little better than a number 2, with a broader point and softer lead. They weren't half-bad. The shapes looked recognizably human, not a child's moon-circles, but studies that showed skill and motor control. All of them had hair sketched in roughly. Long feathery hair swept off to the side. Some were slightly more detailed, more worked-over, with serious attention given to the shape of the face. The ovals had no features. It was eerie, faces without eyes and lips, not a smudge of human expression.

"Well, that's creepy," Abbie said.

"Creepy?" Lipschitz said, surprised. "I guess in this context."

Yes, in this context, Abbie thought. A serial killer of girls drawing blank faces. I will hereby qualify that as creepy.

"I was just happy that he'd begun to look outward and reconnect with other humans, even on a pictorial level. When I first started working with him, his drawings were . . . inward. Demon eyes. Rage-scrawls, I call them." Lipschitz paused. There was another sheet tilted in his hand, and he was looking down at it thoughtfully.

"What's that?" she said.

"This?" Lipschitz handed the sheet across to her. "This was last week."

Abbie took the paper. Just one face, taking up most of the center of the page, with an inch of white space on each side, and at the top and bottom margin. Much more detail here. The face had eyes, almond-shaped. A pert nose, flared at the end. And the hint of two full lips, drawn faintly, the top one shaded in, the bottom one just traced.

"The hair, the eyes, the shape of the face," she said. "It's Sandy."

"Could be. The beginnings of her, anyway. And he drew her face normal size."

"What's the significance of that?"

"Well, it's not a *completely* accepted interpretation, but the consensus is that the life-size face indicates he's thinking of Sandy as fully human, on an equal level with him. He's literally not minimizing her image."

Just the eyes gone, Abbie thought. A human being slipping back into your memory, a human being that you killed. How did that feel?

"Did he talk about her a lot?" she asked.

"Yes. Sandy and his daughter."

Abbie sat back. "I didn't know he had one."

"Oh, yeah. She'd be about nineteen now. Spent the last eight or nine years with the mother. Marcus has a lot of guilt about her, growing up without her daddy. Some anger, too. I gather his wife got full custody."

"Apart from his memories, did Flynn have hallucinations?"

"Yes."

"Can you tell me anything about them?" Abbie asked.

Lipschitz leaned back in the chair and it creaked under his weight.

"They were both visual and auditory. As I said, he saw faces. Not only of his victims. He visualized his own daughter, Nicole . . . hung. He was very upset about those instances, naturally. He hadn't seen Nicole for years, but he began to dream about her death."

"Do you think those fantasies of Nicole's death were a way of atoning for his crimes?"

Lipschitz smirked. "That would be classically Freudian, I guess, but I don't think it's that simple."

"What about the auditory hallucinations?"

"At night, he'd hear voices asking about Sandy. *Where is the girl? What did you do with Sandy?*"

Abbie shivered despite herself. "'What did *you* do with her'?" she said. "Was Marcus a split personality?"

Lipschitz clucked. "We haven't used the term split personality in about two decades."

"You know what I mean."

"Did he have dissociative identity disorder? No, I don't believe so. This was part biology, having to do with brain injury. But it could also be Marcus coming to terms with what he'd done. It was like a horror movie for him, a flash of gore. Each session, he'd describe more details. And the voices perhaps reflected his horror at what he'd done, as well as his efforts to remember it."

"Were the hallucinations getting worse?"

"Well, more intense. His brain was healing, rewiring itself in certain ways. Things were coming back. But Marcus . . . Marcus is still a confused soul."

"Did he have visitors?" Abbie asked.

Lipschitz smiled. "*No one* visited Marcus. He was the infamous Hangman, after all."

"Groupies? Serial killers often have them."

Lipschitz shrugged. "That you'd have to take up with admin. They monitored his mail. I wasn't aware of any. But Marcus was . . . he was fragmented. He hid things from himself, let alone me."

Something buzzed in Lipschitz's pocket. He seemed grateful for the distraction.

"If you don't mind."

Abbie stood to leave. "I need to see Hangman's cell."

Lipschitz studied the screen of his iPhone. "Damn nuisance," he said, placing the device on his desk. He looked up at Abbie. "Um, what did you say?"

"Hangman's cell. I'd like to see it."

"Why? They had a tac team sweep it already. They didn't find a thing."

"If you could humor me, I'd appreciate it."

Lipschitz picked up his desk phone. "A guard has to bring you down."

9

Abbie had to wait forty-five infuriating minutes for the new guard shift to come on. She spent the time checking Flynn's prison file: he'd had no visitors in five years, not a single one. He'd gotten letters, apparently from wannabe groupies, but never answered them. He'd been largely cooperative and had been granted "basic earned privileges"—including the right to have pencil and paper in his cell.

Finally, a short, squat, thinly whiskered guard arrived to take her down. Hangman's cell was on the second floor of the prison. There was a straight line of eight cells along the corridor, five feet from a railing that looked down on the public area, the same number across the gap on the other side. The sound of the other inmates—gossiping, calling out to each other—echoed down the row. Abbie glanced over the railing at the cement tables below, painted a light green, those prison kinds of tables that are built right into the floor and can't be taken apart and used as weapons. After the last cell in the group of eight, the wall angled left and there were six cells in a semicircle facing a guard booth that had Plexiglas windows on all sides. One guard kept an eye on the twenty-two cells from an office chair inside the booth. Hangman's cell was number 16, the first after the turn.

She went to the cell window, the only opening in the beige metal door except for a slot for food and for handcuffing. The guard stood behind her.

It was probably 6 x 8 and unremarkable in every way. There was a single cement bunk, with a thin mattress on top. A blanket had been folded at the foot of the bed with a pillow at the head, the way the guards fixed a cell when it was empty. A lid-less toilet was affixed to the wall in the opposite corner, with a stainless steel mirror above it. There were no posters or drawings taped to the walls.

If the room had held any indication that it had once held a human being inside, they'd been scrubbed away. She had an image of Hangman running across fields near Warsaw, a mindless automaton, a bald berserk thing, its face smoothed out like a mannequin, running and stumbling over the rows of corn stubble.

Abbie turned and looked from the door of the cell to the guard booth. There was an older guard in a brown uniform with tan epaulettes sitting in the chair, staring glumly at nothing.

"Listen, how long you going to be?" the guard behind her said.

Abbie stood there. Something, some misaligned thing, was bothering her. She couldn't leave until it was gone. "I don't know."

"Well, I got prisoners to take down to chow in D wing. When you're ready, call Ortiz over there, and I'll come get you."

Abbie glanced at the older guard behind the glass, and nodded.

"Holler if they get too *nnnnnaasty*," the man said, and his laughter echoed back to her as he walked off.

Abbie headed to the last cell before the wall curved into a semicircle, the one just before Hangman's. She ducked her head down. Inside a thin white man with wrinkly, tattooed arms and greasy hair to his shoulders was laid out on his cot, facing the door, and reading a tattered paperback. Abbie read the title—*The Fate of All Mankind*—before the inmate dropped it to his lap and stared at her.

"How you doing?" Abbie said.

The man's eyes were watery. He looked like an old biker with emphysema.

"Ah'm okay." Southern accent.

"How long have you been in this cell?"

"Two days. Got caught shoplifting again."

Abbie nodded. "You have a good night," she said. The man looked almost disappointed when she pulled back from the bars.

"Hey!" he called out. "What are you looking for? This ain't my first time through this place."

Abbie considered that. "Someone who had a cell next to Hangman's for the past few weeks, or longer."

The eyes looking at her with a look a thousand years old. "Try Hector Lopez. He was in 8, next door to Hangman, for a couple of months. He's in 14 now, on account of spitting at Sergeant Platz, the animal."

10

Hector Lopez was young and wiry and dressed in a clean wife-beater and white pants rolled up to the calf. When he saw Abbie standing at his window, he lifted up off the toilet seat where he'd been doing curls with a towel tied around something square and heavy. He walked toward the door with a rolling gait, catlike, smiling.

He whispered something in Spanish.

"Excuse me?" Abbie said.

"Oh! I thought you might be . . ."

"Do I look Spanish, Hector?"

He grinned. "Might be, might be."

Abbie shook her head. "I'm Detective Kearney with the Buffalo PD and I have a question for you."

His teeth were brilliantly white, and he had dimples. He came to the door and rested a muscled arm on the horizontal bar. "The answer is yes, *mujer*. You don't even—"

"Shut up, Hector. I need to know something about Hangman."

Hector's face twisted as if he'd bitten into a lime. His head shot back. "Why you want to talk about that freak?"

"You were celled next to him for a while, weren't you?"

Hector leaned toward Abbie, studying her. The motion caused his biceps to pop. Abbie rolled her eyes.

"Yeah," he said.

"Did you ever hear anything from his cell? Or outside it?"

Hector's face went still, then he turned and strolled back slowly to the toilet. He pivoted, sat on the toilet seat, and picked up the cloth, began wrapping the ends of it around his left hand while he flexed his fingers.

"Be serious, Hector," Abbie said.

"I *am* serious," he said, puffing a little as he lifted the weight up, not meeting Abbie's eyes. "I'm a very serious person, cuz."

"Did you hear anything?"

The eyes were bright, but Hector's face was stony.

"You help me, I can help you," Abbie said.

"With what?"

"If your information helps me find Hangman, I'd say a reduction on your sentence for good behavior. Or transfer downstate. Where you from, the Bronx?"

Hector considered that. He curled the brick a second time, a third and fourth, then lowered it to the floor, picked up the looped cloth with his other hand. "I might have heard a thing or two."

"I'm listening."

Hector's face grew red as he finished the fifth curl.

"You're starting to annoy me, Hector. Is that little curling weight legal? I might have to have one of the sergeants come down and check it out."

Hector's face tightened. He dropped his head, then came back off the seat, but there was no roll in his walk this time. He got to the window and laid his left forearm against the flat horizontal bar.

"What you lookin' for?"

Abbie held his gaze. "What'd you hear?"

Hector rubbed his nose with his finger. "Spooky shit."

"Like what?"

His eyes on hers. Not unfriendly.

"Was it a voice, Hector?" Abbie asked. "Late at night, sometimes?"

He backed off, his face tight with shock. "How'd you know that?"

Abbie felt a thrill of excitement go through her. "What did the voice say?"

"What do you think it was saying?"

"I need to hear it from you."

Hector paused. He dropped his gaze to the floor. "'Where's . . . the . . . girl?' That's what I heard. Usually after lights-out, around this time, come to think of it."

Abbie felt a surge of adrenaline that seemed to lift her heels off the floor. *I knew it I knew it I knew it.* "Very good, Hector. And when you heard these things, did you ever try and see who was saying them? Was it Hangman or someone else?"

Hector shook his head. "Nope. Stayed on my cot."

Abbie smiled. "Come on now. You weren't afraid of some voice talking in the dark, were you?"

Hector stared at her, and the eyes were deadly serious. For a minute, Abbie wondered what he was in Auburn for.

"Who else is gonna know about this?" he asked.

"Nobody."

"You swear, Carney?"

"It's Kearney. And yes, I swear. Now who was it?"

Hector dropped his gaze. He leaned toward the window and lowered his voice. "It was Carlson, man. The dude Hangman just killed? He killed him, right? Carlson was whispering in the man's cell in the dark like some crazy person. *Where's the girl?* What's up with that shit?"

11

Hangman sat on the green bench, dressed in khakis and a bulky blue down coat that was too long in the sleeves, watching the cars pass. He had a Buffalo Bills winter hat on now, the kind with the festive red-white-and-blue ball sewn to the top. The cap was pulled low over his eyes, and a black scarf was pulled tight around his mouth. Steam appeared through the holes in the yarn, and he tasted the wet wool when he stuck his tongue out. His eyes watched the cars, relaxed, waiting. He felt no urgency. He could see in the rhythms of the people walking by and stopping to wave or chat that the news hadn't yet gotten out to the wider public.

He stared at the house across the street, a stately old Colonial whose owners had faced the lower half of the facade with local river stone. He decided he liked the effect. To keep himself from turning his head, he tried to imagine what color he would paint the top half of the house instead of the pale cream the owners had chosen. How the different colors would look in the light of the early dusk, like now.

Hangman heard the bus rather than saw it, and judged the distance at three blocks. His hearing was exceptional, despite having his right eardrum blown out during a fight with a red-haired bully in grammar school, and he didn't need to turn to watch the bus approach. The vehicle had a balky transmission and Hangman heard it shifting up with agonized jerks as it came down the broad avenue toward him.

The bus shuddered to a stop a block away, the stop previous to the one he sat across from. The kids getting off the bus would come toward him. It was a late bus, full of the kids who did theater and sports and other things after school.

It was cold. He cinched the scarf tighter, looked at the house. To keep his pulse from racing, he imagined the house painted a dark olive green. That might work, would give the house a more rustic feel. And then change the shrubbery in front to roses and hyacinths.

The bus started toward him.

The engine, roaring like a tank's, coming down the avenue to his left. His eyes didn't move. It was odd to be hunting again. A feeling of exaltation rose in him, honey filling the marrow of his bones.

The orange of the bus swam into his field of vision, black smoke pouring from the exhaust as it ratcheted to a stop, the brakes shrieking. The feet of the students appeared under the frame of the bus as they exited. Six sets of feet, three of them definitely female, two male, one undetermined. The engine sounded again, and the tall side of the bus was pulled away like a curtain at a theater, all at once, and there were six students standing and laughing in three groups.

From across the street, Hangman's eyes quickly swept over the six figures, their mouths moving in gossip, the thin arms gesturing excitedly. Behind the scarf, he frowned deeply. Then his gaze moved right to the girl moving on the edge of the second group. His heart seized up as he stared at the face behind a scrim of blowing brunette hair that she caught awkwardly with the third finger of her right hand and swept back behind her ear. His eyes were avid now and he watched her step down off the curb and walk toward him with two friends, not even bothering to check both ways before crossing the street, confident of being protected by the world as all teenagers are.

The girl came toward him and he let the scarf fall away, revealing his open mouth, so intent was he on her brown eyes.

12

The entrance to the escape scene was hard to miss. There was a line of cop and sheriff cars tilted down into the ditches on both sides of the road as the van slowed on the country lane. Uniformed men bent over the open trunks of cars, getting equipment out. The sheriffs wore clear plastic caps over their hats and yellow slickers.

Just like Attica in '71, Abbie thought. These grim, square-jawed faces, like the ones of soldiers on Russian monuments to World War II, were the same as those cops. From those newsreels, she'd always thought of the men out here as some kind of other species. Killers, really.

"Here you go," the van driver said as they pulled up to the entrance to a small lane to the left.

"Don't leave me."

The driver nodded as Abbie dropped to the street. She let a car pass—behind the wheel, a fat-faced blond woman with eyes wide as she stared at the cops massed by the entrance before speeding off. Abbie hung her badge around her neck and let it rest on her black wool coat, then strode up the lane, her leather boots squelching in the mud. Cops coming the other way glanced briefly at her, some opened their mouths, then spotted the badge and went back to their conversations.

She walked five minutes before the trees to her left and right, which had huddled above her, their branches interweaving, began to space out and then fell away. The ruts of the lane petered out and she walked onto a grassy clearing.

There was a white van with NY STATE CORRECTIONS written in blue on the side. The sliding door was open and men were watching something in the backseat. Abbie walked over.

A sheriff's deputy turned, feeling her presence as she walked up. He nodded and touched the tip of his wide-brimmed hat. Country manners.

"Hi," she said. "What's going on in there?"

"A re-creation," he said quietly. "Seeing if Hangman could really have gotten out of the restraints. They fixed Williamson up just like he left Auburn and put a key in his mouth. He's our best tech guy."

"Our" would refer to the Wyoming County Sheriff's Department, by the patch on his heavy olive-colored nylon jacket.

"How'd he do?"

"Took him three tries but he got it. The seat belt, believe it or not, played a big part. If it was loose enough for him to lean forward, then Hangman could have gotten the key down to his hands and spit it out. Then he got Fatty Joe's gun. He was a good guy. I knew him."

The deputy brought up his iPhone, and stared at it.

"That a picture?" Abbie said.

"Yup." He handed her the phone. "People've been sending it around."

Fatty Joe Carlson was smiling, standing in front of a late-model Corvette, his arm around a young boy in a football outfit. Abbie peered closely at the image. Carlson was dressed in a richly colored Missoni sweater—the kind with the wavy stripes—and pressed jeans. She spotted the watch on his wrist, which had a distinctive clasp over the crown. A Panerai. She knew the brand, as her ex-husband had bought the classic model for Christmas one year, with Abbie's money.

Carlson's son was wearing a forest green football uniform, pads, and a helmet that seemed impossibly large for him. Across the forest front of the uniform, "School Saints" was written in white.

"That his son?" she said.

"Yeah, Joe Jr."

"He goes to Cortland Christian?"

"Yup. Plays football."

"That poor boy," Abbie said. She released the man's wrist and the phone dropped away.

She meant it. She thought about the boy that Hangman had made an orphan. He's probably been told something bad had happened to his daddy, and that he wasn't going to school tomorrow. Later they'd tell him his father was never coming home and he needed to go to the mall to buy a new suit. Black.

"He drove a 'Vette?" Abbie asked.

The cop's face froze. "What the fuck does it matter what he drove? He's dead."

"I'm just wondering if Hangman could have the keys." No she wasn't.

"Oh," the deputy said. "Sorry. No, he left the keys in his locker at Auburn."

Abbie nodded. She was doing figures in her head. Basic addition. And the figures weren't adding up.

She circled around the vehicle, then walked past it toward the top of the hill twenty yards away. It was a steep crest that gave way, lower down, to pine trees and scrub that formed a dark belt around the middle of the hill. A couple of deputies were deep in conversation, looking out over the flat valley, the wide brims of their hats tilting like ringed planets as they moved their heads.

The grass swished against her boots as she came up to the edge and looked down. Cars swept by on the road that snaked along the base of the hill. An Amoco gas station to the left was busy; she counted all four pumps occupied by cars, two of them official. Cops would be filling up on their way to manning the roadblocks. She followed the road along to the right and there was the black roof of the Warsaw Motel, missing a few shingles.

There was a group of teenage boys, two of them on ten-speed bicycles, gathered in the early evening light out in front of the motel. They were crouched over the handlebars, whispering together and glancing occasionally at the place. Maybe they thought the killer was coming back to the scene of his last crime. Right now, this must be the most famous place in Wyoming County.

So why did the Corrections officer bring Hangman to a spot overlooking the motel where he'd been captured?

Abbie felt the breeze steady on her face, running up the slope and cresting over, a clean fall wind that smelled faintly of pine.

Abbie looked down. Hangman knew we'd find the van eventually. But what if there was something he didn't want us to see?

She sighed and stepped down the steep bluff. A flat rock buckled under her boot heel and went slapping down the hillside, picking up speed.

"Hey," one of the deputies called. "What the hell you doing?"

"Investigating," she called back, turning quickly to place her hands on the grassy slope. She began to crawl down the hill, like a backward crab, eyes darting left and right. Loose rocks went spilling down, sending up little trails of airborne dust.

The two men were looking down at her, their hats appearing as dark saucers against the dying sun.

The hill was covered with scrub and shallow-rooted grass that tore away in her hands. Ten feet down, her left foot slipped back dangerously and Abbie dug the toe of the right one in.

The ground leveled out a bit and she was able to stand. She looked back up the hill. No garbage or trash—it didn't appear the hill was a lookout or a lovers' hideout. The grass waved back and forth, and a small contrail of dust lingered where she'd come sliding down. Abbie turned and surveyed below her. The gradient got even steeper before it flattened out about thirty yards below.

She spotted something shiny five feet to her left and up a bit. She scrambled along the little ledge until she reached it. Shotgun shell, half-planted in the dirt, already rusting, the brass base shining slightly. Abbie tossed it down the hill.

She was turning to assume the crab position when she saw something else. It was down eight or nine feet, a ball of something blue caught in the root of a scraggly purple flower. Abbie's brow creased as she walked carefully toward it. She slid, catching plants with her hand to keep her from tumbling down the slope. A yellow-topped weed came away in her hand and she swung away from the hill, feeling herself tip backward. She went with the momentum and turned all the way over, collapsing onto the hill on her back.

"Careful now," someone cried from up top.

If you were so concerned, she thought, you'd throw down a rope.

Abbie took a breath and turned her head to the left. There it was, rocking slightly in the wind. The glossy blue surface shone in the sun. Paper.

Abbie inched over, her throat dry from the dust. She crouched, her fingers scrabbling in the weeds, inching toward the blue ball. Another couple of inches. Her rib cage felt like it was going to separate at the breastbone. She lunged the extra two inches and felt the thing in her hands. She breathed out, tucked it into her lapel pocket, and began the laborious climb upward.

One of the deputies was waiting at the edge. He bent at the knees and offered her his hand.

"Long way to go for a piece of trash," he said.

Abbie took his hand and he pulled her up with a strong tug. She vaulted up to the top of the hill and almost went tumbling the other way.

"Sorry," he said.

"Might be something better than garbage," she said. "Thanks."

She pulled it out of her pocket and put her thumbs into the center of the ball, then carefully pulled it flat. A glossy photo, ripped along the left side. A line of rowboats was tied to a pier with dark blue water lapping at their gunwales. A man pulling the oars of a rowboat while a woman leaned back on the front wooden seat, a look of rapture on her face.

"Like I said, trash," the man said, then walked off toward the Corrections van.

Something far off rang in Abbie's mind, like a bell. Have I been there, she thought, the place in the picture?

Abbie smoothed the paper out against her palm. The paper crinkled as it unfolded. It was crisp, hadn't been down there in the weeds for long.

Not a photo. A brochure. And she'd seen this brochure, years before. But what was it for?

"Wherewherewhere . . ." Abbie whispered.

Rowing a boat on a lake during the summer. She'd always wanted to do that, had asked her father once, but he said it was for the swells. She didn't get it at the time—"swells," like waves in the water. And rich people.

Abbie whipped out her phone, clicked on the web browser, and typed in "Hoyt Lake boat" in the search box. A website came up. "See the city in a whole new way!" said the banner headline. Underneath the picture unfolded slowly. The same skyline, the same tied-up boats. The same doofy couple.

Hoyt Lake Boat Rentals, Abbie read. Hoyt Lake, in the middle of Delaware Park. In the North.

A surge of panic went through her as she stared at the image.

13

Martha Stoltz slammed the front door of her house on Mill Lane, slung her schoolbag onto the leather couch, and headed straight upstairs. Her mother had asked her, no not asked, *ordered* Martha to scrub the tub the first thing after getting home from school. Martha was determined to get it done so she could have a text-storm with Jenn about what happened in Gym that morning. But first, chores. They were studying Italian fascism in History, and Martha had slowly come to the belief that her mother would have fit right in with Mussolini.

The tub had been a problem ever since her mother had ordered it last fall. It had looked white and shiny when the workmen installed it but it was just about the hardest thing on earth to keep clean. The pebbly surface of the bottom seemed to grip the dirt, and her mother hated dirt. Martha was beginning to think that her mother had OCD or something. She couldn't stand to see a drop of maple syrup on the counter or a streak of dirt—plain, normal old dirt—in the bathroom. She'd even been rehanging the clothes in Martha's closet so that they looked perfect.

The woman needed a vacation, or a boyfriend. A boyfriend would be more fun. Maybe she could go to his house and straighten the clothes in *his* closets and give Martha a break.

Martha flicked on the bathroom light, sighed deeply at the sight of the dingy tub floor, then ducked down to the cabinet under the sink and found the Comet. Her mother would use only Comet, even though Martha told her the spray-and-wait cleaners worked just as well. She peeled back the label and breathed in. It was like sniffing glue, that first rush.

The pseudo-high lasted about ten seconds, then the smell began to turn her stomach. Martha turned back, rooted under the sink for a scrubbing brush, found one beneath a box of tampons, and turned on the bath tap, soaking the sponge as she sprinkled the Comet liberally across the tub's floor.

Martha heard something, like a muffled shout. She paused for a second, but there was only silence and the wind rattling the electricity wires that attached to the house. She bent down and started to scrub.

She worked the brush vigorously, determined to get the cleaning done fast. The sides were easy but soon she was despairing at the ridges between the tiny bumps. Her triceps muscle began to ache, and the tendons in her wrist soon followed. She switched the brush to the other hand with a sigh.

Damn, damn, damn this tub, she thought.

She heard the sound again. Was someone shouting?

Martha spritzed the tub with water through her hand, spraying it to get the foamy residue, the color of sea foam, down the drain. She paused. That sound again. An echo of an echo.

She turned off the water and cocked her head.

The noise, now clearer. It was a dog barking.

"Oh, that bitch," Martha said out loud. She pulled a towel from the rack, rubbed her hands on it quickly, and walked toward the stairs.

"Rufus?" she called out, her voice charged with concern.

Rufus was her dog and he was afraid of the dark. He literally shook when you put him in the closet for ten seconds. Any longer than that he would turn into a writhing ball of terror. It was *unconscionable* to put him in a dark place. But she heard the dog's muffled barking, which could only mean one thing: her mother had put Rufus in the basement again.

Martha charged down the stairs, whipped around and headed for the kitchen. "Damnherdamnherdamn—"

She slid into the kitchen and stopped. The sound was only slightly louder in here. Still an echo. Still far away. Was Rufus trapped down near the hot water boiler?

"Ruf—" she said, yanking back the basement door. A clammy smell came wafting up toward her, and she peered into the darkness framed by the door. She felt a small tremor of fear. The basement had always repulsed her. It was like some kind of tunnel to the middle of the earth. She was always afraid things were going to crawl up into the darkness through a pipe, giant earthworms or eyeless slugs. She knew it was ridiculous, but it didn't stop the feelings.

The sound again, behind her. The barking wasn't coming from down here. Rufus was outside.

She heard her phone buzz in her schoolbag. Mom, for sure, wanting to check on the progress of the tub. God, that woman.

She went to the back door and opened it and looked out over their enormous, overgrown backyard. Rufus had probably caught himself on the fence again, trying to shimmy underneath the chain link and catch one of the skinny rabbits that lived in the brush. His barking, though, was . . . hysterical. Nonstop.

"Rufus!" she called and clambered down the steps, jogging lightly while she tried to fix his position from the barking, growing louder now. She'd forgotten her coat, and it was cold. The wind swept through the trees and the pines danced in rows down the middle of the yard. She didn't like going back there too far. Once you lost sight of the house, it felt like you were in a forest.

"Rufus?"

The dog was squealing. It must have gotten its head down one of the rabbit holes and scared itself to bits. That had happened before.

Martha listened, scanning the trees. All she saw was brown on brown.

"Rufus?" she said, shakily. Then louder: "Okay, boy, here I come."

Her phone rang again.

"*Not now*, Mom." She wasn't going to give her the satisfaction.

Martha wished she'd brought her coat. The wind was really cold and the branches of the scrub brush would scratch her bare arms as she followed the little trail that wild animals had cut through the yard.

She called out ahead.

"Rufus, calm down, it's me."

Silence.

Then, a little further on: "Where are you, boy?"

The barking went higher, the dog's vocal cords straining in fear, and Martha turned slightly left, pushing through a dry pricker bush. *Oh God, don't let him have stepped on a nail or something. Oh, Ruf—*

She pushed past a shaggy, squat pine tree and there was Rufus, or at least his snout, sticking up from the ground behind some swaying grass and brush. He must have tumbled into a hole, and being the little thing he was, couldn't get out.

Martha blew out a breath in relief. Now to get him out and into the warm house.

Rufus stopped barking and began to whine, his snout shaking.

She dropped to her knees. "Oh, Ruf, you dumb little boy. How'd you get down there?" He was in a hole, all right, behind a screen of wiry branches. He'd probably dug it on one of his expeditions, tearing through the dirt looking for God knows what.

Behind the hole was a thick bush, untrimmed like everything back here, that looked as solid as a green wall. It was too cold to go around to it and search for a way in. Martha pushed her hands into the thin mesh of branches in front of her and brought her head in just behind, trying to get a look at what was holding the dog down.

Across from her, a branch snapped.

Martha, startled, looked up. A man in a red mask was watching her. He pulled on a rope that snaked through his hands and something rose up with a ripping sound.

"Oh, God," Martha cried and then the rope caught her throat.

She gagged, her throat closed tight. The man gave a hard tug on the rope, bending over at the waist like he was swinging a pickax, and Martha's feet lifted in the air and she was twirling.

Twirling. Trees. Then blackness. Then the back of her house. Blackness. Different trees.

Martha tore at the rope digging into her neck. She twisted slowly and on her second turn she saw the man with the red mask tying the end of the rope to a big elm.

Spinning, slowly, around and around, the tops of the trees like one woven crown. There the house through the trees, then the green pines, then the man bending to pick up something. A bowling bag.

Around she spun, the sunlight going dark. Two more turns and the man was standing in front of her. The red mask had holes for his eyes and mouth and it was tight on his face. The man reached out and grasped her leg, stopped her twirling.

Martha gagged and kicked, stars exploding in her peripheral vision like fireworks, but it only made the rope dig deeper into her neck.

"You're about sixteen," a voice said. A memory like a streak of blue light came to her in the spreading darkness, a song they used to sing on the playgrounds when she was a girl.

Hangman, Hangman, what do you see?

Lights sparked in her brain and then faded out. Blue, green . . .

Four little girls, cute as can be.

Brilliant red. With a gasp, the rope around her neck slackened and she fell hard to the ground. She clutched at the cord. It was still tight around her neck. Little specks of hot bright light jabbed at her brain. Her breath rasped in through her throat. She couldn't scream, could barely breathe. The rope was still tight, choking off her oxygen, making her sleepy.

The red mask came closer. He was kneeling down, studying her face. The eyes were in shadow.

Martha spit something up. His eyes crinkled in concern and he wiped the spit from her cheek. He turned and she saw he was unzipping the bowling bag; it was an old one, like from the '50s, pale almost yellow leather with tiny cracks and then red, dirty red leather with a gold zipper. He unzipped it slowly, the two sides of the bag parting like he wanted to make the moment last. Martha stared at the mouth of the bag as it opened. Her mind was dazy.

What was inside the bag?

Her head spun, voices singing dreamily to her.

Hangman, Hangman, where do they go?

She heard the zipper tugging along the steel teeth. The sound stopped and she stared at the black gaping mouth of the bag. The man's hand going in.

Down on the ground,

Where the daffodils grow.

14

Abbie was running toward the spot where she'd left the van. Cops streamed by her in their long yellow rain slickers, like dusters in the Old West. She dialed a number on the phone.

Perelli's number rang three times before he picked it up.

"Yeah?"

"I found something at the escape scene," Abbie said. "I think it comes from Hangman. It's a brochure for Hoyt Lake. It's fresh."

"Hoyt? Where'd he get it?"

"Maybe it was in his papers. Maybe the guard brought it to him. But I think it means he's headed for Buffalo."

Silence.

Abbie took a deep breath. "You need to move the perimeter back to the city limits."

Perelli snorted. "Stop traffic coming in from the west? We can't do it. We've all decided to try and trap him up there."

"Because you didn't know where he was heading. Now we know. Roadblock the three exits downtown. It's the likeliest route."

"Not if he comes in on 33. Or on foot. How do you even know the brochure was his?"

"It came from him. It rained here last night, I just looked it up. The paper is dry. No one else comes up here. He's thinking about Delaware Park."

More silence. Abbie knew she only had to think cop-wise. Perelli had to think of the politics of it, of TV stations, of the risk and reward in a larger picture.

"Fuck, you're right," he said. "We'll put up roadblocks on the three exit ramps off 90. Maybe we can do the same on 33."

Abbie waved to the van driver, thirty feet away, smoking by the side of the road. He tossed the cigarette into a ditch and turned back toward the van, with Abbie following.

"One other thing," she said. "The murdered guard was talking to Flynn in his cell, asking him about the last girl."

"What the hell for?"

"Not sure yet."

"Raymond is on his way up to you. Meet him at the prison."

And he was gone.

15

Abbie heard the Saab before she saw it, the turbo pro-
testing as the driver swung into the parking lot. She swung around.
The Saab came whooshing up from between two parked trucks and the
brakes shrieked as the driver pulled away at the last minute, missing
her thigh by about three feet.

Raymond nodded at her from behind the windshield.

She walked to the driver's door.

"Move over," she said.

"I can drive."

"Not my car you can't. Move over."

Abbie got in and shifted into drive. Gravel pelted against the under-
carriage as she swerved in the parking lot and headed toward the exit.
When they were out on the main road, she took the folded brochure
out of her inside pocket and handed it to Raymond.

"This the brochure?" he said. "Goddamn, you white people know
how to enjoy yourselves. I didn't even know they had rowboats out
there."

"What's Perelli doing?"

Raymond whistled softly.

"In about twenty-five minutes, there's going to be the proverbial ring of blue steel around the city. Checking every car coming in. And now it's your case."

Raymond flashed her a smile. Abbie felt her heart sink.

I'm the last line of defense, Abbie thought. The city was going to lose its collective mind, and she would be the poster girl for the investigation. The quiet life on Elmwood Avenue, her sanctuary, seemed like a tiny black-and-white photo quickly receding into the distance. She thought of Mills, her boyfriend, and wished very badly that he was near her, touchable.

The traffic was knotted in lines on 20A. She jumped off at an exit and tried the back roads. There the red brake lights winked back at her from the dark lanes. Night was falling. She caught sight of a huge looming shape—all spindly arms—and thought for a moment that an airplane was falling out of the sky and pitching nose-first into the earth, but realized it was a wind turbine. The farmers of Wyoming County were finally getting some return for the lonely windswept acres.

So Hangman had turned ghost, evading the search parties that were tramping over the corn stubble and gliding past the barricades of the itchy-fingered troopers and town sheriffs. He was resurrecting his legend, turning his image from a pathetic brain-injured gimp 'that had been nearly forgotten back into what he was. A fiend, a killer of girls.

They were starting to respect him again. Hangman would enjoy that, she thought.

"I need you to check the bank accounts for the dead CO, Carlson," said Abbie. "See if there are any large deposits in the last, say, six months."

"Why?"

"Carlson was asking Hangman about the girls," she said.

Raymond's eyes crinkled up in confusion. "When?"

"Before he escaped."

"*Before* he escaped? That doesn't make any sense."

"Sure it does," Abbie said. "Someone else wants information. And they were willing to pay for it."

Raymond hummed. "Getting any financial info right now is gonna be tough. The family and the union won't like us poking around in his personal life. He's the only hero we have right now, you know."

"I know," Abbie said, braking to avoid a slow truck, then accelerating along the breakdown lane. "But if we find out how he escaped, we might get accomplices. Hangman eluded capture for months. If he has an accomplice, they're likely to be less skilled than he is."

"Point taken," said Raymond.

"Who was the lead on the original Hangman case?"

Raymond stared off. "Shit, who was it? I can see him."

"Big Irish guy?" Abbie said. "Red face?"

Raymond chuckled.

"Kearney, you're bad. But yeah, he was a County product. He's retired now. What the fuck was his name?"

He snapped his fingers. "McGonagle. Charlie McGonagle."

"Is he in the County?"

"Yeah, he hangs out at a cop bar on Seneca, last I heard. Del Sasser's Bar and Grill on Seneca."

Abbie handed him her phone.

"Punch it into Google Maps. I need to talk to him."

16

Opening the door sent a wedge of light across the old linoleum flooring. Faces turned from watching the news station where *Hangman: Trail of Terror* ran across the bottom of the screen in red. Three or four of the faces looked vaguely familiar—her father's old friends, perhaps. She knew what kind of place it would be; the County didn't have retirement homes for cops, it had bars. One reason she left Raymond outside. A young woman would be startling enough, let alone a black man.

The bartender, an older man with a short-sleeve dress shirt above a stained apron fraying at the strings nodded.

"Charlie McGonagle?" Abbie said.

"Over here," said a voice.

He watched her approach, his head tilted back at an angle as if she were poisonous and he didn't want to set her off. He didn't put his hand out. Charlie McGonagle was dressed in a black leather jacket, not the motorcycle type but a blazer, a little too big for him. His hands were big and meaty. He had a scar near his left eye, but his face was striking, memorable even, its cheeks pockmarked with old acne craters, the nose sharp and red. His eyes were blue and sly, his hair was the color of old carrots. Dyed, Abbie thought. His potbelly was under control, but it strained the green knit sweater he was wearing. He had a gold chain around his neck and on it was a miniature gold badge.

Her heartbeat dropped down and she nodded. At first glance, McGonagle looked like a bookie or a boxing promoter or a "friend" who comes to ask you when you're going to have the third installment of that money you got from the local loan shark. There were two kinds of detectives when it came to clothes. There were those like her father who dressed like English squires, who took their first big paycheck when they moved up from patrol and went to the best store in town and ordered brown leather shoes that shone like mirrors, Irish walking hats, checked wool pants, and white oxford shirts, ties with a floral pattern or maybe a conservative stripe. Who had a certain mental image of the detective as the prince of the department and dressed to match it. Maybe guys like her father wanted to put as much distance between themselves and the perps on the street, to emphasize that they represented Society with a capital S, so they dressed like what they imagined the gentry to be. Upper-class swells with a dash of boulevard style.

That was her dad. Dressed to the nines to go see a dead bouncer rotting in an alley down near Chippewa.

Something twinged in Abbie's chest. She'd forgotten for just a second that her dad was dead. It happened to her once or twice a day. She caught her breath; it was like a rib had shifted and brushed her heart.

Then there were the other kind, those like McGonagle, who dressed closer to the men they chased. Who wore leather and gold chains and black, always black. They wanted people to know they were associated with the hard men in the city. A whiff of danger and uncertainty. They *wanted* you to look at them and not know for a tantalizing second or two which side they were on, whether you were about to be greeted with a gruff "Buffalo PD" or smacked in the mouth. Men like McGonagle enjoyed blurring the lines. They were comfortable with evil. Maybe they even saw the humor in the chase, or the futility.

Both types could go bad. She wouldn't judge him. Yet.

"Yeah?" A deep, gruff voice.

"I'm Abbie Kearney from the PD."

The voice came reluctantly, each word parsed, heavy. "I know who you are. I want you to know that I respected your father greatly. I didn't get a chance to tell you that at the funeral."

She didn't want to think about her father or the funeral now, but a surge of warmth pressed through her heart. The County was at its finest when it was mourning, seemingly the only time it was permissible for the Irish to express actual emotion. The elaborate bouquets in the shape of a harp (from the Irish-born) or a shamrock (from those who thought that's what the Irish liked) from people he'd given a break to twenty years before, the burly men taking her hand and pulling her in for an embrace, sobbing while they stroked her hair, the matronly women with voices too choked by emotion to speak. The filmy eyes of old widows whose walks he'd shoveled or whose sons he'd gotten plea-bargained for bashing some guy's head in . . .

If they knew anything, the Irish knew grief.

"Thank you," she said.

"That's the only reason I'm talking to you."

Ah, that's the County I know, thought Abbie. She said, "I thought the fact that there's a serial killer on the run might be a motivator, too."

"I won't joke about that fucking cockroach," McGonagle rasped. "You have to catch him."

"There are probably two thousand people actively looking for him right now. We'll get him."

"Not unless they get very lucky."

Abbie sat on the stool next to McGonagle. "Why do you say that?"

"Because I tracked him. And he was the most careful criminal I ever came across. He loves killing too much to risk it. He has a story written in his head, like a play. You've just seen the opening goddamn act."

"You never had a chance to interview Hangman about the murders, did you?" she said. "He was in the hospital for months, and then went right to trial."

"That's right. But some killers want to get caught. They get sloppy or cocky. None of that happened with him."

"Where do you think he'll go next?"

"Where the girls are," McGonagle said. "The kind of girls he liked. He'll stay in the North."

Abbie made a face. "The North is going to be locked down. I doubt if there'll be a girl out alone."

"There are always girls out alone, Kearney. It's not 1954 anymore."

"He won't look elsewhere, like the County?"

McGonagle chuckled, took a gulp of his amber-colored drink. "Not unless he wants to disappear. There's no one who'd take him in."

"His family might."

"True. But do you think they're not being watched right now? If they buy an extra half-dozen eggs at the Wegmans, it will be noted."

Abbie thought about that.

"What about Sandy, the last girl?" she asked.

"What about her?"

"You never found her, obviously. Do you have any theories of what happened to her?"

"I might. Do you?"

"Three possibilities," she said. "One, Hangman killed her and buried her, but that would be a departure from his MO. Two, he put Sandy somewhere and was going back to her. But the search for her was pretty thorough—"

"It was more than thorough."

"And she was never found," Abbie said. "Or three, he had an accomplice and passed her off to him before he was caught. The accomplice disposed of the body."

"The second man theory," McGonagle said. "I spent many a night on that shit, I can tell ya that."

"And?"

"Hangman didn't have many friends. He had co-workers, acquaintances. But friends? No. And the percentages on serial killers working in tandem is pretty low."

"But it exists. The Hillside Stranglers. Charles Ng and Leonard Lake."

"Yeah, and the Copelands," McGonagle said. "No shit."

"Did Flynn have any girlfriends after he and his wife divorced?"

"A few one-night stands. No one he confided in. And I know because I spoke to all of them."

The bartender came over and tipped his head backward toward Abbie. She shook her head.

"No previous arrests?" she asked McGonagle.

"He had a couple of drunken incidents in late '06," McGonagle said. "That's when he was out of control on Chippewa Street, running around yelling his head off. He was brought in as an EDP, checked out and released."

An emotionally disturbed person, Abbie thought. Was he contemplating his murder spree the year before he started it? Was he trying to drink away the urge to kill?

"Let me ask you something," she said. "Did you ever see money in this case?"

"What do you mean?"

"Money where it shouldn't have been. Anyone have more in their bank account than they should have?"

McGonagle hummed to himself. "Some of the victims' families were pretty fucking well-off. But I never saw anything out of the ordinary. Hangman was paying his bills, getting along. Why do you ask?"

Because I found an $80,000 Corvette owned by a Corrections officer. Who also wore a Panerai watch, which might not be unusual in Miami or New York but is a rare brand in Buffalo. Whose son was in Catholic school instead of the local public school. A CO who made $45,000 a year, tops. In Wyoming County, that could only mean two things: Carlson was dirty or lucky.

"Just a thing that came up," she said, changing the subject. "No one heard the shot when Hangman tried to kill himself?"

"The motel manager did."

"How soon did the first person enter the room?"

McGonagle cleared his throat. "Only two people in the Warsaw that day. One guest at the opposite end and the manager, doing repairs four doors down from Hangman's room. Someone clogged up the toilet by flushing a wig down. The things you remember. The manager heard a shot, but figured it was a hunter or someone taking target practice in the woods. A few minutes later the cop pulls up and finds Hangman."

"You checked his car, of course," Abbie said.

"Of course. We checked all the cars in the motel lot. Hangman liked to transport in his trunk; we found fibers from the second girl's clothes."

"That's not in the file."

"Some things aren't," McGonagle said, taking a drink from his beer. "We had the perp, we had the case locked up. Life moves on."

"But if he rents the room," Abbie said, "he'd want to have her in close proximity, so he can go and get her quick. Unless the killing site was somewhere else."

"Yeah, maybe the room was just for him. You can drive yourself crazy."

You could, she thought. Trying to follow the logic of a regimented serial killer without knowing the scenario in his head could lead you to madness.

"Anything else?" McGonagle rasped.

"Hmm?" Abbie said, distracted by her thoughts. "Oh, there was a notation in one of the tip files, two callers saying that if they found Hangman, he would be a PSK."

"Yeah."

"What does it mean?"

"A daughter of John Kearney doesn't know what PSK means? What is the world—"

"Maybe I blocked it out," Abbie said. "It happens with parts of my childhood."

"You're a funny girl, Abbie. Maybe too funny for your own fucking good."

"What's it mean, Detective?" Abbie said.

"It's an old County term that's used for anyone who, let's say, does something unforgivable. It means that if they found Hangman they wouldn't turn him over to the cops. He'd be a PSK, a public service killing."

Abbie caught her breath, then let it out. "That's lovely."

"Just the neighborhood's way of saying that they'd take care of him."

"And to think I moved away."

His laugh was like an old pebble rattling down a metal chute. "Ah, the old breed. You'll be sorry when we're gone."

Abbie rolled her eyes.

"Anyway, you can't say that anymore," McGonagle said. "But believe me, if Hangman shows his face, he *will* be a PSK."

Abbie pulled the torn brochure out of her pocket and placed it on the bar. The bartender, a toothpick between his lips, set McGonagle's drink next to his empty and watched her unfold it.

"This mean anything to you?" she said.

McGonagle leaned forward and studied the picture in the dim light from the Genesee Beer sign and a dirty amber light near the TV.

"Nothing. What is it?"

"Something I found near the escape scene. It's part of a brochure for the rowboats at Hoyt Lake."

Even in the half-lit bar she could see the blood drain from her face. "One of Sandy Riesen's girlfriends, it was," McGonagle said, staring at the photo.

"What about her?" Abbie asked.

"She told me that Sandy had told her she was going out the day she disappeared. And when the girl asked her where, she said, 'Rowing.'"

A cell phone rattled to life and jittered along the bar toward the rail. McGonagle grabbed it with a large paw. Abbie's phone buzzed in her purse. She reached for it, but saw the pallor of McGonagle's skin deepen as he answered the call. He hitched his right hip up and put the phone back in his pocket, then lowered himself out of the chair.

"Where are you going?" Abbie said.

"He got another one. Dead."

She felt something bloom in her chest like an old sickness.

Abbie swore, closing her eyes. She pulled out her phone; it was Perelli calling. She hit "Talk."

"Where?" she asked.

"Where do you think?" Perelli said.

"The North? *Already?*"

"Get there now." Perelli hung up.

Two men at the other end of the bar got up and turned to leave. One nodded at McGonagle. Abbie felt the air of the old tavern electric with that thing her father had with his cop friends. Irish telepathy.

McGonagle raised two fingers at the bartender, who gave a barely perceptible nod. Then the old cop turned to look at her, his face gray as old asphalt.

"He's come home," he said.

17

She ran to the idling Saab. Rain was falling in a silver mist.

"It's 42 Summers Street," he called as she hopped in. No time to kick Raymond out of the driver's seat.

They were off and racing toward the 90 headed downtown, the skyline a ragged smudge through the rainy windshield.

"What do we know?" Abbie asked.

Not much. A young girl had been found up in a tree. The radio was a jumble of voices, the dispatcher trying to discipline them. They were ten, twelve minutes away.

The rain was a shadow of gray on trees and the facades of houses as Raymond steered the Saab off the ramp and gunned it through downtown Buffalo on the way to the North. When they approached the house of Martha Stoltz, Abbie could already tell the place was going to be a goddamn crime-fighting convention. A quarter-mile before the GPS showed her arriving at the address, the sides of the road had been spotted with squad cars, deputy cars, unmarked cars from four, five different jurisdictions, even fire chiefs and civilian cars with blue lights on the dashboards. And then the sides of the elm-lined avenues became choked with vehicles, bumper-to-bumper. Finally, at the entrance to the Stoltz house itself, the lawn was chock-a-block with cars jack-knifed in crazy directions, a calligraphy of terror. She didn't even have to check the house number. The sidewalk was thronged with men in uniforms, like there was some kind of bizarre costume party spilling out from inside.

At the thought of a trampled crime scene, Abbie felt anger rise in her slowly, like steam knocking up the pipes.

"I know what you're thinking," Raymond said, looking over at her. "But it's Hangman. You're not going to get a pristine scene, Kearney."

Abbie took a deep breath.

You're not solving a crime, she said to herself. You're solving a criminal. There's a difference.

This was the biggest deal to hit Buffalo in years and everyone and their CSI: NY–watching cousin would want in. She'd have to be diplomatic.

You are the lead detective now. Play nice, smile, and *be diplomatic*.

Raymond glided up to the house and she jumped out. The Stoltz home was a Tudor, painted cream with dark red trim, the color of kidney beans. As she hustled up, details ticked in her head: Shades drawn, parents probably not home yet. New landscaped front garden with a curving stone border. Typical North house, money spent tastefully. Third house from the corner, a main street that would have seen plenty of traffic. A risky move to come in from the front. She wondered what was out back, if the yard reached all the way to the groves of Delaware Park, which offered countless entrance points and hiding places.

Abbie grimaced, then slipped through the crowd toward the side of the Stoltzes' house, where a flagstone path led toward the backyard. There were men smoking in the driveway but no perimeter established out here. She prayed someone had choked off the entrance point to the actual location where the body was.

At the side of the house, there was a waist-high wooden fence, literally of the white picket variety. Extension cords snaked out from the side door of the house, one linked to the other, like thin snakes with mice in their gullets. A phosphorous glow in the backyard lit up heavy-limbed trees.

There was a slim uniformed cop with a mustache and wire-rimmed glasses standing in at the gate to the backyard. He had a gaggle of men in front of him and he was talking low, his shoulders hunched forward like he was telling a secret or giving his team a play in the huddle. She didn't recognize him.

He saw her coming, held up a hand to the man he was talking to, and took a step across her path, presenting himself.

"Kearney," he said.

She read the nameplate. "Livingston. You the doorman?"

"Yep. I've kept everyone away from the body, so far."

Raymond came up on her side.

"Good, let's keep it that way," Abbie said to Livingston. "No one in unless I ask for them. The techs on the way?"

"Yep."

She took a deep breath. Forget about going in without preconceptions, she'd have to do a speed investigation first, and then a more in-depth one later if she needed to. She had to shotgun the process, focus everything on two questions: where is Hangman now and where might he be going next?

"What's your feeling, was it him?" Abbie asked Livingston. Normally, she'd ignore the theories of those who got to the scene before her, but now she needed to expand the pool of opinion. She sensed the other cops behind her, trying to catch a word of the conversation, like water building up behind a dam. She didn't want to turn and look, address the crowd. That was Livingston's job.

Rain was speckling the cop's glasses, made him look like he was crying. He grit his teeth and nodded. "I'd say a hundred percent. It's too early for copycats, and she didn't get up there on her own."

"House show any signs of entry?" she asked Livingston.

"Not as far as I can tell. I did a quick walk-through to see if there was anyone alive inside. Front door locked, back open, door ajar. The mother is on her way here. She was in Albany on business, some banking thing."

"Did the mother know any of the earlier victims' families?" Abbie asked.

"None we know of. The girls didn't share the same grammar school and seemingly no social contacts."

"Had she heard Hangman escaped?"

"Oh, yeah. She's the one who called *us*."

"What?" Abbie said.

Livingston looked at Raymond.

"I set up the protocol," Raymond said. "For the schools. We knew it was coming."

Raymond explained. It was late in the afternoon and children were just arriving home from school, unaware that a deranged killer was on the loose. About a quarter of the city's teenagers had failed to pick up their parents' calls. So the police lines were jammed. A call had come to Buffalo 911 forty-five minutes before from a Mrs. Stoltz, who'd been well on her way to hysteria. She'd been calling and texting her daughter for the last hour at five-minute intervals, without any answer. The operator had asked Mrs. Stoltz questions from Raymond's protocol:

How old is your child?

Sixteen.

Where do you live?

The North.

What color is her hair?

Brunette.

"They were getting fifteen hundred calls an hour in dispatch," Raymond said, "with every paranoid mother in the city phoning in, asking if their kids were safe, could we check on them. So they worked out a triage system. Girls first, teenagers between fourteen and sixteen, brunettes, then girls from the North. Narrowing it down. We sent a patrolman out and he saw her up in the tree."

Abbie felt a cold chill. Every cop had an MO they hated. For some, it was shootings, though they were the bread-and-butter of Homicide. Those cops hated to see the holes blown in the human body, the casual destruction of the flesh. A big-bore bullet tended to aerosolize the blood inside the wound, sending it out into the surrounding air in a fine mist that you could still smell when you walked into the murder room. Some Miami cops called it "getting Febrezed."

Other cops got queasy at the sight of a slashing, because deep down they hated knives. It was the way the mind worked, tossing up your gravest fears onto the Technicolor screen inside your head. Suicides in bathtubs, the bodies all swollen up, could stop you eating for a couple of days. Bludgeoning had its detractors, too: the bones turned to jelly, crackling like loose ice cubes as you lifted the body.

Abbie hated hangings. The unnatural angle of the neck, the bulging eyes. They had the hopelessness of the suicide along with the echoes of old-time executions, the ones depicted in crude woodcuts from the Middle Ages. Hanging was how they dispatched witches, when people still believed in spells and hauntings. They were rituals of punishment. They gave her the creeps.

"Why'd the girl go into the backyard?" she asked.

Livingston turned to look at the dark trees looming behind the house. "We found her dog back there, down in a hole, its voice nearly gone. My guess? She was coming out after him."

Hangman dug a hole? He really wanted her outside, Abbie thought.

"Let's do the yard, Raymond," she said. Abbie nodded to Livingston. "You come, too."

"Hold on," Raymond said, turning to survey the crowd. "Mackleveigh," he called.

A fat, silver-haired sergeant turned. He'd been talking to some other cops and his hands were caught in some expansive gesture.

"Yeah?" he said, turning.

Raymond frowned and nodded him over with a quick nip of the head, like *Hangman on the loose and I gotta spell shit out?*

The sergeant came over, walking like John Wayne.

"Mackleveigh, you're the doorman now. No one in until we give the all clear."

The sergeant seemed pleased. "Got it."

Raymond took Abbie's elbow and guided her forward. He unlatched the white picket gate and they walked through, the hum of conversation beginning to fall away. Abbie reached down and grabbed her phone, punching in something as they walked.

"You, too?" Raymond said. "Just like my daughter."

"I'm not texting my BFF, Raymond, I'm seeing how Hangman came in."

Raymond stopped, gave her a quizzical look. "Wha-at?" he said softly, coming around her to look.

Abbie punched up Google Maps and entered the address. The little circle appeared and there was the pictorial map, laid out in tans and yellows. Abbie hit the button on the upper right for the satellite view and the picture changed to black and green, spotted here and there with silver flecks of houses. As Abbie pinched and zoomed, the picture darkened and the houses bloomed bigger.

Abbie stared at the photo, then pointed to the property line near the park. "Here it is. It's a really long backyard, backs up all the way to Delaware. I'll give you three to one that's how he came in. The street would be too risky, even if word was just getting out that he'd escaped."

"Mm-hmmm," said Raymond.

Abbie frowned. "But did he choose the house because of the easy access to the backyard or was he coming here anyway and tailored his approach to what he found?"

Was there a kill list or was it random?

"Chicken or the egg," Raymond said.

They started walking again and turned the corner into the yard, clearing tall bushes that hugged the back of the house.

There was Martha. The girl was up in the trees like a scarecrow, shrouded by low-hanging branches and leaves. In the quiet of the backyard, Abbie could hear the groaning creak of the branch, the rope straining under the unexpected weight of the girl. Her head was pitched forward, her long brunette hair spilling forward and covering most of her face, with the thin line of her center part like a pale centipede. Of her face, only an ashen forehead and one eye, open wide, were visible at thirty feet.

Abbie moved closer.

She was dressed in a low-cut sailor's sweater, the blue and white horizontal stripes that only thin girls wore, because it gave them a little more bulk. The waist of the sweater ringed tightly around her waist, a good fit, but the neck hung away from her breastplate, probably because the angle of the girl's back caused it to hang loose. She wore jeans, expensive ones, expertly faded down the front and with some copper-colored stitching on the seams. Martha had one black ballet flat on, the other down under her bare foot, the nails of that foot recently painted a rather daring shade of crimson. She had long arms, the wrists raw and splotched hanging out of the ends of the sailor shirt, the left hand open, the right one half-shut. There were three red scratches, all aligned, above her left breast, as if something had raked her skin downward. A tall girl, a little gangly, with style making up for the new height that thinned out her frame and probably mortified her, a growth spurt at the worst time . . .

It was like when the boys and the girls played together when Abbie was growing up, swapping toys out of a sense of novelty. By the end of the day, the G.I. Joes ended up in some ridiculous situation—their guns taken out of their hands and parasols jammed into the round little hole that formed their hands, or a pot of tea hanging from the green plastic arm. And the Barbies, in her experience, always ended up dead, hung with a shoestring more often than not, victims in some tribal war game the boys had made up. And what better hostage than a pretty girl, her feet pointed downward and a tangle of mussed-up hair over her face.

That's what Martha looked like. A teenage girl should be jittery with life, but she was so motionless that she seemed to have imparted stillness to the rest of the yard. A magic spell.

"We have to get her down before they start taking pictures from the other houses," Abbie said.

Raymond frowned. "You want me to get some tarps, string them from these branches?"

Abbie took a deep breath. If it was a normal investigation, sure. It would give her a chance to study the body, visualize the crime, sweep every square inch for fabrics and minutiae. But time was short.

"No, give me a few minutes and then we'll have the ME bring her down and take her away. What's the ETA on the mother?"

Raymond glanced at his watch. "An hour."

Abbie looked him in the eye. "Whatever you do, do not let the mom back here before the body comes down. She will never forget it if she sees this. I don't even have to say that, do I?"

Raymond blew out a breath. "No, you sure don't."

"Get the canvass going. Perelli is sending every uniform not patrolling, so we've got the manpower to do the whole neighborhood. Anyone who saw *anything*, I want to talk to."

Abbie strode forward, lifting her feet and bringing them down on the rain-slicked leaves, not wanting to kick them and cover something the killer might have dropped. She came to the hanging tree, saw it was a rough-barked elm, thick. There were no notches or spots in the bark. Martha's foot swayed back and forth at the height of Abbie's chin, a cold wind stirring from the direction of the park.

Abbie took Martha's right hand in hers and studied it. The hand itself smelled strongly of a detergent—she caught the scent without even bringing the hand up—and she could see green crystals smeared along the palm. No marks of a struggle, nothing defensive.

Abbie walked around the body, looking at the rope. It was an old one, thick-twined, the color of olives spotted here and there with something dark like motor oil. Probably stolen from Martha's or a neighbor's garage. It was looped twice over the elm's thickest low branch, then the section on the opposite end of the noose was tied tightly to an elm standing alone about ten feet back of Martha's swaying feet. The rope had blended into the background; it was a dull autumn color, similar to the moss-covered bark of the trees and the dead foliage. Martha, rushing out to rescue her dog, had probably never seen it.

Abbie spotted the hole. It had been freshly dug, the dirt thrown back away from the house in a half-circle, only noticeable if you looked for it, otherwise just looking like dark spots on the leaves covering the ground. The girl had obviously heard the dog barking and been lured out.

Why didn't he keep her for a few days, like the others? Was he over-eager, unable to control himself after staring so long at blank walls? Like a tiger that's been caged for years being set back in its old hunting grounds and spots a deer—a deer so young that it's forgotten or never learned about the predator that once haunted this place.

She walked around the scraggly bushes that partially screened the hole and knelt at its edge. It was about half the size of a manhole cover. The shovel was lying about ten yards away, its long tan wooden handle pointed away from the hole.

"What kind of dog was it?" Abbie asked.

"Schnauzer," Raymond said, coming up behind her. "Why?"

"Think about it. If he was going to dig a hole to the right depth, and not waste precious minutes by going too deep, he'd have seen the dog first. He'd have to get inside the house or at least close enough to get a glimpse. Too deep and you can't hear the dog clearly. Too shallow and it runs away. So either he knew the dog or he got up close to see it."

Raymond frowned. "So, what you're asking is, if he got so close to the house, why not take the girl inside?"

"Exactly. He took his time—and added risk—by luring the dog out and setting up a fairly elaborate death mechanism. Why not just take her in the house, in her room?"

Raymond kicked a leaf. "Because he was crazy to start out with, and then he took a bullet to the brain. You asking for common sense from someone who's double-fucked in the head?"

Abbie glanced at him sideways, a look of disappointment on her face.

"All right, that shit was weak." Raymond sighed. "You say what?"

She turned to stare into the hole. "The things that drove him five years ago still drive him today. The rope and the noose are important to him. He couldn't find a place inside to stage a hanging, and he didn't have time to get her to his usual spot, if that's even available anymore."

"And he wanted her dead very, very badly," Raymond said. "So he took the risk."

Abbie stood up, brushed off the thighs of her slacks. "This is what I need in addition to the regular canvass. Find the bus driver from her school route and ask if he spotted anyone along the way, either standing on the sidewalk or trailing the bus in a car. Get someone to Nardin Academy, see if anyone was lurking at the school, anyone out of the ordinary. See if anyone called the school asking about the girl *before* she got on the bus. Start talking to the neighbors."

Raymond had pulled out a little leather notebook and was taking notes with a small silver pen.

"Wait," Abbie said. "What time is it?"

Raymond turned his wrist: "6:53."

"Good. That's peak jogging time back there in Delaware Park. It's empty during the day, but right about now you get the after-work runners who cover a few miles on the trails and paths. Put two uniforms on the main jogging paths and flag down everyone who comes by. Ask them if they spotted anyone or anything unusual. I want to know what Hangman is wearing and if he's on a bike or using a car, and also, is he alone or accompanied? If he's accompanied, get a description. When you've assigned all that, come back to me."

18

It took Raymond a few minutes to delegate the different tasks. Abbie stood, studying the body and the yard, and thought. Why was Hangman stalking the North? It wasn't where he'd grown up. The houses out here were big, older, well maintained, Tudors next to Victorians next to stone French country mansions. Some of them had names as well as numbers, like The Priory or Lane's End. The air seemed thicker here, the sounds of car doors closing and voices carrying from the next street held in a kind of luxuriant oxygen-rich stillness. Quaint ethnic restaurants, not cheap pizza joints, lined the main strips.

A memory came to her, unbidden. She'd come to this neighborhood when she was doing her alumni interview for Yale, her senior year at Mount Mercy Academy in the County. She remembered the outfit she'd worn: a Donegal tweed skirt and a severe black sweater, gray tights and her favorite black pumps, modest but still an extra inch of height when you really needed it. They were her "I'm Getting Out of Buffalo" clothes. She'd driven herself; she didn't want her father to take her, wanted to start the separation process right then.

For Abbie, the North was lawyers, gated communities, Protestants, schools like the Nardin Academy or Nichols, playing fields full of clean-limbed young people in sweaters playing exotic games like field hockey

or lacrosse, unknown in the football-mad County. When she was growing up, it was a place populated by another race of people—people very
much unlike the hot-blooded, quick-to-anger Celts she lived with.

The Yale alum who interviewed her had been a pediatric surgeon
with thinning hair and bright, perceptive eyes. He'd taken her through
his house, an old Colonial with threadbare Oriental rugs, showing her
photos of his college friends he'd kept for forty years, pictures of him
rowing lightweight crew on the Charles River when they raced Harvard, his junior year abroad "digs" in Prague, reunions full of men in
fitted suits, *another world*. She'd warmed to him in the house, felt like
she was being welcomed into a new family. Walking through the hallways lined in hardwood, she'd said to herself: *Yes, please. I'll take it, all
of it. I can move in right away.*

The surgeon had treated her like an equal, like someone who already
belonged.

And then at the end, he'd said something odd. "You know," he'd
said while they were sitting on his leather couch with a fire roaring in
the overlarge hearth, "when I heard there was a candidate from the
County, I thought it was a mistake. I was sure I was going to open the
door and . . ." His eyes opened wide and his face tightened with an
expression of mock terror. He threw his hands up.

And Abbie had stared at him with hatred. You expected what, she
thought, an animal? Some drunken half-wit? She'd felt a hot surge of
loyalty to the County, maybe for the first time in her life.

But she'd swallowed, counted to three, and kept her poise. "What
did you expect?" she said brightly.

"Who knows!" he cried out, his hands slapping on his thighs.

And then: "I have to tell you," he whispered, his hand on the couch
between them, leaning toward her. "I double-checked with the SAT
people. You know, just in case."

Abbie hadn't understood at first, but felt her heart go icy anyway.
Something in his tone had changed.

"You checked my SATs?" she said.

The surgeon's eyes were fish eyes cold now, deepwater fish eyes.
He'd called about the SATs to make sure she hadn't sent another student to take the test instead of her, a Nardin girl or some Jewish whiz

kid from the rich suburbs. Bitterness flooded every cell of her being. Her SAT scores were her ticket out, the most precious things she possessed.

Abbie had hissed at him to go fuck himself, slammed the door behind her, and run to her father's car, parked at the curb. Then she'd burst into tears. Two weeks later she'd aced the interview for Harvard and never looked back.

Let it go, she thought now. Their kids are dying.

But does the killer feel what I felt toward the North? Envy? Or is it just pure rage?

In the Stoltzes' backyard, McGonagle appeared at her elbow, still dressed in the leather jacket. She flinched. He was like a ghost, an all-knowing ghost.

"What are you doing here?" she asked.

"Everyone calling me with so many fucking questions, thought I'd come answer them face-to-face."

Abbie narrowed her eyes. "That's bullshit."

He laughed. "Okay, so it's bullshit."

"Is there something—"

McGonagle held up both hands in front of him, as if he was trying to calm an angry bear. "I'm here to say that Hangman is an open wound with me and my friends. You understand? He should have died five years ago. We want him caught and put away. Nothing's more important than that. So anything you want, you come to me and ask. Did you hear what I just said? The word I used was *anything*."

Abbie couldn't help herself. Her head tilted back almost luxuriantly and she laughed.

So here it is at last, she thought, the invitation to the shadow force, aka the Murphia, i.e., the Network, that lawless society of cops, ex-cops, and God knew who else that she always knew existed but who everyone denied even hearing about. Cops helping out cops. Favors for the boys. Specializing in everything from parking tickets to, apparently, serial killer investigations. The world her father walked in and was worshipped by.

The Network was what the County had instead of money.

"Aren't you supposed to be wearing a black hood or something, or at least a green silk sash and a shillelagh?" Abbie said.

McGonagle smiled grimly. "Don't fucking flatter yourself. You're not wanted."

"Then what is this?"

McGonagle frowned and gave an almost imperceptible shrug of the shoulders. *It means whatever you want it to mean.* "Let's just call it a seventy-two-hour-pass, huh? You need a phone call made, it will be made. You need a door opened, we'll make sure it's unlocked when you get there. When Hangman is found, the pass expires."

Abbie glowered at him.

"Does the name Stacy Jefferson mean anything to you?"

McGonagle's face went perfectly still.

Stacy Jefferson had been the first female black detective on the force. She'd been a local girl, from the tough-if-not-lethal Bailey section near downtown Buffalo. She'd had two solid parents with city jobs and she'd made it to the Violent Crimes division in 2004, her childhood dream. She'd won awards for her outreach to the black community, but she wasn't window dressing. Abbie had heard she was a detective's detective—a bulldog with skills. Then a year after she joined Violent Crimes, she'd gotten caught driving a Ford Mustang up from South Carolina with a half-kilo of cocaine tucked inside the door panels. She'd fought the charges, claiming a conspiracy. She'd lost badly, been kicked off the force, and was doing serious time downstate.

Abbie had heard the real story from another female detective at a barbecue that summer, after the cop had one too many piña coladas. Stacy Jefferson had caught a case involving the head of the Common Council, Buffalo's city legislature. It was a corruption case: a black council member who'd arranged for his secretary ("the only thing she could dictate," said the drunk detective, "was their sexual positions") to live in one of the new condos being built off of Delaware for needy but worthy families. The white Mercedes convertible parked in the driveway had alerted the secretary's neighbors that she was hardly needy, and a quick check of her work record had turned up her connection to the city council. Jefferson was assigned the folder.

Jefferson had the secretary dead to rights, but the detective knew it was the council member who was pulling the strings. As soon as she started down that road, however, she'd been stonewalled. She couldn't find any paper trail linking the condo to the politician; the wiretap was clean; the secretary teary but silent. So Detective Jefferson had turned to the Network. She'd asked a white detective if he could talk to the donors to the councilman's campaign, see if they could cull one of them from the pack, get them to admit who was funding the secretary's lifestyle. That was her guess: a rich donor paying for the condo. It was then that Jefferson's new boyfriend had turned up in her life, sweet, handsome, and a graduate of the same high school she'd gone to. Jefferson had agreed to drive his car back from South Carolina. She'd been pulled over at the city line for a broken taillight and suddenly Jefferson's badge didn't work for getting off minor traffic offenses. The dope was found by a German shepherd, and the boyfriend turned out to be an ex-con released early from Attica. He disappeared, along with the case against the council member.

"What about her?" McGonagle said.

Abbie laughed and shook her head. "What you're forgetting is that I'm a second-generation cop. Jefferson was naive. I'm not."

"We didn't fuck Stacy Jefferson. Her jailbird boyfriend did."

"Yeah, and I heard he's working for a construction company in South Carolina owned by a Buffalo cop's brother."

McGonagle smiled. "Everyone deserves a second chance, Abbie. This is America."

Abbie studied McGonagle. "How old is she?"

McGonagle squinted and turned his head. She felt, almost as a physical shock, the potential for violence in him. "How old is who?" he growled.

"The teenage girl who got you to offer me the special member's pass for blacks and women."

McGonagle's face seemed frozen. Then he looked away. "You're a fucking witch, you know that?" he whispered.

Abbie waited. After a moment, the retired detective spoke again.

"My granddaughter. Moira. She's fourteen. Red hair, and probably out of Hangman's demo, but who's gonna take a fucking chance with that? There are a lot of Moiras out there."

Out of the corner of her eye, Abbie could tell he was studying her.

"There are things you're going to understand thirty years from now," said McGonagle. "The cases you want to solve before you die. I don't want to go out with Hangman still on the books. He's unfinished business of the worst kind."

Abbie thought about it. "No thanks," she said finally.

McGonagle folded his arms. "I understand where you're coming from, but this isn't the time to be all lily-white about things. We don't have time on this one."

"I'm not being lily-white. And 'we' doesn't exist. This is my investigation."

She heard his voice drop. "Abbie?" he said.

McGonagle had taken a step or two toward her and the streetlight behind him threw his face into shadow. He moved chest-first, like a soldier.

"You'd call the shots," he said. "We can do it clean, too."

"Go home, McGonagle."

He stood there, looming, dark-faced, then turned on his heel and walked away.

19

Abbie saw Raymond leading a band of men—deputies, uniforms, detectives—through the gate, lining up at the back edge of the deck. The faces were turned her way, anxious, noses chapped red from the wind, eyes solemn. They were going to walk the yard looking for clues.

Raymond sidled up to her. "Gonna fuck up my Ferragamos."

Abbie grimaced. "Why'd you dress for a first date anyway?"

Raymond looked at the line of men, still forming up. "You wanna know why black detectives dress nice? Because when one of you ofays sees me running down the street with a gun, I want you to think, 'Was that Billy Dee Williams I just saw?' That way, I don't get shot, see? Cuz who's gonna shoot Billy Dee?"

Abbie smiled. "I want you to go slow back there. Got it?"

Raymond nodded, then turned and called out, "Gentlemen, listen up. We're going shoulder to shoulder . . ."

She moved away, toward Martha. There was something she wanted to look at before the techs arrived. The right hand. It bothered her.

Abbie found a heavy wooden box, an old apple crate with metal corners pounded into the wood, lying upside-down at the base of a moss-covered tree. She hefted it and carried it to the body, swaying in the wind. She put it down at Martha's feet.

Abbie gently held Martha's right arm as she stepped up, to keep the body from twirling away from her. When she was steady on the box, Abbie reached out and felt in the girl's pockets, her fingers swishing inside until she felt the seam at the bottom. The left pocket yielded a Starbucks receipt from 12:14 that afternoon. Abbie pulled out an evidence bag and slipped it inside, then placed the bag in her front pocket. But it was the right hand that intrigued her. She cupped it in hers. The fingers were curled inward. Abbie brought the hand up and looked at the fingernails. A little blood under fingers two and three, possibly some skin cells mixed in—that would be for the techs to decide. Was Martha trying to grab her attacker, was that why the hand was curled like this? The hand had been doing something at the time of death. But what?

The hand was empty. Abbie looked around the ground in a circle. Nothing but dry leaves and broken twigs.

The scratches above Martha's left breast would correspond with the right hand reaching up. Maybe she was clawing at the rope, a natural response to being strangled.

Abbie reached forward and began to pat the body. The sweater was light wool and she could feel Martha's cold skin beneath. Nothing around the back. She moved her hands to the front of the body and felt the outline of a bra. Abbie tried not to look at Martha's eyes.

Her hands descended toward the girl's waist. As it moved down, Abbie felt something clumped under the material. She looked around and saw the line of cops moving toward her. She waited until it passed, the men parting on the left and right of her, and moved on. Then she lifted the hem of the sailor's sweater and placed her hand underneath. Cold flesh. And then, to the right, something else. Paper.

She pulled it out.

A crumpled piece of paper, torn in half. A vein beat in Abbie's neck; she took a deep breath. She stepped off the apple box, the wind ruffling in her ears. The paper was wrinkled, lined in blue like school loose-leaf, no punched holes. The writing was in black ink. She spotted five letters as the wind lifted the top flap of the paper. *ished.*

She took the corner and slowly unfolded it.

Three and a half lines in a haggard scrawl.

This life is so terrible.

Darkness is everywhere. The evil-doers are not punished.

They are not your children.

I live where

The last line was cut off.

Abbie stood, her mouth slightly open. Then she took her phone out and took a photograph of the note.

Raymond had spotted her. He came walking back as the line of men trudged through the undergrowth. "Two Frito-Lay bags and some empty Jack Daniel's wine cooler bottles so far. Not much of a party."

Abbie handed him the note. "I found this under her sweater. Maybe Hangman left it there, or maybe she snatched it from him."

Raymond brought the note up and read the contents, then whistled.

"Bring it to the lab," Abbie said. "First test it for fingerprints; if Hangman's getting any help, maybe they left their prints on this. Then fibers. See if they can tell us what he was wearing, maybe he kept the note in his pocket. Then handwriting. Tell them I want a comparison with anything they have on Marcus Flynn from the original cases. Also, scan it for impressions from writing that was done on pages above this one, if it came from a notebook full of these pages. Got it?"

No humor now. Raymond nodded and walked off.

They are not your children. Something tugged at her memory, like the world's tiniest fish nibbling on the world's thinnest line. So faint.

And, even more tantalizing, *I live where*

What in God's name did it mean?

20

Abbie waited at the gate for the results of the neighborhood canvass to come in. Cops milled around in the side yard, sneaking glances at her face, and looking away quickly when she locked eyes with them.

Someone talk to me. Please. Give me something.

Her phone rang. It was Perelli, calling with the financial info on Carlson, the dead CO that Hangman had killed in his escape. Carlson didn't show any large deposits into his bank account, just a biweekly payment of $1,843 from New York State, his net wages. He moonlighted on occasion at events and bars in Buffalo; he'd even done security for a few R&B and hip-hop acts that had come through town and didn't want to pay to fly their bodyguards from New York or L.A. It was a grand here and a grand there. Small money.

There were regular withdrawals from Geico insurance and payments toward his mortgage, which he'd refinanced in 2011. He paid most of his credit cards off in full every month and had only a couple of thousand dollars on a MasterCard that was being carried forward. In late 2010, Carlson had been sanctioned by the courts for not paying alimony to his wife, one Rita-Claire Montcrief, now a resident of Atlanta, but after having his wages garnished for six months, he'd come up with the outstanding balance in full and hadn't missed a payment since.

It was all very normal. But it didn't answer the question: how does a Corrections officer afford a fully loaded Corvette and a Panerai watch? She told Perelli to find out where Carlson had bought the Corvette and see how he'd paid for it. Perelli had grumbled about remembering who outranked whom in this department, but she reminded him that he was only passing on her requests to someone who did the actual work, so to stop bellyaching. He snorted, then filled her in on what Buffalo PD was doing.

Marcus Flynn's last residence, an apartment in a slowly decaying block off Niagara Street, was being staked out. The houses of the detectives who'd worked the case were being watched, in case Hangman wanted to exact revenge. Search teams were being assembled to sweep the city, checking backyards, abandoned buildings, Dumpsters, vacant businesses, and storage sheds for any sign of the killer. Detectives were being given night-vision goggles and thermal-imaging equipment and would be assigned to the North. All burglaries and break-ins were being treated as possibly Hangman-connected unless proven otherwise; no clothing had been reported stolen, but it was impossible for Perelli to believe that the killer was still wearing his orange prison jumpsuit. And Marcus Flynn's most recent photo, from Auburn, was being shown on local TV, as memories had faded and it was possible he could walk around without being recognized.

Despite all that, they hadn't gotten one verified sighting of the murderer.

"What about potential victims?" Abbie asked Perelli.

"We've told parents of teenage girls not to let their kids out alone under any circumstances," he answered. "We've called all the high schools and made sure they instituted a pickup policy where every girl has to be seen getting into their parents' cars. No walk-homes alone. No buses. Their parents' cars only."

"That's good," she said. "Restrict his opportunities. Maybe it'll flush him out."

"We've got extra patrols at the malls. Teenage girls tend to congregate there, though what kind of mongrel would let their daughter go shopping today, I don't know. And you'll never believe what the big seller at the Galleria is right now."

"What?" asked Abbie.

"Hair dye. Mostly blond, a few reds."

Abbie said, "Huh." She'd never thought of that, but it was clever. "Who's buying it, mothers or daughters?"

"Mostly mothers. Dyeing their kids' hair."

"I'd do it, if it was my daughter."

Perelli's voice cracked with exhaustion. "Abbie, give me something. Soon."

Abbie felt a wave of heat across her vision. "It's a five-year-old case, and I've been working it for six hours, Chief. Do you mind?"

"All right. Just do what you have to do."

"How about martial law?"

Perelli laughed grimly. "I've thought about it. Listen, we checked on purchases of red masks. A few little stores still haven't checked in, but we're getting close to Halloween and I've got a few hundred devil and monster masks with some red on them, sold at Walmart and other places. Most people paid cash. Tracing the buyers just ain't gonna work."

Abbie rubbed the back of her neck. The muscles were starting to tighten, the first sign of a knockdown headache. "It was a long shot."

"Anything else?" asked Perelli.

"One other thing. In the main case file, there's a reference to folder 3CW. It's missing. Do you know what was in there?"

Perelli sighed.

"No idea. Take it up with McGonagle." He hung up.

21

Abbie saw the cops up and down the block fanning out, knocking on doors, chatting with people on their porches. One elderly woman three doors down and across the street had her hand to her mouth and Abbie saw her jaw shaking with sobs.

She found Dr. Lipschitz's card and called him. Voicemail after five rings. She left a message, saying that something urgent had come up and could he call her immediately please.

Abbie kept the phone out, clicked on "Photos," and brought the screen close. She studied the note she'd found on Martha's body. Except for "They are not your children," the note seemed straightforward. Hangman was imprisoned, his life hellish. He was killing "the evil-doers" out of a deep black despair.

But who was Hangman talking *to* in the note? Was he so insane that he believed that killing the girls was really getting revenge on evildoers? Perhaps he was truly schizophrenic after all, and the "your" he referred to in the note was actually a voice in his head?

The phone buzzed in her hand, and she snapped up the call after the first ring. Lipschitz.

"You've seen the news?" she said.

"Yes," Lipschitz said.

"We found a note at the scene."

"Bring it to me," he said quickly. "I'm at 26 Spring Street."

A few minutes away.

"I'll be there in five," she said.

Twenty-six Spring was a small old wood-frame house dwarfed by rust-colored office buildings on both sides. Light gray paint with pearl white trim. She dashed up the steps and found him waiting for her in the doorway.

"Come in," he said.

Abbie walked into the front room, which he'd made into a private office—gray-and-white wallpaper, two leather chairs and a desk, a bit messy—and fished for her phone.

"How old was the girl?" Lipschitz said grimly.

"Sixteen."

He grunted. "This is terrible. In so many ways."

Abbie hit the menu button on her phone and tocked the photo button. "Mostly one. Another dead girl."

Lipschitz shook his head. "I have eight patients at Auburn, and there are six thousand in the New York State system alone. I have to think of them as well. Things will get worse not just for Marcus, but for every psychiatric inmate in the system. Funds will be cut in the goddamn legislature, I guarantee you, and guards will be that much quicker with their truncheons. My drug budget is so low I can barely afford Post-its, but it will go lower, believe me. It's a disaster for all of us."

The note came looming up. She handed the phone to the psychiatrist. "The sooner we catch him, the less damage he does."

Lipschitz sighed. He walked quickly to his desk, laid the phone down, and stared at it, rubbing his head.

"*This life is so terrible,*" he read. "*Darkness is everywhere. The evil-does are not punished. They are not your children. I live where . . .*"

Lipschitz's face flushed red.

"I can't tell you much. It's depressive talking, fairly garden-variety. Darkness is a common theme among depressives, and you have to remember that the way they keep prisoners, with twenty-three hours of artificial light, doesn't help. I didn't expect this; I thought he would be more exuberant, perhaps more manic. Marcus always showed signs of a latent manic-depressive cycle."

"What about 'They are not your children'?" Abbie asked.

Lipschitz rubbed his temple with his hand. He nodded, as if to say, *I know, I know.*

"Something about that line . . ." Abbie said. "It connects to another part of the case. At least I think it's another part of the case. There's something familiar."

Lipschitz snorted in frustration. "He never talked about the relationship between the children and their parents. It's out of the blue."

Abbie frowned. "Who are the evil-doers?"

"Don't jump to conclusions, don't assume that he's seeing the *girls* as evil. He might not be referencing them."

Abbie's brow crinkled. "Then who?"

"He wouldn't tell me. God knows what he'd imagined to justify the killings. But Marcus . . ."

Lipschitz shook his head.

"Doctor?" Abbie said impatiently.

"It sounds so grotesque," Lipschitz said. He took a deep breath, his voice rising: "He claimed he was saving the girls. From something worse than death."

"What is worse than death?"

The psychiatrist slumped in his chair, staring bleakly at the phone. It buzzed.

He looked at the text, then handed it to her.

"You'd better go," he said.

It was from Raymond. *Come now.*

Night had fully fallen by the time she got back to the house—9:34, the Saab's clock read. She pulled up in front, tires squealing on the rain-slicked leaves that coated the gutters. Raymond, standing on the front porch, spotted the Saab and hurried over, ducking raindrops.

"Anything?" she said.

Raymond leaned his arm on the door. "One of the uniforms got a hit on a neighbor. But it's a weird one."

"What do you mean?"

"I mean it's *weird*, Kearney. The house is four down on the side street due west, Oakland, which means her yard backs up on the back corner of the dead girl's lot. Her name is Melissa Chopin. Now get this: the woman says she has information, but she'll only talk to the lead detective. She's not even saying if she saw something, and she sure as hell won't say *what* she saw. She's high-strung, you know, talking about *preconditions*."

Abbie screwed up her face. "Sounds like a lawyer."

"Bingo."

Abbie felt her pulse quicken. Lawyer or no lawyer, the possibility of an eyewitness had perked her up immediately. "I'll talk to her. What are the preconditions?"

"You have to enter and leave through the backyard; Chopin doesn't want any of the neighbors seeing a detective coming through her front door. If a squaddie pulls up in front, even an unmarked, she's gone. She says she'll only give this information once, and then the family will be unavailable 'from that point forward.' You believe this shit?"

"That we can get around. But why?"

Raymond rolled his shoulders like a boxer loosening up for the fight.

"Whatever they saw over there scared the living hell out of 'em. They're packing up as we speak, according to the uniform, and they ain't leaving a forwarding address. She'll talk to you in thirty minutes. You got one shot, Kearney."

22

Abbie was famished; she hadn't eaten since breakfast, and she could feel her blood sugar falling off a cliff. She needed to eat something before talking to the mystery woman. There was a pub at the corner of the Stoltzes' block that she'd spotted coming in. Abbie hurried there at a half-trot.

The place was bustling, men in wool coats at the bar crouched over burgers and fries, harried waiters rushing to and fro with a please-don't-speak-to-me look on their faces, families with extra chairs pulled in around the small round tables, and the sound of jingling silverware mixing with the TV news turned up loud. Abbie noticed four or five parties who'd eaten and had the dishes cleared but were huddling over post-dinner drinks, dawdling, trying not to be noticed. They don't want to go home, she thought.

People are hunkering down. Better than sitting at home jumping at every creak from the tree in the backyard and every moan of the wind.

A small black-edged TV blared from above the bar. Abbie took one of the few available seats, a rotating leather stool with metal studs along the edges and listened to the broadcast, waiting for the bartender to finish pouring a series of cocktails.

The news channels were in a frenzy, with text running along the bottom of the screen and mobile news vans out on the roads interviewing housewives and business owners along the "Trail of Terror"—the westward line from the Auburn prison to the center of Buffalo. The *Trail of Terror* again, remembering the TV at the bar where she'd found McGonagle. My God, thought Abbie. It's not a goddamn hurricane.

The reporter was a striking young black woman with bright red lipstick and a long camel-hair coat, holding the microphone in a hand covered with a thin leather glove. She was only a few blocks away, on Bryant Street in the North, where the red comet of the Trail of Terror ended. Her eyes were bright with excitement. "The escape of Marcus Flynn, the killer known as Hangman, revives haunting memories for many Western New Yorkers," she intoned to the camera. "They recall the nights of fear that gripped this city in 2007 when four young girls disappeared off the streets. Many people I've spoken to talk about staying awake all night, tying pop bottles to strings and attaching them to their front door, as a kind of early warning alarm in case Hangman tried to enter their houses. Teenagers remember spending weeks inside their houses, forbidden to go anywhere. Cops worked double and triple shifts, some falling asleep in their cars and not showering for days on end. But those were the lucky ones. For those who weren't so lucky, like the families of the victims, the memories are even darker."

Don't do this, Abbie thought. Don't ambush the dead girls' families and ask them how they're feeling.

Abbie caught the bartender's eye and quickly ordered a turkey club and a Diet Coke to go.

Somehow the TV reporter had found the father of Maggie Myeong, the third victim. He hadn't been ambushed, though. Walter was standing next to her, his hands by his side.

The noise dropped an octave. Abbie glanced down the bar. Most people had turned to the TV.

Walter Myeong was a short Asian man with a long, broad, saturnine face. Abbie would have put him in his late fifties, but in her experience, grief can age you fast. He had thinning black hair and long sideburns going gray at the bottom. He was dressed in a black overcoat and white striped shirt and striped red tie. The only people in Buffalo who wore ties when they didn't have to were people in the North.

The reporter asked him how he was holding up.

Myeong's eyes were small and nervous, darting here and there, first looking into the camera and then away. "My family is doing as well as they can. There's nothing Marcus Flynn can do to us that he hasn't done already. We do want to know how he got away and why we weren't informed that he was being moved from Auburn."

"You weren't notified?"

"No. No phone call." A vague clunkiness with the English language.

He turned to look into the camera, squinting at the bright light. His gaze was odd, lost, almost childlike.

The reporter pulled back the microphone. "Mr. Myeong, there have always been rumors that the fourth victim, Sandy Riesen, might still be alive. As painful as those are, do you think there's any chance that Mr. Flynn might now lead authorities to where . . . ?" She paused.

"To her body, you mean," he said softly.

She felt the people around her take a half-breath.

"You believe Sandy is dead?" the reporter asked. My God, what a she-wolf, Abbie thought.

"Of course she's fucking dead," said an old woman next to Abbie who was wearing a faded green raincoat.

"I don't know," said Myeong. "But I can tell you one thing. I don't want Mr. Flynn killed. If this escape proves anything, it shows that his cognitive abilities, they are returning. Perhaps the memory, too. We've never believed that he was unable to remember what he did to our daughter."

"Why does he want him taken alive?" the bartender said, shaking his head. "I hope they shoot Hangman like a rabid dog."

The older woman worked over a plate of chicken wings and spoke between bites.

"If she was your girl, Jack, you'd do just what he's doing. He wants to know details, and so would you."

The bartender frowned and looked down at the ground, thinking. Abbie looked along the bar at the rapt faces, their skin shining slightly in the glow of the TV. The city was just now reentering the tragedy that Hangman had visited upon them, fitting back into the paranoia that only a killer on the loose can create. But Walter Myeong had never left it.

Abbie's eyes went back to the TV.

"—the prison was responsible?" the reporter asked. "Do you think the authorities at Auburn were negligent in letting him escape?"

"I can't say for sure," Myeong said tiredly. He turned to the camera. "But when they catch him again, I want him interrogated about my daughter and the others. To find out the truth once and for all. I want to emphasize this. We want Hangman captured alive. A dead man won't do anything to ease my family's pain."

Abbie studied Myeong's face. Why was he insisting on Hangman being captured alive? Either Myeong was a Christian to the marrow of his bones or he really believed that the killer was withholding information.

"That poor man," whispered the old woman to Abbie, bumping her elbow gently. "Can you just imagine?"

"There you have it," the reporter said, turning back toward the camera. Abbie's eyes lingered on the father of the dead girl. He looked down at the ground, but at the last moment he tilted his chin up and stared into the camera, his eyes filled with pain. And just before it cut away to the anchor, Abbie swore she saw Walter Myeong nod.

She wanted to ask the bartender to rewind the video, but it was live and the crowd would have probably lynched her.

"I know where that girl is," said the old woman.

The bartender eyed her.

"Margaret," he said, and there was a warning in the gravelly voice. He was carrying a turkey club stacked high on a thick white plate. He set it in front of Abbie.

"Actually," Abbie said, "it's to go."

The bartender's eyebrows tilted up. He left the plate on the bar. "You sure about that?" he said, leaning in. "We're going to stay open as long as it takes. Dollar shots at midnight."

Abbie smiled. Was it a pass? Or a warning?

"I'm sure," she said.

He shook his head once and took the plate back.

The old woman next to her. "I wouldn't go out there," she said, "for a million fucking dollars."

Abbie turned to her.

"I get paid to," she said. "Where do you think Sandy is?"

The woman's eyes were milky and she studied Abbie's face, as if trying to recognize her.

"Don't be telling stories, Margaret," the bartender said as he wrapped up Abbie's order.

Abbie looked to the old woman. She seemed fearful, but there was a glint of defiance in her eyes.

"Where?" Abbie said.

"Hoyt," the old woman said softly.

"Hoyt Lake?" Abbie said, feeling a thrill of fear. "Why there?"

The bartender set a plastic bag on the counter. "She's senile, don't listen—"

"Shush," Abbie said. "Why Hoyt?"

The old woman looked at her hands, studying them. Then she looked up again.

"Don't you know the story of the Madeleines?"

"No," said Abbie. "I don't."

The old woman smiled.

"It's happened here before."

"Horseshit," said the bartender.

"It's happened," said the woman.

That's all the woman would say.

23

Abbie ate half the sandwich and a few French fries in her car before hurrying back to the Stoltzes' backyard. Two thickset men in forest green windbreakers, the one turned away from her with "Erie County Medical Examiner" written on the back, were wheeling a gurney ahead of her, and the wheels kept getting stuck in the mud.

"Pick it up, gentlemen," she said.

The man turned. "Excuse me?"

"I said, *pick it up*. People are getting home and I don't want the whole neighborhood seeing that poor girl hung up in the tree."

The far worker—mustache, flushed cheeks, flannel under the windbreaker—made a face.

"I don't work for you, lady."

Abbie stopped. "If you make me do your job, you're not going to have one tomorrow. Pick . . . . it . . . up."

They picked it up.

Raymond came hustling up behind her and pointed his left arm straight out. He was wearing a trench coat now—fitted to his lean body—and the arm was spattered with rain.

"Second house from the back. It's got a vinyl fence, tan and white, only one over there. There's a gate you can go through. She said it'd be unlocked."

"Got it," Abbie said.

"One more thing. Chopin doesn't want her name on any radio calls or on reports. Like I said, preconditions. Shit, you might find Johnnie Cochran waiting for you when they open the door."

Abbie made a face and headed toward the gate. She could only see the second story of the house over the level top of the newish fence. She half-ran through the layers of leaves and twigs and reached the gate a little out of breath. The latch was a lift-and-pull device in black steel. She lifted it and the gate drifted toward her.

The yard was neat. A trampoline cloaked in black netting sat at the center, and there was a slide-and-swing set dead center, the colors on the plastic beginning to fade from exposure to Buffalo winters.

Young kids, Abbie thought. I'll bet that's why we're going through the cloak-and-dagger routine. She hurried around the swing set and glanced at the house.

A woman stood behind the gray-green glass of a set of French doors, her arms folded tight over her chest. She was watching Abbie, the first floor in darkness behind her. Her face was ghostly, unreadable behind the shimmering reflection of the lights on the glass.

The door moaned as she approached and there was Mrs. Chopin, dressed in a charcoal pantsuit, an ivory silk shirt at the neck, holding it open.

"Mrs. Chopin?"

"Yes. Detective Kearney?"

"That's right. May I come in?"

Melissa Chopin hesitated. Her lips were pressed so tight that they were nearly white. "I guess."

Abbie nodded and entered the darkened dining room. The floor was hardwood, broad planks, expensive. The dining set was sleek metal with thin-backed leather chairs. There were soft footsteps from the floor above.

"My husband is upstairs packing," Chopin said, her arms still crossed over her chest. "The patrolman told you about our conditions for talking?"

"Yes, I wanted to—"

"They're nonnegotiable. Let's get that straight from the beginning."

"If I can save a girl's life, do they become negotiable? You have a child. I would hope they would."

Vertical lines at the corner of the woman's mouth. A woman with barely an ounce of fat on her. Burned away in vitality or anxiety or whatever.

"That's a very manipulative way of putting things."

"No, that's my job," Abbie replied. "But tell me what happened and I'll see what I can do."

The woman was tight roping the line between civility and barely controlled hysteria. Abbie wanted to keep her this side of the border for as long as she could, but she couldn't let witnesses dictate the terms of the interview.

The woman nodded once and turned toward the dining table. Chopin pulled a chair back and sat down, putting her head in her hands. Abbie went around the other side and slipped into the chair facing her.

"My son," Chopin said from inside her cupped hands, and that was all for a few seconds.

"Yes?" Abbie said.

Chopin turned her head up and her eyes drilled down into Abbie's. "He stayed home sick today. Croup or something that sounded like it. I had meetings downtown, I couldn't stay with him. Maria, our maid, was baby-sitting."

Abbie nodded. She wouldn't even ask the boy's name. That would set the woman off like a pin pulled from a grenade. "How old is your son?"

Chopin opened her mouth, then closed it. "Seven," she whispered. "Only seven."

"Go on."

"He was upstairs in bed, for most of the day. I was checking in about every other hour."

I'm a good mother, Chopin's body English practically screamed. But I wasn't here. How could I not be here?

"He got a little restless, so he got out of bed to play."

"Upstairs in his bedroom?" Abbie prodded gently.

Tiny nod.

"Does his bedroom look out over your backyard?" she asked.

Same again.

Twenty yards, Abbie had counted off on her walk over, counting one stride per yard. Add in another ten yards for the Chopins' backyard. The boy had been thirty yards away from Hangman putting Martha Stoltz up in the tree.

"Did he see something at the Stoltzes'?"

"Ye-es."

"Can I talk to him about it?"

"No."

Abbie frowned. "Mrs. Chopin, I know what you're thinking. Your boy saw something horrible and, what's worse, you weren't here to explain it to him . . ."

"He thinks it was Halloween."

"Excuse me?"

"My son, Ja—" She stopped. "He loves Halloween. He's had his costume for a month now. He's going as Ben 10."

"Okay," Abbie said. "I don't want to hurry you, but every second helps us—"

"He thinks everyone loves Halloween as much as he does. That's what he believes. So he thinks what he saw was someone practicing for it."

"What did he see?"

"A man in a red mask walking through the leaves. He was carrying a bag. J-j—"

"Let's call him John," Abbie said.

The woman nodded gratefully. She listened for a moment to the sounds of movement upstairs, her face lost in thought. Then she looked at Abbie. "John called it his medical bag. He thought the man was playing Dr. Frankenstein. And he watched. He watched very closely."

"Because he loves Halloween."

"That's right."

"He saw the man dig a hole?" asked Abbie.

"Dig a hole? No. He didn't mention that. He saw the man waiting in the trees and there was a rope tied in the tree above him."

So the hole was already dug, and little Johnny witnessed what happened afterward.

"And the girl came out of the house?"

"I know the family. I never much liked them, but I know the mother over there and Martha was a nice girl."

Abbie nodded soothingly. "So Martha came out," she said again.

Melissa Chopin closed her eyes and made a hissing noise between her teeth. When she looked at Abbie, the veins in her eyes had turned crimson. She brought her hand up to her mouth and pressed her fingers to her lips.

"Ma'am?" Abbie said.

"Yes. And the man played a trick on her, is how John put it. He caught her in the noose and pulled her up. He held her there for a few seconds and then he let the rope out and . . ."

After twenty seconds of oxygen, the brain is stunned, Abbie thought. Martha was basically incapacitated.

"He talked to the girl. She was grabbing at the rope. The masked man turned away and got his bag. The girl . . ."

Abbie waited.

"She was dancing on her toes. That's what J-j— . . . John said. And then the man pulled something out of the bag."

"What was it?"

"A book. And a mask. That's when he got scared."

"I'll bet."

Abbie frowned.

"Your boy didn't call for the baby-sitter, Maria? Did she witness any of this?"

A fast shake of the head. "No, that little bitch didn't see a thing. That's why I just fired her."

"What did Hangman do with the mask?" Abbie said.

"He put it on Martha. Then the man opened the book and showed her a page."

The note, Abbie thought. It was ripped out of a book. It was part of the ritual, not meant to be seen by us.

"The man made her read it," Chopin said.

"How does your son know that? He was thirty—"

"He opened the window. He wanted to hear what Dr. Frankenstein said to the girl. He thought . . . he compared it to his school play. They're doing a Halloween one this year. They're calling it *Spooks and . . .*"

Abbie touched her arm, calling her back. "Ms. Chopin, what did he hear?"

Mrs. Chopin took a deep breath.

"He heard the girl scream and say *No, no, no.* And he began to pull the rope higher. So then Martha looked at the page and she started to read. He let her down long enough to finish."

"What did Martha say? Did he remember anything?"

"Yes."

"Did he hear the part about 'I live'?"

The woman looked at Abbie sharply. "That was the last thing she said. How did you know that?"

"It doesn't matter. But that's the part I'm most interested in. Did he hear it?"

"Yes."

Chopin looked down at the paper that was molded to the inside of her palm. "Martha said, 'I live where *the kings abide.*'"

What kings, Abbie thought.

"He's sure about that?" Abbie asked.

She nodded, a snap of the chin down.

"And he knows the word *abide*?"

"We sounded it out. He's sure that's what she said. He's very smart, Detective." The woman sucked in a breath, her arms still crossed over her chest. "And that's when he pulled the rope up and she dropped the paper. She started jerking on the end of that rope. My son knew it wasn't pretend anymore."

There was a bump from upstairs, something being moved. Maybe a suitcase being brought down hurriedly.

The woman looked up at the ceiling, her skin as pale as a ghost's. "John started to scream," Chopin said. Her eyes dropped and met Abbie's.

"And that's when Hangman spotted him."

I'd be leaving, too, thought Abbie.

Abbie stood on the Stoltzes' porch, waiting for Raymond to report back on the final canvass. *I live where the kings abide*, she thought. What the hell does it mean? Has Buffalo ever had kings living here? She pulled out her phone, clicked over to the web and Googled the phrase.

There was a link to the Santa Rosa Cycling Club in somewhere called King's Ridge. A review of a movie called *Riding the Bullet*, based on a Stephen King story. "When a man finds out his mother is dying and tries to hitchhike a ride to the hospital," the plot summary read, "he's picked up by a stranger with a deadly secret." Abbie moved on to a long essay on Jesus, King of Kings, riding a donkey into Jerusalem. Did "the kings" in the note have something to do with Christianity? Perhaps it referred to a church or convent in the area?

Abbie frowned. The boy who'd watched Hangman said "where the *kings* abide." Kings plural.

She clicked on the next page of Google results. Blog posts on what kind of transport kings used throughout history. Then cycling sites and fantasy book reviews. It's possible there was a clue buried here, but if Hangman was obsessed with a Tolkien novel, it did her no good anyway. She needed an actual physical location where Hangman might be hiding.

She tried adding "Buffalo" to the search terms and came up with a Wikipedia page on the Buffalo Soldiers and some articles on the L.A. Kings hockey team. Dead ends, all of them, as far as she could tell, after clicking through for a few minutes.

Abbie looked up. Damn it. I've eavesdropped on the ritual that Hangman uses with the girls he kills and we still can't get a fix on him.

Where do kings abide?

Something's missing. Abbie thought back to the NPR show she'd been half-listening to in her garden when the alert came in on Hangman's escape. The one on the Higgs boson and dark matter. One of the guests had said that dark matter could change the appearance of things in the visible world. It slowed certain molecules as they zipped through the universe, brought their speed down enough so that humans could see them. But other molecules, it let them go past, undetectable. There were entire dimensions of the universe that we couldn't perceive because the nature of dark matter cloaked them.

Some dark *thing* is warping the facts of the case, Abbie thought, distorting the shape of the crimes, tearing things apart and reordering them in false shapes. I'm only seeing what it allows me to see.

She quickly tabulated a list in her mind. One or more of these things is not what they seem:

The A on Maggie Myeong's hand.

The way Flynn escaped.

Carlson's Corvette.

Carlson whispering to Flynn in his cell.

The Madeleines, whatever that was.

The phrase, *where the kings abide.*

If Abbie could remove the dark matter, or accurately account for it, the clues would line up and she would see Hangman clearly. *I would know his mind and see where he's going.*

It was 1:16 a.m. No other sightings were coming in. Her eyes were drooping. She checked in with Raymond a final time, telling him what Mrs. Chopin had said, then headed home to sleep.

"Tomorrow morning," she said to Raymond. "Meet me at the top of City Hall, 7:30."

"You jumping," he said, "or throwing someone off?"

24

The next morning, after a chocolate croissant and a cup of Earl Grey from the boutique bakery two blocks down, Abbie headed to Police HQ. She took the stairs to the second floor and grabbed a pair of old Zeiss binoculars from the Property Desk, strung the case's leather strap over her shoulder, then hustled back down, the battered case banging against her thigh. Exiting onto Franklin Street, Abbie rounded the corner and Niagara Square, resplendent and near empty in the morning light, across from her. On the other side of the square was City Hall, thirty-two stories high. In three minutes she was across the square and into the lobby, with its Art Deco murals. She got on the elevator and hit the button for 25.

The old, tiny elevator, which smelled of wood polish, climbed steadily, shaking slightly. A woman got on at 14 pushing a cart filled with folders, got off at 20. The elevator resumed its climb. At 25, it eased to a stop and she pushed the door open.

A sign said "Windows on Buffalo" and pointed to a stairway. Abbie pushed through the door, ran up the three flights of stairs, and found herself on the open-air observation deck, facing downtown. She made her way around the narrow parapet to the left, her hand on the stone half-wall that kept people from falling down into Niagara Square. She took out the binoculars, set the case down on the cement floor, then began scanning the streets below, block by block.

A few minutes later, Raymond appeared behind her. He was wearing a black blazer and tan slacks, his buckle shoes polished to a high gloss.

"What's the idea?" he said.

"Looking for castles," she said.

Raymond hummed.

"*Where the kings abide*. Ain't no castles out there, Kearney. You know that. Shit, this is Buffalo."

Nevertheless. She just wanted to see Hangman's territory, the groves and lanes and woods he hunted in. To survey it.

Abbie brought the glasses up again. North Buffalo came swinging into view, the lone line of Elmwood Avenue straight ahead. Delaware running parallel to the right.

"He's here somewhere," she said. "But he's getting help."

"I'm starting to believe you," Raymond said.

Abbie glanced over. Raymond sighed and looked away.

"You were right about the guard," said Raymond. "He paid cash on the Corvette."

"*Cash?*" Abbie said.

"Got the Goodyear Eagle performance tires, too. Eighty-two grand plus."

Abbie whistled softly, turning her gaze back to the binoculars. She swept the little side streets, the stone houses looking like another world from up here. "That's serious money."

"True, but prisons are dirty places, Kearney. He could have been bringing in meth for prisoners, turning the other way for conjugal visits that weren't on the schedule. You know what I mean."

"I *know* that. I asked about that when I was up there. No one had heard a thing."

"But he's a martyr at this point!" Raymond protested. "Nobody's gonna step up and say, 'You know what, I remember the guy bringing in a load of meth for the Aryans.'"

"Were there any tickets issued up near Auburn, before the escape?" Abbie asked.

"Two," Raymond said, leaning on the parapet and looking down.

"One for blocking a driveway, the other for a broken taillight. Both hunters after snipe. The deputies up there talked to both guys and looked through the cars and their houses. They were both locals, and they'd both bagged legal birds; the evidence is in their meat lockers, and I made sure the deputies checked. Doesn't look like they had anything to do with the escape."

It's too perfect, Abbie thought. She flicked the binoculars toward Delaware Park. The dark matter is bending the beams of light around something big. An optical illusion.

"What did you think about the North, growing up?" she asked Raymond.

"The North?" Raymond said softly. "That's where the *real* white people lived."

Abbie laughed. "I'm not really white, Raymond?"

"No, cuz you ain't rich. That's the magic ingredient."

Abbie brought down the binoculars and turned to him. The wind was whipping through the gaps in the parapet, shrieking a little. "I ran cross-country against them in high school," she said. "The Nardin girls would talk about going to Switzerland for vacation. I'd barely been out of the state."

Raymond smiled.

"Yep. My Aunt Erdy was a nanny in one of the mansions on Delaware. Millionaire's row, baby. One of the kids she watched asked her if they used her head to clean the pots."

"No."

Raymond grimaced. "She changed families. From the next one, she used to bring us back food after they had parties up there—slices of cake, tasted like heaven. She even brought back clothes for me to wear, too. I said, No, ma'am, I'm not wearing some white boy's hand-me-downs." Raymond stared northward. "Got a beating for that."

Abbie scanned the park again. She saw tufts of burgeoning green, leaves beginning to turn ocher and flame-red. Lots of groves, dark archways underneath the small brick bridges. A million places to hide. "That's what I'm thinking about," she said.

Raymond shook his head. "About Aunt Erdy?"

"In a way. What would you do if you saw a white guy walking around your neighborhood?"

"Watch him," Raymond said quickly.

"Exactly. Strangers out of their element get noticed. Yet Hangman is moving around the North and no one sees a thing. He's the most famous stranger in Buffalo history, and yet he's there like he belongs."

Raymond turned and looked north.

"Who's hiding him, Raymond?" Abbie said.

"You fucking got me."

"He must *have* something on someone who lives out there," Abbie said. "Before they caught him the first time, was Hangman really this good?"

"If he hadn't taken himself out, we'd probably still be looking for him."

Abbie grimaced. They *were* still looking for him. "Has anyone talked to his ex-wife?" she asked.

Raymond huffed. "Ginnie Payne? We have a detail out front of her house, just in case. Believe me, that asshole isn't shacking up with *her*. She'd slice him up, then call 911. There's been no contact for years and right now she's got the TV on, following the news like everyone else. We went through the house top to bottom. There's no sign he's been in touch."

"Who do you have there?"

"You know Markowitz and Shaney?" Raymond said, a mischievous look in his eyes.

"No."

"They're ding-dongs. Fat and slow, the kind of cops you wonder how they made the force. They're usually giving out parking tickets, but we put them in a squad car out in front of Payne's house on Sycamore Drive with a box of donuts and a couple of extra-large coffees."

"Now why would you do that?" Abbie said. "Hangman might want to take a shot . . ."

"I hope he does. We got two detectives in the house across the street. A couple of uniforms—real cops—are camped in Ginnie Payne's second bedroom. A few of our SWAT guys placed discreetly around the neighborhood. Hangman will get in if we want him to, but he sure as hell won't get out."

Abbie was impressed. "I want to talk with her."

"Like I said, she hasn't had any contact. And Perelli wants everyone to think the clowns in the black-and-white are the only attention we're paying."

Abbie gave him a frosty smile. "I think you're forgetting who's lead on this, Raymond."

"You pulling rank?" Raymond said with a wounded look.

"Looks like it."

He gave it a few beats.

"Pull up out front and go through the front door. Wear your badge around your neck and leave your jacket open so people can see it. You'll have to be very visible entering and leaving the place. We want it to look like we're doing a shitty job of protecting Ginnie Payne."

Abbie bent down and grabbed the binocular case, slotting the Zeisses in. She handed them to Raymond. "I'll be there in twenty."

Raymond looked down at the leather case. "One more thing."

"Yeah?"

"Do me a favor. Bring some Danishes or something in your purse for the guys inside."

Abbie's eyes narrowed. "Sure thing, Raymond. Can I vacuum while I'm there, too, maybe dust a little?"

"It's just so we don't have to send a delivery guy later. The less attention we draw to the place, the better."

Abbie blew out a breath. "Agreed."

25

Dead streets. Empty playgrounds. Basketball courts with the metal chain nets swinging in the wind. The only time she'd seen the city this empty was during Bills play-off games or when big lake-effect storms were approaching.

A thick-bodied redhead pushed a stroller down Chapin Parkway, one of those thousand-dollar contraptions that looked like they'd been engineered by NASA. They walked slowly. Abbie watched them go. Something tingled along her spine, a feeling not a thought. She shivered.

She drove down Delaware Avenue, swung a left onto Sycamore Street. She pulled up in front of 76, a small '20s-era stone cottage trimmed in white, with a black-and-white out front. A cop car out front had steam wafting out of its muffler.

A car door clunked three doors down. Abbie saw a woman dressed in a Burberry coat ferrying three small children toward a Honda minivan. There was no one else on the street.

Abbie got out, grabbed the Danishes and bagels she'd picked up at a Tim Horton's, and walked to the black-and-white. When she was even with the passenger door, she tapped on the window.

The cop in the front seat had a napkin on his lap and, balanced on top, a donut with a dab of gleaming jelly at its side. He jerked away from the window, startled by Abbie's sudden appearance. Abbie read the nameplate. Shaney.

He rolled down the window. "Kearney," he said, a little abashed.

Abbie had gotten used to being recognized by people she didn't know, especially cops. "Anything interesting?" She ducked down to nod at the uniform in the driver's side. He held a cup of coffee and raised it to her. His nameplate read Markowitz.

"Channel 7 was by a couple of hours ago," Markowitz said. "Besides that? Nothing."

"How is Ms. Payne?"

Shaney shrugged. "She's up and she's down. Looking out the window every five seconds. Her daughter's twenty now, she thinks maybe Hangman got out to take a shot at her. Which makes no sense. The girl's away at college."

"You haven't gotten on the radio about my visit, right?"

"Right," Markowitz said. He had a mustache that looked like a high school boy's first attempt at facial hair.

"Good," Abbie said. "I'll be out in a little while."

"Those Danishes?" Shaney said.

"Yeah," Abbie replied, walking away. "They are."

26

When she answered the door, Ginnie Payne was showing the strain. Her face was powder-white, her eyebrows and hair stark black. She resembled a bird, one of the predators, a hawk or a falcon. Even her sweater was the deepest black. The tendons on her neck strained through the flesh like smooth rope. She looked at Abbie with a pulsing intensity, then pushed the door open.

"Detective Kearney."

Abbie walked in, following the trim woman into a small living room. The TV was on, tuned to one of the local channels. Abbie saw that they, too, were doing live Hangman coverage.

"Thanks for talking with me," Abbie said.

"I hope it helps," Ginnie said, turning as she sat on the cream-colored leather couch. "At least more than talking with the other idiots they've sent over."

Abbie sat across from her on a matching seat. The room was taste-fully done up in sleek, leather-and-steel furniture. It looked like a showroom and smelled like a lemony cleaner. Obsessive dusting was clearly Ginnie Payne's release.

"I hope it will."

Ginnie Payne tilted her chin up, her eyes dropping to take Abbie in from head to toe. "You look better than you did six months ago."

Abbie smiled ruefully. "Thanks. I guess."

"I thought you handled it . . . well. That's why I agreed to talk to you."

"Your situation is even more difficult, I'd imagine," Abbie said.

Ginnie made a face. "It is. I won't deny it. To be the ex-wife of a serial killer is something I never prepared myself for." She tucked her chin in toward her chest, and looked down at the floor.

"The dreaded Hangman," Ginnie whispered bitterly. Her lips curled around the words, as if they were rotten, soured. She thought for a moment. "And now he's brought it all back, as if the first time wasn't enough."

"Do you think there's a chance he'll come here?" Abbie asked. "Do you feel threatened?"

"I do. I didn't the first time, obviously, because I didn't think Marcus was the killer. I never even suspected. I was an observer like everyone else until he was caught. And then the inquisition began."

"You were separated from Marcus, divorced, for what, three years before the killings started," Abbie asked. "Why an inquisition?"

Ginnie Payne studied Abbie's face, her eyes aggrieved. She stood up and walked to the window, pulling the drapes apart to stare at the street. She shook her head in disgust. "I saw three of my neighbors loading their families into their cars this morning. They don't want their precious daughters to even be close to Hangman's wife while he's out there." She turned back to Abbie. "Buffalo is in many ways a very— how shall I put it—old-fashioned place. Old-fashioned as in medieval. I once loved the killer, so I must have loved that part of him that killed the girls. It's unimaginable that I didn't know he was capable of these things. And then there's Nicole."

"What about her?" asked Abbie.

"I won custody in the divorce. Marcus had threatened me several times and grabbed me violently one night around Christmas, when I'd spent too much on a gift apparently. My lawyers convinced the judge that he wasn't stable enough to share custody. So when it was revealed that he was Hangman, a rumor went around. He killed those girls because he was angry at not seeing his daughter. He couldn't reach Nicole so he strangled . . ." She stopped. "I still have Nicole. I shouldn't be bitter. There are four . . ." She looked up. "No, five families without their children today. I shouldn't be bitter. But I am."

"People blamed you for the murders because you won custody?" Abbie said.

"Yes. They did." Ginnie Payne's eyes met Abbie's. "You stopped your brother from killing, Detective Kearney, and so they forgive you. But I *created* mine. That's what they think. So I must suffer."

"When it comes to their children, people aren't rational," Abbie said. "They think of curses and blood and fate. But Ms. Payne—"

"Ginnie. Please."

"Ginnie, time is short. You know that. Is there anything you can tell me? I've read the files, I've gone through your interviews. Do you have any idea where Marcus is going?"

A look of exhaustion swept over Ginnie's face. "None. Is Marcus angry enough with me to try something? I don't know. We got divorced for the most boring and normal reasons. We married too young, we were incompatible, there were money pressures, and he lost his temper and got physical with me. But I didn't divorce him because I saw the potential for him to kill young girls. I just didn't. Why can't anyone understand that?" Her mouth twisted into an ugly grimace.

"Did you have *any* communications with him when he was in prison?"

Ginnie shook her head. "None."

"What about friends that might be helping him now?"

"I can't think of one. They all abandoned him after he was caught."

Abbie frowned. "There was *no one* who might have come around in the years since? A close friend?"

Ginnie shook her head. "I'm telling you—"

"Think, Ginnie. Forget the stock answers that I know you've been giving."

Ginnie put her fingers to her temples and pressed. "Oh, God. He had a couple of friends from UB that would look him up when they passed through town. They were nice guys, I liked them. Unlike his high school friends, you could hold a conversation with them."

Abbie remembered them from the files. Both living out of town during the original murder spree. They'd been checked out thoroughly.

"Was there anyone else?" she asked.

Ginnie closed her eyes. "No."

Abbie blew out a breath. "What about Sandy? Did he ever talk about her?"

Ginnie tilted her head, frowned. "Yes. Toward the end, before he got caught, he did. He was strange, really animated."

This was the first time Abbie had heard it. The file mentioned nothing about a close connection between the killer and his cousin. "What did Marcus say?"

"He'd gotten into his head that she was being abused. That's all he cared about in the week before she disappeared."

Abbie felt as if she'd stepped on a high-voltage wire. Abused? Was that what Lipschitz was referring to when he said Hangman was saving his victims from a worse fate?

Ginnie went on, "He would mutter these dark things about protecting Sandy."

"Who did he think was abusing her?"

"He didn't say. Marcus—well, he had a savior complex since he was a boy, as far as I can tell. He wanted to be out rescuing the innocents of the world, starting with animals when he was a boy, then moving on . . . to girls. That was his cover, I think. He could quote you statistics about thirty percent of young girls experience some form of abuse by the time they reach sixteen, *blah blah blah*. He even wanted to home-school Nicole. But all along, he wasn't rescuing them, he was getting them for himself. It's so diabolical I can't even . . ." She reached up her hand and covered her mouth for a moment, then dropped it. "Marcus kept parts of himself hidden. When I first met him, I thought he was an open person, like me, someone who was looking to get away from a difficult childhood. His was difficult because his father was a drunk and his mother was a cold woman who died and left him alone in the world. But what I learned is there's always some kind of inheritance; you never escape the people that your parents were. Marcus was secretive." Ginnie shook her head, then rose off the couch and walked to the window. Her voice grew scornful as she looked out. "Is this a joke or something? Performance art? How many donuts can two cops eat?"

Abbie got up and stood behind her. She saw Shaney lifting what looked like a bear claw to his mouth.

"If you were Marcus, where would you go?" she asked.

"Don't ask me that."

Abbie grabbed her arm and turned her slowly. The woman was sleepwalking. She had to wake her up. "Right now Marcus is out there and by now he's probably found another girl. He's studying her habits. He's writing down the times she leaves the house and when she gets back and how many people are with her each time and what she weighs, because he's going to put her on the end of a rope. Do you understand, Ginnie?"

Ginnie made a sick sound in her throat. "I didn't sleep last night because I understand."

As Abbie watched her, Ginnie walked slowly back to the couch and slumped onto it, bringing her hand up to rub her temple. "For six years, I lived with this animal."

"And my brother skinned a man alive."

Ginnie looked up, searching Abbie's face.

"We've both been close to horrible things," said Abbie. "And we will never be the same. Never."

Ginnie nodded.

Abbie took out a card and a pen from her bag and circled the cell phone number on it. She laid it on the table by the window. "This is my number. If you have any kind of feeling, any memory that comes to you in the next few hours, I want you to call me. I will not be doing anything except looking for Marcus until he's back in prison. Anything."

Ginnie grabbed Abbie's fingers with her two hands and squeezed them. Her face looked gaunt. "Please catch him. Just not for that girl, but for me and Nicole, too. We're not going to make it. Please, Detective."

Abbie felt the woman's hands shake in her own. *Just make it stop. Give me back my life.*

She knew how that went.

Abbie's mind was on Sandy Riesen. Why had no one told her about the abuse?

She left the Danishes and bagels for the cops upstairs, and headed back outside.

27

Leaving Maggie Payne's house, Abbie's mind was churning. She drove home slowly. The Saab was making a funny noise again, a whirring coming from the engine. Not now, please, not now.

Abbie climbed the stairs of her Victorian and slid the key in the lock, but the door just opened without her turning it. That Mills, Abbie thought. He acted like he lived in some Canadian fishing village where you could leave your doors open and only baby seals would come walking through to nestle in your spare bed.

Mills was splayed out on their leather couch watching an English soccer game. Arsenal against somebody else. Mills loved Arsenal.

"Hi," she said.

"What's going on, babe?"

Abbie sighed. She wanted to tell someone about the case and about McGonagle's offer to help, unofficially. No, she wanted to tell her boyfriend. But her boyfriend was also a cop.

"Did you eat?" he said. "I brought you a gyro."

Abbie smiled. "Thanks, Mills."

He smiled and shook his head. "Why do you still call me Mills?"

Abbie squinched up her eyes. "Because that's what I called you when we first met, dummy. I'm sentimental."

"Is that right?"

"I am. Really I am."

She walked over, sat on the couch, and leaned into him, wrapping her arms around his chest. He reached around and gave her a squeeze that left her breathless for a second.

"This case . . ." she said.

"I wish I could be out there with you."

Abbie smiled. "Headline in *The Buffalo News:* 'Detective's Hunky Boyfriend Helps Her Catch Hangman.' Thanks but no."

"It'd be good for my career," Mills said. "And my chick options."

She gave him a kidney punch, and locked eyes with him. Her eyes slowly grew more troubled.

"What is it, Abbie?" Mills said.

She pulled away and relocated to the other end of the couch. She watched the soccer game in silence for a few minutes.

"So there's this cop named McGonagle," she said finally, feeling tense as a coiled rattlesnake. "He's in touch with the Network."

They'd discussed the Network before. There was a version of it in most decent-sized cities in the Northeast, but nothing like the octopus-like organization that seemed to infiltrate every corner of her hometown. Mills had been fascinated. They had nothing like it in Niagara Falls, just a couple of corrupt state reps whose crimes basically added up to free rent for their relatives.

"Uh-huh," Mills said uncertainly.

"He offered to help on Hangman."

Mills went still for a second, then blew out a breath and slumped back into the leather couch. He stared at her, his tousled hair low over his eyes.

"You can't."

Abbie hugged her arms closer. "I know that. But maybe there's a way to get the information without . . ."

"There's no such thing as an experienced virgin," Mills said matter-of-factly.

"Don't be gross," Abbie said.

"You know what I mean. Either you are or you aren't. Either you're with them or you're not."

"I guess."

She frowned. Seconds ticked by, filled with silence. Abbie swung her legs up on his lap. "Rub my feet?" she said.

"Gladly," he said, and his smile was instant and warm. Abbie reminded herself for the thousandth time to keep this one around.

"Just the feet, mister."

Mills laughed and slipped her foot out of the black Tory Burch flats she was wearing. Abbie smiled and sank further into the leather. She wanted to sink into the couch, to disappear from the world for ten or twenty minutes. She reached over and pulled one of her fancy throw pillows over and pressed her face into it. She could feel Mills's thumb press the arch of her foot, a known trouble spot, pushing right up to the edge of pain, and she groaned slightly.

Strong hands on a boyfriend are worth one million dollars, she thought. But there was something she was trying to blot out, to not think about, and of course it came welling up to her out of the darkness of the pillow. The redheaded woman pushing the stroller. The image floated into her brain and stayed there.

What do you want, Abbie thought sleepily. Babies have nothing to do with this case. Go away, go away.

But the image was trapped in the front of her brain. She couldn't get rid of it, as much as she tried to focus on the foot rub.

Did it have something to do with the note she found on Martha Stoltz—*They are not your children?* Or the original crime spree? Or . . .

Abbie's mind churned. The image refused to disappear. It was unwavering. Persistent.

After enjoying the foot rub and hurriedly eating half the gyro, Abbie hurried next door and knocked on Ron's door. Her watch read 1:45. Something stirred above. She heard feet on the stairs, soft crumps growing louder.

"Abbie," Ron said, pulling the door open.

"Is Charles home?"

Ron glanced at his watch.

"He's on a plane, coming home from a conference in Chicago. Some retarded—"

"Have you ever heard of something or someone called the Madeleines?"

"Not the cookie, right?" Ron said dubiously.

"Not the cookie. Something to do with Hoyt Lake."

"Oh, *that*," Ron said tiredly. "You've come to the right place." He pulled the door full open. "Come on in."

Abbie followed him across the small foyer and down a dark hallway into the kitchen.

"Wait here, hon," Ron said before disappearing into a back office.

They'd had the kitchen redone in old French country style. As Abbie waited, she turned on the coffeemaker and heard the water begin to circulate.

Two minutes later, Ron emerged from the office with a pamphlet.

"Found it," he said.

"What is this?" Abbie said, looking at the unadorned cover, which read *Legends of North Buffalo*.

"Charles gives it out on his North Buffalo tour. The Madeleines is on page 3. I remember because it's one of the only juicy pieces of gossip in there."

Abbie opened the booklet and flipped to page 3, "The Myth of the Madeleines" printed in bold at the top of the page. She began to read to herself.

"At the turn of the twentieth century, as Buffalo approached its apogee of mercantile power, local historians began to record a series of rumors that appear connected to the unease the new riches brought. Thousands of young men and women were flocking to the Buffalo area from all over the country, to work in the factories, restaurants, and stores that were the inevitable result of the city's new prosperity. In a striking past echo of the American situation today, the sudden influx of wealth produced a socio-psychological unease about the men who possessed it. The Madeleine stories were one of the results . . ."

Abbie skipped a paragraph of sociological theory and picked up the narrative again.

"The rumors vary in details but the main story line is consistent: a young woman named Madeleine arrives in Buffalo to work in one of its shining new factories. Her origins are unclear: usually the Midwest, but sometimes the poor Southern states. She begins talking to her co-workers about a suitor she's met, a 'man of some prominence' in the community, though she won't tell anyone his name. The woman, though taken with her new lover, appears troubled by his actions. The myth cites his possessiveness in some cases, his capacity for violence in others. She appears with bruises on her face or arms but attributes them to accidents in the factory or at home. Finally, she fails to show up for work one day. A check of her lodgings at the rooming house finds no trace of her. Her best dress is missing. The girl has disappeared without a trace. The last anyone heard of her, she was going rowing on Hoyt Lake."

Abbie looked at Ron.

"Hoyt Lake," she said.

"Keep reading," he answered, with a smile.

"Hoyt was a popular excursion spot for Buffalonians during this time. On Sundays and holidays, the paths were filled with promenading couples from all over the city. But during the week it was the province of the rich whose mansions backed on the park. Boats could be rented for a nickel an hour. The rumor goes around that Madeleine was taken out on a boat and dumped in the middle of the lake by her powerful lover, who'd grown tired of the girl. Her body was weighted down so that it didn't float to the surface.

"If the rumor is to be believed, there is more than one Madeleine in Hoyt Lake. The myth always ends with the same image: if you go out onto Hoyt on a particularly clear night when the moon is full, and you row your boat to the exact center of the lake, you can look down and see a litter of white objects on the lake floor. The bones of the Madeleines, the disposable women of Buffalo's boom."

Abbie flipped over the page and skimmed the rest. It was mostly theories about where the rumor came from.

"—derives from a shared anxiety about the expendability of workers in the new economic landscape—wealth inequalities spur a reflexive doubt—intentions about those who sit at the pinnacle of power . . ."

She folded the pamphlet and put it into her pocket.

"Is that all there is, rumors?" Abbie said. "Did anyone ever find actual bones in Hoyt Lake?"

Ron pointed at her, tipping forward. "The exact question I asked Charles. Do you know what he said? That no police in 1910 were going to dredge Hoyt Lake in order to convict a millionaire of murder. So, no real bones." He walked over to the coffeemaker. "Wouldn't that have been something?"

"When is Charles home?" asked Abbie.

"Six o'clock or so. He'll go to UB first, then come home. I'm making him sea bass. You game?"

"Can't," Abbie said. "I want to have a look at Hoyt Lake."

"Don't fall in," Ron said cheerfully.

28

A freezing mist had moved in from over Lake Erie and she rolled up the window to keep out the cold. The big, two-story houses she passed were swathed in fog, which occasionally parted to reveal a mansion against a backdrop of white. She turned into Delaware Park and drove slowly along the curving road. The park, too, was abandoned, except for an occasional jogger. This is where the local high schools came to practice for their cross-country races, and she saw one group of female students, the hoods of their sweatshirts pulled up over hidden faces, as they whipped by on the right in tight formation. There were no stragglers. On their sweatshirts, just above the heart, she recognized the crest of Nardin Academy, the best girls school in the city.

Despite her lingering resentment toward the North, Abbie felt the urge to step out of the car and clap for these girls, to be their one-woman cheering section. Good for them, carrying on as if nothing had happened. Stiff upper lips.

The Saab swept slowly by the backstop of a baseball diamond, only the top of it visible in the whiteness, and then over a bridge, tiny Hoyt Lake on her right, the wind turning the water's surface rough like a crocodile's skin. She passed over the bridge and on her right the mist parted and a stand of birches appeared. Birches were rare in this park, and their white thin trunks caught in the mesh of fog always seemed to her like the bones of the local Indian dead, sucked from their burial grounds by the mist and now hanging midair like an accusation.

Abbie saw Hoyt Lake emerge to her left, slate blue under the white clouds. It was small, a modest lake for a modest city. She parked and opened the door of the Saab, stepping out into the cold. She leaned against the car's curved hood. Where would Hangman go? Where the girls were, obviously. What if the girls were all being kept inside? He'd have to find a stray, or he'd eventually have to get inside a house. He hadn't escaped from Auburn to keep his head low and go live under a false identity in the Midwest. He'd escaped to kill in the place he'd most likely be caught. He was here.

From what she could see, there were very few unescorted girls in the city of Buffalo. There would be even fewer after everyone absorbed the news of the Martha Stoltz murder. Some girls would be going to school Monday morning. If I was the parent of a teenage girl, Abbie thought, a fifteen-year-old brunette, what would I do? Keep her at home and skip work to watch over her? Escort her to school and believe there was safety in numbers?

The sound of footfalls and bird cries emerged from fog, sharp and distinct, but the runners and the starlings that gave them off passed by unseen. It was impossible even to judge how far away the things making the sounds were. There was only a shifting white curtain, sweeping ahead and back as the wind swept it along.

Two minutes later, Raymond's black Ford Crown Victoria rolled out of the mist like a dark-hulled Viking ship. He stepped out of the car in a black-and-yellow-checked sports coat and wide, mustard-colored slacks. He pulled the sports coat's wide lapels up around his chin.

"Next time, I'm choosing the meet-up spot. Some nice jazz—"

Abbie smiled. "I was thinking about something my father said one time. He told me there are really only two classifications for murder. Normal or abnormal."

Raymond sighed.

"Class in session now?"

"Shut up, you might learn something," Abbie said in her best imitation of a County detective.

Raymond looked away, stared at the white mist for a moment. "Okay," he said.

"The normal murder means that you tailor your investigation by what you see. Say you have the body of a man with a necklace clutched in his hand. He's been stabbed multiple times, several times in the face and eyes. Some checking reveals he's been divorced twice and his friends report that he and his current wife have been having problems. He lives in the suburbs but he was found downtown in the Chippewa district, where every other establishment is a bar, many of them frequented by college students from UB or Buff State."

Raymond's eyes were thoughtful.

"So the necklace belongs to some chick," he said. "Some chick the vic knew. He gave her the necklace, most likely. There was some kind of argument . . ."

"And he snatched the necklace back. And the woman stabbed him. Assume the wounds to his face were not accidental but were inflicted because the killer wanted to disfigure the man, make him unattractive to other females. Assume stabbing at the eyes meant that he'd been looking at those other women and this was the killer's revenge."

Raymond nodded. "I got you."

"You focus on the single most likely reason for the things you see: jealousy. The killer would be found somewhere in his romantic history. Do that first. Focus on the most obvious explanation."

"That's eighty percent of my caseload."

Abbie nodded. "But an abnormal murder, that's different. Here it's the clues that *don't* make sense that are the important ones. The weird signs, the outliers."

Raymond watched a male jogger appear out of the mist and trudge by, puffing like a train. The man passed without a nod. "So what is Hangman?"

"Well, the escape has a bunch of normal elements. Marcus Flynn was a prisoner and all prisoners want to escape. He saw a chance and took it. He was a serial killer who started killing as soon as he'd escaped and in the same MO as before he'd escaped. He'd been successful at not getting caught, and they'd been unable to catch him in the hours since his run began. All to be expected."

"But what you're saying is that the abnormal things, they interest you more?"

"They do," said Abbie. "I think that's how we'll catch him. Someone was paying Joe Carlson to find out what Hangman knew. That's odd. Think about the facts connected to that piece of abnormal information."

Abbie held up her hand, then uncurled the index finger.

"Fact: Hangman was drawing pictures of Sandy, which were displayed on the walls of his cell.

"Fact: The drawings were getting more and more detailed, indicating his memory was coming back. Flynn's drawings could be seen by anyone in the prison. Like Joe Carlson. Who was being paid by someone to watch him.

"Fact: Just as Hangman was beginning to get his memory back, he escaped."

"The timing," Raymond said.

"It's interesting, isn't it?" Abbie said.

"So you think there was a second man, who paid Carlson to keep an eye on Hangman."

"I do."

"Who?" Raymond asked.

"No idea. But the important thing is to think of this as an abnormal case. The clues that are in plain sight are what Hangman knows we know. The clues that someone attempted to hide, those are the ones that matter."

"The second man has money," Raymond said. "So who does that point to?"

"It's a pretty short list. The victims' families. The people in the North."

Somehow, as the rest of Buffalo was ravaged by layoffs and foreclosures, the North had remained a green oasis where the residents made their fortunes by mysterious means. Few people in the County or anywhere else had the cash to buy $80,000 Corvettes. The second man had to be from the North, or the richer suburbs. Amherst, Williams-ville.

"Who do we start with?" Raymond said.

"There's a lot of things happening around Sandy. The missing girl. Her father's rich and he was Hangman's uncle. There's one other thing—his home backs up on Hoyt Lake."

Raymond shot her a bug-eyed look. "Stop playin'."

"It's true," Abbie said. "So I'm going to have a talk with Frank Riesen. He's a twofer—he might have information on his daughter's disappearance, and he might be the second man. Then I'm going to talk to Walter Myeong, Maggie's father. Less tantalizing, but still rich."

Abbie nodded to Raymond, who popped off the hood of the Saab and walked toward the Crown Vic. Abbie jumped in her car, did a slow U-turn, watching for more joggers, then whipped the Saab into a straight line and drove through the park, the white mist parting in front of her and whipping over the windshield as she pressed the gas. She exited the park and took Delaware Avenue downtown, drove eight minutes before finding Riesen's business address.

29

Abbie stared at the low-slung building, sleek and metallic-looking, that housed Riesen Properties, LLC. It looked like a just surfaced submarine, with rivulets of rain sliding over the surface. She parked across from the building, hustled across the street, pulled open the dark glass door and strode in.

There was a hush to the building, accentuated by low-burning golden lights set low into the dark walls. A feeling that made you want to whisper. In Abbie's experience, that meant money.

No directory was posted in the entrance, just a smoked glass door to the left. Pulling it open, she found herself in a wide reception room with padded leather benches along one wall and a glass-and-metal desk straight ahead. A young woman glanced up from a shiny Apple laptop and smiled.

The receptionist had light brown hair streaked with gold pulled back in a bun, a tailored business suit in cream, and a black silk blouse. Strangely tanned for the season, she wore scalloped gold earrings, a plain gold chain necklace tucked behind the silk collar, and no wedding ring. Her green eyes were appraising, noncommittal.

Abbie walked toward the desk, pulling out her ID as she went. "I'm

Detective Kearney from the Buffalo Police Department," she said as the woman glanced at the badge. "I'd like to speak to Mr. Riesen."

The receptionist nodded, smiling. "He's not available," she said in a faintly accented voice. Abbie couldn't locate the origin. Boston? London, a long time ago?

"When might he be available?" Abbie said. "It's urgent."

There was a leather appointment book at the corner of the desk. Abbie looked at it, but the woman only leaned back in her chair. She was in terrific shape, you could see by the way she held herself. "He's in a business meeting with a client. I couldn't say when he'd be available to talk. His schedule is very tight these days."

Abbie took that in. "I'm investigating the Hangman case."

Abbie couldn't hear any sounds coming from the street. It really was like being in a submarine a hundred yards underwater. "You heard he escaped?"

The woman's eyebrows raised briefly, and the smile stayed steady on the lips. "I did."

"Every piece of information helps in these kinds of investigations."

"Mr. Riesen's involvement with the case happened a long time ago."

"Mm-hmm," Abbie said, eying the woman. "And you are?"

"I'm Katie Siegel, Mr. Riesen's personal assistant."

"Ms. Siegel."

"Katie, please."

Abbie almost laughed. She found herself in some kind of duel.

"Katie. Mr. Riesen seems to have given you a lot of leeway in deciding whether he talks to certain people. Like the police searching for his daughter's killer, for instance."

Katie's face hardened. "He—"

"And it seems you've been told beforehand to brush us off."

Katie's eyes were unreadable. It struck Abbie that she was good at her job, and that job involved saying no a lot. "I have been given instructions on how to handle Mr. Riesen's time, yes."

"And I didn't make the cut?"

Katie smiled and shook her head softly. Her politeness was exquisite.

"Can I ask what kind of deal he's negotiating?" Abbie said.

"It involves a commercial property in Toronto, but I don't see how that can possibly matter."

"I'm trying to see what the stakes are. How much he might possibly make in the deal. I'd like to measure that against the chance that he might help me save a girl in the next couple of days, see what the current price of a teenage girl is these days. Or does it fluctuate due to market conditions?"

The smile was gone now. "Mr. Riesen lost his daughter, Detective."

Abbie leaned across the desk. "Yes, I know. Which makes me wonder why I'm talking to you and not him right now."

Up close, Katie's eyes were extraordinary, a kind of luminescent green flecked with gold. "Perhaps it's painful, Detective Kearney. Perhaps he doesn't see what's to be gained by going through it again."

"What's to be gained is saving another father from going through the same thing."

Abbie thought she detected a flicker of worry or sympathy in the eyes, but it came and went so fast it was hard to tell.

"I'll tell Mr. Riesen you came by."

"I'll tell him myself," Abbie said. "I *will* be speaking with him." She placed her card down on the leather appointment book and turned to leave.

Abbie drove toward Niagara Square, thinking of the image from this morning that wouldn't leave her. The redheaded woman pushing the stroller. It was back again. She could see the woman leaning into the wind, the stroller's big, ten-inch back wheels turning as if in slow motion.

Was it the stroller? No, there were no strollers or prams or rocking cribs in the case. But there were children. The North's next generation was being killed off.

What did the note say? "They are not your children."

When she'd thought of children, she'd thought of teenagers. Their habits, their clothes—Martha's raw-skinned hand sticking out of the blue-striped sailor's shirt—their vulnerabilities. But these teenagers had once been infants. Is that what stuck with her about the baby in the stroller—their innocence?

No, it wasn't anything so airy-fairy. It was something concrete.

Okay, it wasn't the stroller. What else went with babies? Diapers. Onesies.

Abbie pulled to the curb, pulled the trunk release button, and got out of the Saab. She walked back and heaved the hatchback open. There was the case file where she'd left it. She pulled it out and flipped to the evidence pictures as traffic whipped by on her left.

Sandy's silk scarf, shiny in the photographer's flash.

Charlotte Breen's green wool V-neck sweater.

Maggie's rumpled Guess jeans.

No, no, and no. There's nothing in this case that is even tangentially infant-related.

She shuffled impatiently to the next page. It was a close-up of Maggie Myeong's hand, the inside left palm.

The A inside the square had been crudely carved, the cross-line of the letter going outside the box. Drawn hurriedly, even frantically.

Abbie's eyes fluttered. Her body felt light, as it always did when a piece of the puzzle fit into place.

The A inside the square. The infant in the stroller.

The two images seemed to align in her mind. The second unlocked the first.

It was a baby's block. It had to be.

30

Katrina Lamb sat in her homeroom in the chilly west wing of Nardin Academy, the swirl of female voices bouncing off the tile floor and getting lost in the high-ceilinged room. She was thinking of Drama Club, which met every Tuesday at four. This being Tuesday, Katrina was getting worried. There was a rumor going around the school that had apparently started the moment the girls had arrived that morning. Katrina had heard that all after-school activities, including clubs and sports, were going to be canceled because Hangman was still on the loose.

She listened to her friends' chatter, their four desks scooched close to each other, and hoped this wouldn't happen. The steam from the old iron radiators made hissing noises as it floated into the classroom.

Katrina wanted to go to Drama Club. She'd been chosen to play Cordelia in *King Lear* and their second and very important rehearsal was scheduled for this afternoon. The club had voted to do *Lear* because for the past three years the members had chosen the most awful plays you could think of, including, two years back, *South Pacific*. But if the club was canceled, it would mean another week before Katrina would get the chance to speak the lines she'd been practicing nightly.

She'd decided to move Actress to number two on her life's ambitions, right behind Oral Surgeon, which is what she'd always wanted to be. If she took science courses at Harvard and tried out for the Drama Club, she'd have four years to decide which was for her. But now Hangman was getting in the way. Everyone in school was talking about how insane he was, where he was hiding out, and when the police would catch him.

It was 2:49, and they were still waiting for the principal, Ms. Ferrote, to speak over the intercom and let them know if after-school activities were canceled. Obviously, the killer had thrown the principal into a spin, just like everyone else, because she was fifteen minutes late getting on the intercom and Katrina was supposed to be in Spanish, not hanging around here with her friends. She stared down at her white capri pants and blue cable-knit sweater and wished she was wearing the long flowing dress that was Cordelia's costume.

"Did anyone see *The Voice* last night?" Bea asked.

Katrina frowned. "I don't watch that show," she said.

"Why?" Bea said in a shocked voice that had no real shock in it.

"Because everyone gets so excited by the new voice and then a few months later you can't even remember her name. It's so fake. I hate fake excitement."

Bea nodded. The hissing of the radiators was making them sleepy.

"I guess you're right," Bea said.

Julia leaned in. "So if Hangman was going to grab some Nardin girl . . ." she began, her voice low.

Katrina looked over at her.

"Who do you think it would be?" Julia finished, looking at the others in turn, a look of serious concern on her face.

"That is in poor taste," said Katrina.

Julia made a face.

"No, it's not, it's just being proactive." She ducked her head down, and looked at Katrina. "So who do you think? I know who I think would get it."

"You know who I think?" Katrina said.

"Who?" asked Julia.

"You."

"Me?" she squawked, clutching at nonexistent pearls on her neck. Her throat flushed red.

Bea and Katrina laughed.

"Yes," Katrina said, studying Julia with mock solemnity. "Because you're so nosy. You'd see something in your backyard, like a man in a red mask, and you'd just have to go investigate. Is that true or not?"

Julia looked at her dubiously. "I'm inquisitive. There's a difference."

"Which is?"

"I'm nosy, but I'm smart about it," she declared.

Katrina rolled her eyes.

"I think it would be Kris Shepherd," said Bea, twisting her red-gold ringlets and looking out the window. "She's odd. I think Hangman chooses odd people to target."

Katrina made a face. "What makes you say that?"

"Because it's not *normal* to get murdered by a serial killer."

Their half-smothered giggles rang sharply against the polished floor. The homeroom teacher, Mrs. Taylor, looked up.

"Girls?" she said.

They lowered their heads and tried not to catch each other's eyes. After a minute, Mrs. Taylor went back to reading a book. Crackling noises came from the intercom, but the principal's voice failed to emerge.

"God, when is she going to give her speech?" Katrina said. "This is torture."

"Maybe she's waiting to announce that they caught Hangman," Bea said. "She's just now getting all the details so that everything can go back to normal."

Julia frowned. "Getting back to potential victims," she whispered, "*I'm* thinking the Indian girl, Anandi."

Katrina shot her a look. Anandi had arrived from India the previous year. There were Indian girls in the school, three at last count, but they'd been raised in the States and had fit in more or less seamlessly at Nardin, especially Shooki, who was Katrina's third-best friend. But Anandi was different, still more Indian than American. The other girls whispered that she smelled like hot spices and that in gym class she'd stood on the sidelines during volleyball and refused to participate. Some wondered if she had crazy tattoos, even though Katrina had assured them this was not the case.

"Julia," Katrina said now, shaking her head sadly. "Really?"

"What?"

"Don't be mean."

"I'm not. I'm being entirely scientific. Or what's that word? Forensic. I have three reasons." Julia presented her hand to the group and held up a finger. "One, she's brunette. Hangman always goes for girls with brown hair."

"Ha," said Bea, tossing her golden red hair. Katrina again rolled her eyes and turned back to Julia.

"Two. She has no friends. Therefore, she's always alone. That's what detectives call 'opportunity.'"

"You don't know that she's alone at home," Katrina said, interested in the question despite herself. "Maybe she has, like, five brothers that she lives with."

Julia shook her head. "I know from reliable sources that she's an only. Three, her house's backyard faces the park. I think he's hiding in the park."

"*My* backyard faces the park," said Katrina. "Am I going to get murdered?"

Julia ignored her. "All in all, Anandi is an excellent candidate. I heard she's always on the Internet. The Internet has really become a way for these creeps to get their victims. Maybe Hangman learned all about computers in prison and now he's in a Starbucks looking at profiles on Facebook, narrowing his list."

"God, Julia," Bea said. "They had computers five years ago, when he got caught. It's not like they were just invented."

"I feel sorry for Anandi," Katrina said. "Her life here isn't very easy. Why choose her, just because she's a loner? Why does everything have to be a popularity contest?" She wondered for a moment if her own popularity would falter if she made a complete ass of herself in Drama Club, and it was as if she felt a little tremor in her belly, like when you go over a bump on a roller coaster.

"I'm just saying, think like Hangman does," Julia said. "He's not going to go after a girl who has like a million friends she walks home with. That's not his MO."

Bea snickered. "MO? Who are you, Inspector Clouseau?"

"I've been studying the case, yes. Isn't it creepy to think that he's out there"—Julia nodded toward the window, which looked out over the Nardin playing fields—"looking for his next target? I hardly slept at all last night."

The intercom crackled to life. Katrina looked at the clock: 2:55. She would miss Spanish, for sure.

31

Walter Myeong's home was on a corner lot on the eastern fringe of the North. It was a large house, squat, symmetrical, with pale yellow bricks flecked with tiny lines of black. The brick gave the house a dingy look, but old-money dingy. Abbie parked the Saab in the driveway and got out, started up the flagstoned pathway toward the front door, painted a deep crimson.

The name Myeong in the North was jarring. When she was growing up, she thought that the North was populated exclusively by people with WASPy names: Rich (the makers of Coffee Rich, a hometown product), Ellicott, Pratt. It'd taken her years to realize that the North she'd carried around in her mind was a figment of the County's imagination, that in the intensity of its racial memory, the County had recreated the geography of Ireland right there in her home city. The County was the South of Ireland: Catholic, warm, working-class, and righteous in its bones, and the North, like Northern Ireland, was Protestant, rich, and foreign.

But there were all kinds of people in the North now. Myeong was proof.

Out front, there was an old-fashioned lamp held by a black iron pole, as tall as a man. The lamp was lit even in the afternoon light, and she could see a figure in the picture window, bent over, a patch of dark black hair. Beneath the bent-over man was the head of a young girl, looking down.

Abbie rang the bell and heard a gong sound deep inside. She heard murmuring, then footsteps. The door opened a crack and Abbie introduced herself to the sliver of a male face, showing her ID in the fading light.

"Police?" Myeong said, a tiny screech in his voice, as he opened the door wider.

Abbie tucked her badge and ID back into her bag. "Can we talk inside, Mr. Myeong?"

He studied her, sharp worry in his eyes. Walter Myeong wore a light blue button-down oxford shirt, black slacks, black socks and no shoes. He wore unfashionable black rectangular glasses and his face was lined, especially at the corners of the unsmiling mouth.

She heard music from the left, piano.

"Why would you want to come in?" Myeong said.

"Because it's cold out here?" Abbie said, smiling.

"Oh," he said. He opened the door and Abbie stepped into the house. The playing stopped and a young Asian girl appeared in the squared-off archway that led into a living room furnished with heavy leather pieces. The girl was eleven or twelve, plain, wearing the uniform of one of the local Catholic schools.

"Your daughter?" Abbie said.

A disturbed look crossed Mr. Myeong's face—pain and exasperation combined—and he glanced quickly at the girl. "No, this is Shun Wa. My student."

The girl smiled and nodded, then looked questioningly at Myeong.

"Please finish up with the Brahms," he said. Motioning to Abbie with a quick nod of the head, she followed him past the living room into the darkened kitchen, where he flicked on an overhead light. The piano playing resumed, faltered, then picked up a smooth tempo again.

"You teach piano?" Abbie asked.

"Since I lost my job at Dow, yes." Myeong was standing by the sink, his arms crossed. "I take anything I can get."

Abbie's eyes wandered over the room. The plastic containers that looked like they'd held leftovers in the yellow plastic drying rack chimed in her mind with the untended rosebushes in the overgrown garden that lined the front of the house and the single car in the driveway. She didn't feel a feminine presence here, especially not in the living room furniture. The house felt cold to her.

The divorce rate for the parents of children who died, despite the belief that it was far higher than normal couples, was actually less than half. People who lost kids tended to cling together. But maybe Myeong had lost more than his job.

"Do you want to sit down?" she suggested.

He shook his head. "This is fine." His voice was nasal and abrupt. Abbie took a breath. Myeong looked like he was poised for a blow. Whether to throw one or receive one she wasn't sure.

"I know that Marcus Flynn's escape must be bringing back awful memories, but I'm part of the team trying to catch him, and I want your help."

He watched her. "But what brings you here, to *my* house?"

Abbie felt the ground under her grow precarious. Myeong gave off a fragile anger, not uncommon in families of murder victims. The interview could go bad quickly. "I'm talking to everyone connected with the case, Mr. Myeong, not just you. Anything I can learn might help us find Hangman before he hurts another girl."

Mr. Myeong closed his eyes, and rubbed them. "It's been so long, I can't think of anything I could tell you that would help."

"The latest girl, Martha Stoltz. Did you ever hear your daughter talk about her? Was there any connection at all between Martha and your daughter?"

He stared at the kitchen floor. "I went through Maggie's high school yearbook, for sophomore year. There's nothing."

"What about activities?" Abbie asked. "Martha Stoltz was active in her Art Club and swimming."

A shake of the head.

Abbie frowned. "There is the symbol that was found on your daughter's hand . . ."

Myeong flinched as if she'd struck him, the body flexing inward, the eyelids pressing shut a millimeter, just briefly and then it was gone.

"I've never understood what it meant, that A. We spent many hours thinking about this. Was it the killer's initial maybe? As you know, it wasn't."

"You said we—you and your wife?"

He swallowed, then nodded.

"Are you and Mrs. Myeong still together?"

"We're divorced," he said. "After the . . ." He looked at Abbie. "After."

"I'm sorry to hear that. Is she still in the area?"

"No. Her family had been here for generations, but she'd had enough. She lives in London now."

She'd gone far away, about as far as you could. "So the A never rang a bell, even in the years afterward?"

He whispered, "No."

Abbie looked down at her notes, as much to break the rhythm of the No's as to look for the next question. "I noticed going through the interviews that the year before your daughter died you went with her to a hospital in Arizona."

Myeong nodded. "Yes."

"What was that for?"

Myeong looked like he could burn a hole in the ground with the heat of his gaze. "Maggie had problems with her stomach. The doctors here told her they were psychosomatic, that she was worried about her grades. We went to Tempe to the special gastrointestinal hospital there, looking for answers."

"How long were you out there?" Abbie asked.

"Three months."

"And did you meet anyone, especially, that you remember? Anyone she kept in touch with?"

"No. There was no one."

Myeong was a tightly sealed box, sealed from inside. Abbie studied him. She felt sorry for the man. He wasn't good with people, she could see that. He was rigid, and he didn't understand how he came across to others. To women, especially. He'd clearly given up ever trying to master charm or witty conversation. He was stuck as himself and would never change.

"Mr. Myeong, I have to ask you a sensitive question. The killer left a note and in it he said, 'They are not your children.'"

Myeong watched her, his eyes unfocused.

"I'm thinking of the letter A inside the box. I think that it's a baby block, like the ones infants play with."

Myeong flinched, his body twisting back away from her. His eyes sought the floor and stayed locked there. "Is that possible?" Abbie asked. "Mr. Myeong?"

Myeong only shook his head. His eyes never left the floor.

Abbie grimaced. "I have to ask you," she said. "If you have any doubt about who Maggie's parents were."

When the voice came, it seemed to rumble out of him. "Maggie was my daughter!"

"You're sure—?"

"Of course!" he cried. "Of course I'm sure she's my daughter." His eyes were wild now, and Abbie felt he might dash out of the room.

"Does the statement mean anything to you?" Abbie pressed on. "*They are not—*"

Myeong waved his hand in front of his face. "Nothing. He's insane. It means nothing to me!"

After that, Myeong closed down. Grunts and shakes of the head to Abbie's questions. No eye contact. He didn't ask her to leave, only went still and stopped communicating.

She said goodbye to Myeong and walked back to her car. When she got in and turned the key, she glanced left and saw him leaning over the girl at the piano, his head a foot above hers, both of them silhouetted against the golden glow of a floor lamp.

Of one thing she was sure: Walter Myeong had known or figured out a long time ago that the image on his daughter's hand was of a baby block.

Her phone rang as soon as she put the key in the ignition.

"Hello?" she answered.

"It's Lipschitz."

"Doctor."

"I want to tell you something that might have to do with the case. Someone offered me money for summaries of my sessions with Marcus Flynn."

Abbie's eyes went wide. "When was this?"

"About a year and a half ago. I got a call one night and they said that if I photocopied the notes from my twice-weekly sessions, and just happened to leave the notes in an envelope in a certain book in the public library near here, I could go back the next day and the envelope would be back in the book. But with two thousand dollars in it."

Four thousand dollars per week. Sixteen thousand dollars a month. Indefinitely.

"Who was the caller?" she said sharply.

"I have no idea. I hung up on him."

Abbie grimaced. "Can you tell me what he sounded like?"

Lipschitz paused. "A white male, older. Over forty, I'd say. I didn't spend a lot of time on the phone. I was offended, and of course I said no. No accent. That's all I remember."

"Why did he want the notes?" asked Abbie.

"Didn't tell me."

"What did you think?"

"It could have been anything, but I assumed it was one of those serial killer groupies. They collect anything they can get: letters, artwork, I mean anything. That's why I didn't mention it before."

"Did he call back?"

"Yes, twice. I just hung up in the middle of his spiel."

Abbie started the car and swung it around, heading toward downtown. "Doctor, I want to subpoena your phone records from that period. Will you agree to that? It would go faster if you said yes."

"Whatever you want," Lipschitz said. "I didn't think this could be related, but I'm not the detective."

"This helps."

She hung up and said a quick prayer that the man with all this extra cash was stupid enough to use his own cell.

32

Abbie drove to the house of Mrs. Chopin, to see if there was anyone lurking nearby. Hangman had an eyewitness to one of his murders; he wouldn't like that. The mask implied a deep desire for anonymity. And he might not know the family had left.

The street was mostly empty of cars. As she cruised past Mrs. Chopin's address, she saw the curtains were pulled and there was a copy of *The Buffalo News* lying on the welcome mat.

Abbie drove through light traffic toward Delaware Park, then headed back to Riesen's building. She parked across the street in the parking lot of a 7-Eleven and pretended to watch the traffic pass by. But really she was focused on the front door of the submarine building. The amount of money involved in the case was growing, and Riesen was the richest man in the files. It was time to talk to him face-to-face.

Abbie tried to clear her mind, but the call from Lipschitz had stirred something up, had linked up with possibilities that had been drifting like loose threads, forming thoughts and then dissipating. Almost against her will, the threads had bound themselves into an idea, but an idea so far-fetched that she rebelled against it. But with Lipschitz's call, it wouldn't go away.

What if Frank Riesen, desperate to find out where his daughter was buried, had gone looking for a way to reach Hangman? What if grief over his missing daughter drove him to contact Joe Carlson? Riesen might have paid Carlson to stand outside Marcus Flynn's cell and ask the question over and over, in the dimness of the hallway at night, with lights out, *Where's the girl?* Riesen could have paid Carlson for this service, and tried to bribe Lipschitz to see what Flynn was saying in therapy. Abbie could imagine herself doing the same thing if she were wealthy and had been robbed of her daughter. What good would millions of dollars do if your child's body was under some desolate hill, covered with moldering leaves, leaching its flesh into the soil?

She shivered and turned the key in the ignition until the vents roared with hot air. She turned the switch to low and left the engine running.

Men like Riesen know that money can find paths around obstacles. It can hire assemblymen, influence mayors, even break through stone walls if need be. Did Riesen imagine that Hangman would blurt out the truth one day, and Joe Carlson would be there to listen?

Or perhaps Riesen had sent Joe Carlson to Hangman's cell to torment him. Never let the bastard forget the name of his last victim. Auburn was a modern facility, not the hellhole that Attica was. Maybe Riesen thought Flynn had it too easy, getting three hot meals a day and a remorse-free existence.

Hangman had tried to erase the memory of what he'd done to his own cousin by firing a bullet into his brain. But maybe Frank Riesen wouldn't let him forget.

Her idea sent a chill of nausea through her. She fended it off—thinking through ridiculous theories just exhausted her. But the more she tried *not* to think about it, the more she did.

Abbie leaned over and flicked the radio over to Band 9. The neighborhoods around her, all over downtown and the North, had been carved into search grids. Teams were moving from street to street, sweeping west to east, which meant they'd started on the shore of Lake Erie and were headed toward her, parked on Elmwood Avenue. They were checking backyards, rattling the doors of garages to make sure they were locked, rousting vagrants, poking inside toolsheds. The reports were terse. An unlocked basement door on West Huron Street.

An abandoned storefront along Fell Alley. An old toolshed off of Niagara Street. The teams checked in as they went in, then called out "Clear" when they left.

Somewhere at Police Headquarters, a cop was checking off the buildings on a big map of the city. Abbie imagined a dark wave sweeping across Buffalo from the lake. At night, the beams of flashlights would flicker at its edge like flashes from an electrical storm. But they weren't finding anything.

Anyone could listen in to the search. HQ believed that the odds on Hangman getting his hands on a police radio were low, but Abbie wasn't so sure. He'd already escaped from an experienced CO and found himself a victim in record time. Who knew what Hangman was capable of? Perhaps he was listening in, just like Abbie, moving just ahead of the search parties, then looping back around to the streets they'd already cleared.

Abbie considered calling Perelli with a suggestion. Have the teams stop where they were, surreptitiously load into cars and vans while staying off the radio, drive a mile to the east, and take up the hunt from the other side of the city, pushing back toward their last position from the opposite direction, all the while giving updates on the radio as if their location hadn't changed. That way Hangman, if he was keeping just ahead of the dragnet, would run straight into the searchers.

She listened to the police radio for a minute, trying to distract herself. But the idea she didn't want to think about kept lurking in the back of her mind.

What the hell. Let's follow it all the way.

What if Riesen, mad with grief, had gone one step further, and paid Carlson to take Hangman to the spot of the girl's disappearance? One last shot at getting an answer before Hangman disappeared into the dungeon of Attica forever.

As one of the guards entrusted with transporting prisoners from one New York State facility to another, Carlson would get the schedule of transfers ahead of time, perhaps by a week but at least a few days. What if he told Riesen that Marcus Flynn was being transferred? Maybe Carlson had even come up with the idea himself, since his golden goose was leaving and here was a chance at a final payoff.

If Riesen couldn't find a guard in Attica to bribe, the transfer would be the final chance, maybe forever, for someone to demand from Marcus Flynn what he'd done with Sandy's body. Abbie couldn't think of any other reason that would account for Carlson being up there on that hill.

Of course, it could just have been Carlson's personal vendetta. Maybe the guard was a frustrated cop, like so many COs, who thought he'd solve the case the Buffalo detectives couldn't close: the whereabouts of Hangman's last victim.

Maybe a lot of damn things, Abbie thought.

33

Hangman waited in the dark. The garage smelled of lawn mower, a mix of old grass cuttings and oil, and damp newspapers. The garage was old, a one-car wooden shack separate from the house, a Victorian he'd been watching all day. He could hear the noise of cars passing in the street, faintly. Not much traffic, a nice quiet block.

He felt safe. The day swelled with potential. He wasn't lucky, he was just smart and now it was going to pay off. He'd had strict criteria for what he'd been looking for. There were thousands of people looking for him, but this was no excuse for lowering his standards.

He'd wanted an unattached garage, and luckily most of the older homes near Delaware Park had been built with them, offering him a range of targets. He'd wanted a woman, and that had been easy enough. The old-money families of the North were so traditional; he'd watched the men leave in the morning for their law offices and corporate suites downtown, leaving behind a neighborhood of females. But Wendy Lamb didn't even have a man in the house.

Even better.

Once he'd seen her at the doorway the day before, fumbling for her keys, her hair a mess, he'd caught his breath. It was wonderful, really, the way things worked out.

He checked the dead guard's fancy watch. It was 3:22 p.m. Wendy would be leaving her house soon.

Hangman breathed deeply, enjoying the smell of the garage. It was as if the odors of summers past were pressed into the oiled wood as into the leaves of a book. There, a hint of mink oil, the kind used to break in a new baseball glove (he used to use the same oil himself as a Little Leaguer, to soften up the leather). Was there a boy living in the house, or had he gone off to college, as all good children of the North did? Was he imagining things or did he even smell a whiff of Coppertone? There was an old beach umbrella in the far corner by the bikes, and that could still have some faint chemical traces of the suntan lotion in its folds.

His senses were wholly aroused. He felt he could sniff the air and smell a woman's perfume from a hundred feet away.

He heard footsteps, *there*. Heels on pebbled cement. Wendy was on the path from the house to the garage. He imagined her scent—something rich. Creed. Or Chanel. There was the clatter of a screen door slamming against the frame. She was in a hurry, not stopping to turn and close the door softly. He turned and moved to the garage's darkest corner, near the bumper on the car's passenger side. He crouched down, a short piece of rope held across his right thigh.

The garage door jerked and began to open, a metallic drone filling the garage. Late afternoon daylight poured into the space, and Hangman crouched lower by the bumper, moving toward the passenger door. Wendy walked into the garage, head down, dressed in a black cloche coat, a rough yarn hat, tan slacks, and patent loafers. He tried to time his footsteps with hers, along the other side of the car, but he hardly needed to. Wendy seemed distracted as she reached for the door and pulled it open.

His heart raced as he slipped around the car, stalking her from behind. Wendy leaned into the car, putting her purse into the passenger seat. When she straightened up, she turned to find him standing there, right in the open driver's door.

He caught the first scream like you would a terrified mouse. Just a short burst escaped at a high pitch before his hand was over her mouth. It had been risky but really a little fun. He pulled her toward him as if they were embracing, slammed the car door shut with his left hand, and shoved her head back until the bones creaked and he felt her eyelids flutter with pain. Her eyes were open so wide that it looked like they would pop out, and her flabby body against him was filled with a wild, flailing power. But Hangman had been expecting this, and he was far too strong. He had her trapped against the car now, and he ground against her bucking body as if he were in lust, while he stared deep into her terrified eyes.

Hangman pressed his fingers into her throat, watching her face contort from a few inches away. The rope slipping over her head, the hair all mussed and the terrified eyes. Gorgeous. He pulled his hand away and she didn't even have time to cry out before the rope was tight around her larynx, closing on moisturized skin with a velvety *thrwiiirrp*.

The woman groaned and her body went into a kind of spasm. He found the keys in her palsied, shaking right hand and pulled them slowly from her grip. Her strength ebbed; he felt it sink away. A thin line of foam appeared in the right corner of her mouth and he pulled back on the noose, twisting the rope to finish her off. As she let go of a guttural moan, he pressed the button on the keychain's remote. The garage door clattered to life and began to close, slowly sinking the space back into darkness.

34

The 7-Eleven across from Riesen's office wasn't busy. From the parking lot, Abbie watched customers stop in for milk or cigarettes and quickly leave. It began to rain lightly and the traffic lights sent long, wavy reflections down the slick streets. Abbie watched the lights change on the asphalt, her frustration building. She listened to the flow of the radio traffic, switching between the search teams on Band 9, and the regular dispatcher on 8.

Shivering in the driver's seat, she turned the key in the ignition. The Saab's engine purred to life and Abbie turned the heat up all the way. She shifted her body left and resumed watching the front door to Riesen's building.

A car pulled in to the 7-Eleven, and two teenage males got out, one fat with an acne-pocked face, another tall and craggily handsome, talking loudly, and headed into the convenience store. Abbie watched them go, arguing about which beer they were going to buy.

Another Friday afternoon in Buffalo, she thought. Some people just go on living their lives.

Raymond texted her. "Negative on phone calls to Lipschitz," he said. "TracFone, a disposable. Used for calls, never again."

Abbie slapped the Saab's dashboard.

"One break!" she cried. "One goddamn little break . . ."

She called McGonagle. As he picked up, she could hear bar sounds: clinking glasses, a droning TV.

"You heard about the note Hangman left at Martha Stoltz's house?"

"Yeah."

Of course he had. McGonagle heard everything. The Network was working at high efficiency.

Abbie felt a strange intimacy talking to the retired detective. There was nothing like the intensity of two cops working the same case. The same dread, the same fear of failing. It brought you close to people you'd never get close to in any other way.

"Did the words mean anything to you?" she asked. "'I live where the kings abide'?"

McGonagle exhaled. "Nothing."

For a fleeting second, she was tempted to take up the old cop's offer of full access to the Network. It had a hundred eyes, this thing, a thousand hands. It heard dog whistles, spoke languages she hadn't mastered yet. Save a life, she thought.

But she couldn't say yes. One step in that direction and she would become a greasy shadow of her father.

"McGonagle."

"Yeah?"

"What was folder 3CW?"

Silence.

"What fol—"

"Do not bullshit me," Abbie said sharply. "It was paper-clipped to your final case file so I know you were aware of it."

Nothing.

"McGonagle?"

"It was an abuse report on Sandy Riesen."

"CW is for Child Welfare?" Abbie said in a shocked voice.

"Yeah."

"What did it say?"

"It said they could find no evidence that Frank Riesen was abusing his daughter, okay?"

Abbie sat up straight in the seat. "*Riesen* was the one accused of abusing her?"

"Yeah. Someone wrote a letter to Child Welfare weeks before Sandy disappeared. Said he'd witnessed her with her shirt off and there were bruises . . . It was all bullshit. A fucking witch hunt."

"Go on," said Abbie.

"Bruises and whip marks across her back. Child Welfare looked into it, interviewed her teachers, classmates, even her gym coach. Some had noticed a few bruises but the girl played field hockey. So Child Welfare closed the case without any findings."

"And then just after that, Sandy disappeared."

"Yeah."

Abbie stared at the submarine building, half-sunk into the shrubbery, as if it was surfacing.

"Do you think he was beating her?" Abbie said quietly. It was as if McGonagle was sitting next to her in the passenger seat.

"No."

Abbie's head was spinning. "What happened to the folder?"

McGonagle gave out a low laugh. "It fell through a crack somewhere in the evidence room. Shit happens."

35

The entrance to Nardin Academy looked like a medieval castle, with a high-domed doorway set between a pair of crenellated towers, all in light-colored limestone. No girls gathered out front waiting for their parents, as would be the case on almost any other day. The wide stone pathway between the street and the doorway was empty but for a few strands of crepe paper in green and white, the school colors.

Two female teachers stood guard at the door this afternoon, peering through the dark glass as each new car arrived in the driveway that fronted the school, opening the door a crack to confirm the car's identity. Then they would turn and speak to someone inside. A girl would quickly emerge and hurry toward the car, get in, and the vehicle would zoom off. It was a system the girls had taken to quickly and without much fuss.

There were a line of cars out front by 3:45, smoke funneling from their exhaust pipes and drifting up into the dripping branches of the oaks that lined the campus. The cars were mostly German, many were SUVs, big ones lumbering up the drive and sitting to wait thirty yards from the door. Nardin was one of the best private high schools in Buffalo, its students from the richest and oldest families in the city. There were college stickers on the back windows of several of the cars: Bowdoin. Harvard. Stanford. Fingernails with French manicures tapped on the leather steering wheels.

A white Mercedes SUV with tinted windows turned off West Ferry Street into the academy's entrance, pulled up behind a Honda Pilot, and parked, the engine continuing to run. The door of the academy cracked and a teacher stared out. She turned her head, keeping the door open a few inches. Almost instantly, Katrina Lamb emerged from beside the teacher, said something quickly to her, then hurried down the steps.

Katrina was annoyed, to say the least. Drama Club had been canceled, as she'd feared, and the principal had informed the students that all extracurricular activities were being put on hold until the crisis was over. When Katrina reached the wide stone pathway, she frowned and folded her arms over two large books that formed the bulk of her homework, staring down as she walked. She hurried down the pathway and pulled open the rear door of the Mercedes.

"Hi, Mom," she said glumly. She placed her schoolbag on the leather seat and pushed it across, then got in after it. She waved to Ms. Crumpworth, the teacher at Nardin's door, and pulled the door shut.

Her mother said nothing, just put the car in drive and drove slowly toward the gate. She had her black coat on, the one she wore in the coldest weather, and her stupid Alpine hat, the knit one with the ear flaps. Katrina wished she wouldn't wear it; it was crunchy and weird and it looked like her mother was trying too hard to be young, which she clearly wasn't anymore. Maybe Katrina would get her a nice new one for Christmas, a black faux fur. That would match the coat.

The SUV made a U-turn and exited the way it had come in, then made a right on West Ferry.

"Ugh, could you change the station please?" Katrina said, making a cranky face. The radio was playing classical, which Katrina hated.

Her mother didn't move. Katrina couldn't see her face in the rearview mirror. Her mother must have knocked the mirror getting in, because it was tilted up and toward the right.

"I mean, really?"

Her mother said nothing. But a few seconds later the music changed and soon the radio was playing CHUM 104.5. Alicia Keys. She must have hit one of the buttons on the steering wheel.

"Thank you," Katrina said, sitting back.

The car made a right turn toward their house on Sycamore.

Katrina sat back and watched the bare trees of the North whisk by through the darkened windows that made everything outside seem as if it was in dusk. The car was warm and she began thinking about the clay pot she was making in Art Club. She'd decided on peonies as a decorative motif, but what if she did something original with the stems? An idea came to her cleanly, as if it had been waiting for her since morning: she'd weave a few letters into the design of the stems as they curled up from the bottom of the pot. Her initials, KL, interwoven with her father's, RL. It would be symbolic. It would be part of her birthday gift to him, with an understated message of love, expressed in a way that fit her personality. Their initials woven together. Unbreakable. Unlike her parents' marriage.

It would be . . .

Her expression changed from one of almost childish delight to confusion. Katrina brought her face closer to the tinted window. "Hey, where are we going?" she said wonderingly.

Her mother had passed their street and was driving along the western border of Delaware Park. Katrina saw joggers running along the trails, their breath puffing out in clouds as they moved along. There were young moms pushing their running strollers, taut in their black Lycra.

"Do you have to get the dry cleaning or something?" Katrina said.

The Mercedes swept on, doing 35 mph. A car honked far away.

"Mom?"

Her mother didn't turn. Katrina watched as she reached to the console of the dashboard and hit a button there. *Clunk.* The four doors of the Mercedes locked.

Katrina didn't hear the sound. Her eyes were on the steering wheel, on the hand extending out of the sleeve of the black coat that had hit the lock button and that was now resting on the wheel's black leather.

It was a large hand. A man's hand.

Her bones turned to shafts of ice.

36

The wet asphalt reflected the ghostly green of the pale sunlight. Abbie took a sip of Lime Diet Coke. When she looked up, Frank Riesen, wearing a trench coat and dark pin-striped slacks, was stepping out of his white Buick Roadmaster, parked in a corner of the lot. He'd pulled in so quickly she'd barely caught it.

Abbie pushed the Saab door open and nearly tumbled out of the car. From twenty yards away, she heard Riesen click the button on his keychain and the *chunk* of the Buick doors locking. Abbie sprinted across the street without looking left and right.

Riesen heard her footsteps. Turning, his face was contorted with a spasm of terror before his eyes focused and his body noticeably relaxed.

"Mr. Riesen?" Abbie called, bringing her ID up as she covered the ground between them. "I'm Detective Kearney."

"I know who you are," he said, frowning.

Abbie came up to Riesen and took a deep breath. "Then you know I came to see you. I wanted to talk to you."

He had the features of a nineteenth-century senator, she thought, a Daniel Webster. The lines in Riesen's face were deep and his eyes were blue and bright.

"If I thought I could help, I'd be happy to," he said. "But I can't." He began to move around her.

Abbie swiveled and walked with him. "Why don't you let me be the judge of that?"

He glared at her in silence, then stepped around her.

"You know he's out there," she said, her voice a little ragged.

That stopped him. He almost said something but thought better of it. Riesen composed himself and then spoke to her in a clipped voice. "Your department promised to do everything it could to bring back my daughter. That was a long time ago."

"This is another chance."

"This is not another chance," he said, walking briskly past her toward the door of the submarine building. He seemed to be shaking slightly. Abbie followed Riesen and dropped into stride with him.

She touched his arm, then gripped it tight when he wouldn't stop. "Mr. Riesen, I'm scared he's going to kill a girl today. This afternoon."

Riesen whipped his arm down. "I believed you people once," he whispered. "No more."

She felt the anger come off him in waves. "I am sorry about your daughter," she said.

"Leave me out of this," he said, practically spitting the words at her. Instead of walking into his office, he turned back toward the Roadmaster and reached for his keys.

Abbie tried to reply but couldn't. She heard the Buick's door slam shut, heard the engine roar to life, heard its tires whisper on the asphalt as it sped out of the lot.

Her mind was awhirl. As Riesen had reached up and grabbed her arm, she'd gotten a good look at his right hand. The fingers were clear in the late fall sunlight. And on Frank Riesen's pinkie was a signet ring with the letter S curled on it in medieval script.

Unless Frank Riesen had, in his grief, gone to a jeweler and ordered a duplicate, this was one of the two rings Sandy was wearing when she was kidnapped.

37

At 6:45 p.m. Frank Riesen emerged from 19 Chapin Parkway in North Buffalo. His face was lit briefly by a light affixed to the side of the home's tall scarlet red door. The house itself was light gray and looked like a French country house, with eight windows set in the front facade, four upstairs and four down. The lawn was immaculate, and the path to the front door was lit by a series of lights framed in oxidized metal. There was a white Buick Roadmaster parked in the driveway. Riesen hurried toward it, hitching up the collar of his expensive trench coat against the cold.

From fifty yards away, parked across the street and a block down, Abbie leaned forward in the Saab's driver seat for a better look. Riesen pulled open the Roadmaster's door, and the inside light once again illuminated his face. The Buick started up and began backing out of the driveway.

Abbie turned on the engine and fastened her seat belt. A minute later, the Buick's lights came slicing out from the driveway and headed north. Abbie let the Buick go a full block before following. A one-car tail was the most easily spotted. She'd have to lie back and pray that Riesen didn't make any sudden turns. The Buick headed downtown toward City Hall and the web of highway entrance and exit ramps nestled there.

"Where's the traffic?" Abbie said into the empty car. The Saab was exposed. She needed cover, and when a taxi turned right ahead of her, she dropped behind it.

The Buick's brake lights flashed ahead and it slid under a yellow light. The taxi stopped ahead of Abbie, but she sped by it and went through the red light, praying Riesen wasn't watching his rearview.

The car turned right on Church Street and swept up a highway entrance ramp. She saw the luminescent letters of the green sign flash in her headlights, "Niagara Thruway North." Abbie followed, grateful to merge into highway traffic. She kept the Buick within ten car lengths as it swept over to the passing lane and surged ahead.

38

Katrina Lamb woke, and she felt the cold air of her breath spread across her face. There was no pain; she felt only pricks, a tingling sensation from her body. She was lying on something that was vibrating, like a washing machine.

Her hands were down there in the dark, miles away. Maybe they were chopped off and she was only feeling phantom limbs. But then she traced a ghostly line of pain across the wrists; her hands were bound together. Something was in her mouth, too. She felt she couldn't breathe and bit down on the gag. It was rubber, round and hard. A cord was tied around the back of her head to keep the gag in place.

Oh God no, she thought.

The vibration became a thump. Something metal behind her rattled. I'm in a car, she thought, the trunk of a moving car.

And then the image of the hand on the steering wheel came back to her. She closed her eyes and screamed into the gag and screamed and screamed. It felt like her eardrums were going to burst because the sound wasn't getting out, it was just echoing inside her head. Her tongue tasted rubber, oily rubber. Realizing she was biting into the gag, she stopped.

A thought tumbled into her mind as the screaming died away: her mom's Mercedes didn't have a trunk. She couldn't remember leaving the backseat of the Mercedes. Hangman must have drugged her and made the transfer when she was unconscious. The trunk smelled of oil and the metal under her cheek was cold as a sheet of ice. Inches away, she heard the axle spinning.

Katrina kicked out with her legs and felt that they were tied together. No, taped. The tape stuck to her skin just above the ankle. It hurt when she twisted it, and she could feel the glue pulling at the hairs on her leg, which she'd forgotten to shave the night before.

The car made a turn and she slid helplessly to the left. Katrina breathed through her nose, trying not to panic. She had to keep calm and not spaz out.

Maybe there was something in the trunk she could use. Something sharp to cut the tape on her hands. The car kept shifting and she could feel things, steel things, clinking back here over the hum of the engine from the front. She kept sliding along with the tools or whatever the metal things that were making the noise. If she could just reach one of them and cut the tape on her hands . . .

What did they say to do, in the movies? Pull out the brake light wires so a cop would see they were out and pull the guy over. She'd seen that on *Dateline NBC* or one of those paranoid shows her mom watched religiously.

She was turned toward the back of the car, lying on her side. The wires would be a few feet ahead of her. But to have any chance . . .

The thought of her mom looped around her brain and came back to her. She tried thinking about the lights but the image of her mother came to her instead. How had Hangman gotten the Mercedes away from her?

Katrina froze. He stole the car, that was all. Her mom was forever leaving keys and bags around where people could take them. Anyway, she couldn't worry about that now. Her mom was *fine*. She just had to get herself loose and she could get to the lights, then she would be free and she could have a mental breakdown then. One disaster at a time, Katrina, she said to herself.

The car turned right and Katrina slid again. Someone outside the car hit their horn and it was so loud that Katrina felt the muscles on her back stiffen. What if someone crashed into the back of the car and crushed her? What if the cops were already pursuing Hangman, and they tried one of those crazy maneuvers where they bumped the back of the car and it went careening out of control and crashed?

She closed her eyes.

The blaring of the horn faded and she could hear only the hum of the wheels on the street. Her ear was pressed to the bottom of the trunk so the metal vibration seemed to thrum in her head, as if her face was just an inch above the road.

She prayed someone would crash into the car. Would cops do that, not knowing she was in the trunk? Would she die in the crash?

She didn't care. Bump it, she thought. Flip the car over! Just get me out of this trunk and away from Hangman.

Focus, Katrina. Block out any negativity from your mind. You have to stop waiting on some guy to save you or you'll be the next girl on the front page of *The Buffalo News*.

She breathed in deeply through her nose, then began feeling around in front of her. Her hands were taped all the way up to the knuckles, so she could only open and close her fingers in a V. It was kind of grotesque, like she was a lobster girl or something, but it was the only way.

Reaching ahead, she felt a nubby fabric under her. Her cheek was lying against bare metal but under her body was a carpet, or maybe old car mats. That's what people did in Buffalo, kept the old car mats in their trunk in case they got stuck in a storm and the spinning wheels had turned the snow to ice. They put the mats under the wheels and it helped the car lift out of the rut.

For a moment, Katrina thought she was going to gag, thinking how dirty car mats were. If you throw up, you're going to choke on your own vomit. *Stop it, Katrina!*

She breathed out through her nose, in and out, in and out. It made a whistling noise, but after ten breaths she was calmer. Katrina laid her hands flat on the floor beneath her and felt around in an arc in front of her body. Just fabric and twigs. Nothing metal or sharp that could cut through the tape on her legs.

Her hand brushed against something plastic that went skittering away as the car turned right. An empty pop bottle maybe. It was a big trunk. She was scrunched near the brake lights but she could feel the space behind her.

She arched her back and her hands went further, the fingers of the right hand feeling along the floor of the trunk. Lobster girl to the rescue, she joked, trying to keep the hysteria away.

An inch further, two inches. One of those tools had to be here somewhere. Her back muscles cramped with the effort. Katrina grit her teeth and her tentacle-fingers crept along the foul-smelling rug a little . . .

She touched something. Not steel or fabric but something else.

Her mind went white with horror. She realized the thing she was touching was bare skin.

A leg. A human leg.

Katrina's eyes went wide and she screamed, whipping her head back and forth.

The leg twitched and pulled away.

39

Abbie trailed the Roadmaster, its distinctive rectangular brake lights flashing occasionally as Riesen drove north toward Niagara Falls. Dusk was beginning to darken the sky. The Buick changed lanes and disappeared behind a chocolate brown tractor-trailer with UPS written on the side. Abbie nudged the accelerator and got into the left lane, searching for the Roadmaster. Nothing.

"Damn it," she muttered darkly, accelerating to the right. As she whipped around a big Ford pickup, she saw the Roadmaster's brake lights disappearing over the hump of the Cleveland Drive exit ramp.

Abbie snapped the steering wheel right as she jammed on the brakes, nearly overshooting the exit. The pickup came within inches of clipping her back as she dove toward the exit, the horn blaring as it shot past, the Saab sliding on loose gravel, nearly going into the guardrail before she straightened it out. Glancing ahead, she saw the Buick making the left on Cleveland Drive and disappearing around the corner. Abbie speared the gas pedal and zoomed down the ramp, swinging the turn just as the light turned red.

She was breathing quickly, her heart racing. The Roadmaster was two blocks ahead now. It rolled under the underpass for the 90. The car's left turn signal blinked on and the big Buick slid up the entrance ramp for the 90 South. Riesen was heading back the way he'd just come.

"Now why would you do that?" Abbie said, tapping the steering wheel lightly with her palm.

She let the Buick zoom up the ramp, then followed once it had disappeared onto the thruway. Once she'd made the 90, she closed the gap to ten car lengths, dropping in behind a black Toyota Prius. She followed Riesen as he retraced his route back to Buffalo, doing a conservative 60 mph, then took the exit for Delaware Avenue. Traffic was thinning out, the work crowd already reaching home. She kept her eyes on the Roadmaster as it navigated the broad avenue. College students waited to cross, on their way to the bars on Chippewa. The Roadmaster zoomed by them, heading northward.

At the main entrance to Delaware Park, the Buick's right turn signal blinked on.

Abbie's face grew puzzled. She wondered for a moment if Riesen was toying with her, leading her on a scenic tour of the Niagara Frontier for some obscure reason.

Riesen's car slowed to 20 mph and slid quietly down the lane shaded by elms on both sides. Abbie slowed even further and watched the car navigate the winding park road. She saw something blue appear up on her left. "Oh no," she said. "Couldn't be."

Two minutes later, Riesen pulled into a parking lot. A sign at the far corner led to a small wooden deck that reached thirty feet over the rippling blue surface of the water. A sign read HOYT LAKE BOAT RENTALS.

Fifteen minutes later, Abbie crept along the shoreline of Hoyt Lake, carrying her portable radio, the volume turned way down, by her side. Her boots sank half an inch with every step into the mud of the soft fringe. The lake was like a black disc laid out in front of her, with two boats floating across the surface, drifting. Behind them, the sky was dark, edged in the west with streaks of orange, the sun disappeared over the horizon. The boat closer to her was Riesen's.

She'd watched him climb unsteadily into it, helped in by the towheaded teenager who was manning the rental shack. She'd watched him push off the dock with an oar, and begin to row, an old business-man alone in a green-hulled boat at 7:30 p.m. on a fall evening. Abbie had jumped out of the Saab and tracked him, ducking behind the weeping willows and small poplars that dotted the shore. To hop in a rowboat and follow would have been foolish. Riesen or anyone else on the lookout for observers would spot her immediately. She had to assume that the reason for coming to Hoyt Lake by such a roundabout way was to see if anyone was following him.

Dusk was settling over the lake, and she could hear voices from the other boat ringing softly off the water. Inside were two teenagers dressed in denim jackets, a lanky black boy and a chubby-cheeked red-headed white girl. They were chatting as the boy awkwardly set the oars in the water and tried to row, the girl sending out giggles of nervousness every time the boat tilted left or right. Riesen was silent, turned in profile, the oars pulled out of the water. He was watching the darkened shoreline.

She checked her watch: 7:32 p.m. The rental shack would be closing soon. She couldn't imagine it would stay open past eight o'clock. Abbie scanned the fringe of land that Riesen was watching, seeing ducks waddling ashore and a jogger or two pass by on the asphalt runner's path, but nothing sinister. Who was Riesen waiting for? Did it have anything to do with the myth of the Madeleines, which said there were the bones of female workers just below where Riesen was drifting? Or was he out on a wild-goose chase?

She heard the plash of oars. Riesen was rowing now, just a couple of strokes. The current was taking the craft toward shore, and he was pushing it back toward the center of the lake. When he'd regained his position, he pulled the oars back in, the wood scraping along the gun-wale.

The teenagers' boat turned in the water, its prow headed back toward the dock. The craft passed within ten or fifteen feet of Riesen's, but he barely glanced at the pair.

Abbie felt a stab of annoyance. Had Riesen led her here on purpose, keeping her away from the true action? What if Riesen was here to throw himself into the lake, unable to bear the reminders of Sandy that were popping up on the local news every ten minutes?

A voice snapped her thoughts back to the radio in her hand. Abbie crouched down, turning her back to shield the sound. She turned the volume down further and brought the radio up to her ear.

"—Team 3. Thirty-four Sycamore off of Delaware. White female, Signal 7."

Abbie closed her eyes. Stephenson was North Buffalo, maybe six blocks away. Signal 7 meant a dead body.

"Tell the chief and get the ME's office here," the voice said. "We're going to check the house, see about next of kin."

Static, with voices calling out in the background. The dispatcher came on.

"Team 3, supervisor wants to know if it appears connected to ongoing investigation."

Just say "Hangman," Abbie thought. Everyone knows what you're talking about. Half the city is listening in right now and your codes aren't fooling anyone. Just . . . say . . . Hangman.

"Uh," the rough voice came back on. "That's unknown at this point."

Abbie felt like throwing the radio into the lake. If it was Hangman, she could be at the scene in ten minutes. But if it wasn't, she didn't want to leave Riesen alone on the lake. The radio popped with static.

Stay or go? Abbie turned and shot a glance at Riesen. He was tilted away from her, looking over the gunwales down into the surface of the water. The boat drifted in a circle. Did he see white bones down there? Were Sandy's among them? Abbie shivered.

The channel was going to fill up with voices fast. She darted up the bank, heading toward a path that curled back toward the parking lot. When she reached the path, almost invisible in the fading light, she brought the radio up. "Team 3, this is Kearney."

She heard yelling through the static. People were piling in already. They were going to muck up her crime scene. Abbie began running.

"Kearney?" The search team leader barked. "All right, go ahead." He sounded annoyed. He wanted to deal with Dispatch only, and not open up the channel to every cop in the city. Too bad. She was the lead here.

"What is the method, Signal 7?" she said.

Waves of static.

"Kearney . . ."

Abbie climbed a steep incline on the path and saw the parking lot. She snapped the button down. "Just tell me."

Blasts of interference, cutting to silence as the search team leader hit the talk button.

"Strangulation."

40

For a moment, Katrina imagined that she was dead, that this was the moment her spirit lifted from her body and she was given one last look at herself, lying on the ground, because she could sense that, yes, she was lying on a rough stone floor. In a few seconds, her spirit would rise and she would gaze down on her corpse and see her lifeless body, a noose tied around the neck and her hands bound.

She was out of the car, she knew that. It was over. He had taken her out of the car and hung her. The lonely death of lobster girl, she thought.

The joke didn't help. Katrina whimpered softly.

Her body felt like it was drifting on a fuzzy cloud. It was almost pleasant. She waited for the moment when her spirit departed. It wouldn't be long now. She felt weird, as if she was grieving for herself. She had the sense she'd been lying on this stone floor for hours.

What will I look like down here? Did he strip me naked? Am I mutilated? She felt strange that she was so unemotional, that the questions didn't send horrific images spinning through her head. Why am I so freaking calm? It wasn't normal.

She felt the flank of her right thigh on the floor, the cold pressing uncomfortably through the thin material of her capri pants. How dead can I be if I can feel my leg? That makes no sense whatsoever.

He must have drugged me again, she thought, and I'm coming out of it now. I'm not in the trunk anymore.

Her left foot tingled far away, and then it was like lights winking on in a city that's just been through a blackout. Little stabs of light all along her back and legs, numb but glowing brighter, as if each nerve in her body was lighting up one by one.

As her mind slowly cleared, fear rose over it like a black wave. Katrina closed her eyes and tried to breathe steadily. She was able to rock her shoulders forward slightly, but she couldn't sit up.

She creaked her neck now and as she did, her gaze swept along the floor. She was in a dark little room with a small window above her head, smudged with dirt, with rusty iron bars outside the glass, just visible in the gloomy light. Katrina could see a wall made of rough stones. For a second she thought she'd been transported to somewhere in Europe, a castle or a dungeon or something like that. Where would you see old stone walls like that in Buffalo, she thought.

She was not particularly claustrophobic and in fact at home she liked to wrap herself up in her duvet as tight as they wrapped Russian babies—she'd seen this in *The Buffalo News* once. The Russians wrapped their babies up tight until they looked like little mummies, with their red faces sticking out on top. It gave them a feeling of security and it prepared them for a life of regulations. She'd used it in a Social Studies paper she did on Russia and she'd gotten an A on it.

The idea of how important that A had been to her then and how stupid it seemed now unnerved Katrina and she let out a gasp. But she caught it quick. Now I'm alone, she thought. I can escape.

Her hands, still taped together, felt the wall just above her head. It was rock, not smooth stone, but actual bumpy, jagged rocks cemented together, like Old Fort Erie that they went to on school trips. The stones were dry and large and Katrina stuck the fingers of her right hand between them, running her fingers along the cement that held them together and she was unable to even scrape off a little.

When she brought her hand away, she felt something on her hands.

She brushed it off quickly. It was an old place. It's like he's taken me to a faraway land, she thought. Dracula's castle.

Think, Katrina. What buildings have I been in that are built of stone? Nardin, that's the oldest place I know. Katrina realized she had no idea when it was built. Think of the letterhead, she thought, it must have a line saying when it was founded. She closed her eyes and pictured the letters the school sent home but she couldn't even visualize the paper. Then she thought of the bills her mother got every semester from the school and, maybe because she always freaked out a little, wondering if her father would send the check, she saw the seal of the school, the weird-looking shield with the two lit torches beside it. She remembered the Latin words, *Pro Christi* something or other, she couldn't recall the rest, and on top the year. Oh, but it was Roman numerals. She could remember the first four or five. M. D. And then three Cs.

So it was from the 1800s. Could she really be locked in the basement of Nardin?

Tiny slivers of light came from her left and Katrina got up unsteadily, first on her knees and then up on her feet and walked toward them, afraid that in the darkness there would be a hole in the floor and she would go plunging down. She felt ahead uncertainly with her feet, waiting to feel them touch down on solid ground before shifting her weight forward. In five steps she'd made it to the door, and she could see it was made of thick planks of wood.

Then she thought of a place older than Nardin: the tombs at Forest Lawn Cemetery by Delaware Park. Katrina rushed to the door, her breath rattling in terror, and pounded on it. What if she was in a crypt with a dead person?

Katrina screamed *Help meeeee!* again and again but there was no response. Oh, please don't let me be in a tomb with a body, I hate dead bodies, I will freak—

Somewhere far off a door opened, and there were footsteps. Someone was coming. Katrina thought, *cops*, and then, Hangman, and she put her taped hands over her mouth to stop from making a noise.

Closer and closer. The footsteps rang out like the sounds of rocks dropped in a well, echoing. Katrina backed up to the far wall, darkness enveloping her. She turned her face to the wall as the footsteps stopped in front of the wooden door.

A key squeaked in the lock. The handle turned. Katrina shook her head back and forth and pressed her hands harder over her mouth, tasting the duct tape. The door rattled slightly in its hinges and then swung free. Air rushed in, foul, musty air.

Katrina turned and saw a boot, a brown boot coming her way, dragging in a single leaf as it stepped over the threshold. On the boot were speckles of dark red.

41

There was only one black-and-white out front of 34 Sycamore. The hordes hadn't arrived yet. Abbie parked the car in front and walked quickly to the porch. A uniform—short, pigeon-toed, nervous—stood there, shifting from foot to foot as he glanced up and down the street.

"Kearney," she said. "Where's the body?"

The uniform grimaced. "Back there," he said, pointing to the driveway.

"The garage?"

He nodded and Abbie was down the steps, running. The one-car garage, door open, was lit harshly from a naked bulb. Black silhouettes moved in front of ladders, shovels, household goods. There was no car. In the corner, she saw a man crouching. He turned, and she recognized Raymond.

"Kearney," he said, standing quickly. "You got here right quick."

The other men—the search team members, she guessed, nodded and walked toward the garage's open door. As they left, Abbie saw a body behind them, the body of a middle-aged white woman. Not a teenage girl.

"Who is she?" she asked quickly.

Raymond blew out a breath. "Looks like the home owner, Wendy Lamb. The address on her driver's license matches the house here. Walks in and BOOM!"

Abbie could hear car doors slam *crump*, one after the other, like a mortar going off in the distance. Soon this place would be swarming with media and cops. "You think it's him?"

"You tell me," Raymond said.

The body was slumped in the corner of the garage next to a pair of old snow shovels. The woman was elegantly dressed. She had a patterned brown-and-yellow Hermès scarf around her throat and a forest green sweater and tan wool slacks. There was a Louis Vuitton bag on its side next to her leg, some of the contents sprayed across the garage floor. Her head was turned away, as if she'd been struck and tossed to the floor, and her left arm was trapped beneath her body.

Abbie bent down. She could make out a line of purplish black around her neck an inch and a half above the sweater's collar. It seemed to grow darker even as Abbie looked at it. "Any other marks on her?"

"Not so as I can tell right now. Looks like this piece of old clothesline is what did it." He flicked the flashlight and the beam moved past the woman's body three or four feet to the left. The garage floor was painted a dark industrial gray. There was a piece of thin, dirty white rope lying on the floor, twisted like it had been tossed there.

"No blood? No note?"

"Nothing."

Abbie reached over and went through the woman's pockets, inside and out. Only a dry cleaning receipt, dated the day before, in the right pocket. Abbie gently eased the Louis Vuitton bag away from her leg and looked inside. Raymond watched as she went through it.

"Wallet's still here," Abbie said, popping it open. The money compartment held a thick band of cash. Abbie riffled through it. Two hundred, two twenty-five at least.

Abbie put the bag aside and reached beneath the corpse, feeling along the cold cement floor until she touched flesh. She tilted her head at Raymond and he took the woman's shoulder and pushed it back gently until she could pull the left hand into the light.

"Here's a ring he didn't take," Abbie said with a sigh. "No defensive wounds. This happened quickly."

A snatch-and-grab, except that the killer hadn't grabbed anything of value. The killing was over in a couple of minutes. There was no staging, none of the ceremonial feeling that the other killings had. Hangman hadn't bothered to do anything to the woman except strangle her to death.

"Where's her coat?" Abbie asked.

"Mm-hmm." Raymond said softly.

"Raymond? I'm almost afraid to ask."

His eyes met hers. They were soft and sad. Abbie flinched.

"Yeah, well, we spoke to the neighbors. Wendy has a sixteen-year-old girl, Katrina."

Abbie turned her head as if she'd been slapped. Raymond reached out and grabbed her shoulder. She turned back, folded her arms across her chest.

"Go on."

"Went to the Nardin Academy," Raymond said, looking at his notes. "Sophomore there. Someone picked her up today in her mother's car."

"It was him," said Abbie. "There weren't enough girls on the street so he found a way to get himself one." Abbie stood up, turned her wrist, and looked at her Cartier watch. "Nardin probably gets out just before four. It's 9:46 now. He's had her for five and a half hours. That's just way too long."

"I hear ya, I hear ya. I've got Traffic looking up her plates now. Should have them in a few minutes."

Abbie felt her heart race, thinking of how much a jump Hangman had on her. Five and a half hours was an eternity.

"He's dumped the car somewhere by now," she said, bitterness in her voice.

"Hey now. Don't turn this freak into Superman. He made a mistake before, and that's exactly how we caught him."

The bare bulb cast a harsh shadow forward as someone approached from behind Raymond. Abbie turned. A potbellied Asian man in an olive green vest, faded jeans, and scuffed combat boots was carrying a padded camera bag and a flash rig toward the body. Abbie recognized Sam, the BPD's crime scene photographer.

"You guys ready for pics?" he said, placing the camera bag on the floor. Unzipping it, he pulled out a banged-up Nikon. She thought about Riesen, sitting in the rowboat on Hoyt Lake. She thought of the Madeleines, the urban myth about the girls dumped on the lake bed. She saw the signet ring gleaming on his fat pinkie finger.

She stepped around Raymond and went over for another look at the woman slumped against the wall. Sam was taking pictures fast in the tight dark corner of the garage. As the shutter clicked and the flash hit the body, Wendy Lamb's face seemed to burn like phosphorous.

Abbie felt anger coursing in her bloodstream like spiky particles of poison. Her hands cramped in the cold, but then the rage washed away and she felt sick. This morning I drove a few blocks from here, remembering how I'd felt humiliated by these rich people in these big homes, because some Yale alum was mean to me. I was feeling sorry for myself about something that happened twenty years ago.

And here you were, Mrs. Lamb, the object of my resentments, getting the life wrung out of you so that Hangman could get to your daughter.

Abbie felt something shift inside of her, like ballast in the depths of a ship.

42

Katrina felt the man staring at her, breathing in the half-dark.

Just keep still and he'll go away. Just relax, Katrina. Her eyelid twitched uncontrollably. Oh God.

The man shuffled forward.

Katrina opened her eyes just a slit, but she wouldn't look at him. All she saw was the boot. She knew the color of old blood on leather. One day three winters ago, tobogganing at Chestnut Ridge Park, her friend Nathaniel had cut his foot on one of the long metal chutes that guided the toboggans down the slope. He'd worn the same Timberlands every year, streaked with the blood.

It's the same color, she thought. Her heart was beating so fast it was painful.

No sound. Just his slow, heavy breathing.

The man didn't go away. He stood there, watching.

Katrina felt the absolute need to know where she was, whether she was in Buffalo or in Fort Erie or in Transylvania.

"Where am I . . . ?" she said.

The boot came closer. Then something dropped three feet from her, hit the floor so unexpectedly that Katrina jerked back.

It was a bowling bag. Red and cream, with tiny cracks that ran along the creases.

She screamed and the sound echoed off the walls, almost deafening her. There's a head in the bag, I know there is. Sandy Riesen's head.

"Where am I?" she repeated, and this time it was clear and loud. She wasn't going to stay quiet. She would fight. Maybe the other girls didn't fight, and that's why they'd died.

Hangman stood there, unmoving. She pulled away from him and painfully twisted her legs under her. She scrabbled her feet along the stone floor. She tried to push back further but she could feel the rough stones of the wall through her blouse.

Katrina brought her gaze up slowly. Hangman was tall, and he wore a dirty gray boiler suit, his face covered by a red felt mask that looked like one of those Mexican wrestlers. His eyes were blue, but Katrina quickly looked away, hating the look in them, like a boy who was going to unwrap his Christmas present—a sicko boy who'd gotten what he wanted.

He was watching her, the door standing open behind him. Beyond the door frame she saw a long shadowy corridor.

She tried to look anywhere but at his red mask. A little gray light filtered into the room now from the window above her. The place she was in was small and filthy, with black grime caked into the seams of the rocks. There was no bed, no toilet, nothing.

God, he can't keep me here. It's inhuman.

"How old are you?" Hangman said. His voice was deep and resonant.

Katrina froze. The voice went through her, echoed in her ears.

"Tell me where I am," she said, staring at the mask. "I want to call my mother!"

He squatted down to study her. The eyes through the mask were blue and intent, two pools of blue floating in all that red. But Katrina met them. She wouldn't turn him into a monster. That's what he wanted to be. She would treat him like the loser he was.

"You're where you belong," he said. The voice was even, but the mask, it made anything coming out of the little black hole cut in the cloth seem . . . terrifying. "Where it all started."

"Why do you want me?" she asked, and her voice only wavered a little at the end.

The eyes stared, blue and horrible to look at, like the eyes of a jackal. Hungry. At last, he said, "Because you have to pay."

"Pay for what?" she said sharply.

The eyes, something passed through them.

Hangman seemed in a trance. He shoved the bag with his right hand and slid it along the floor toward her, tipping as it came closer. Katrina screamed and scurried away. She couldn't stop thinking it was Sandy Riesen's head in there.

"For her," he said, his voice almost singsong. Katrina squeezed into the corner, but she wouldn't turn her face away. Something told her the other girls had turned away. She wouldn't be like them. Whatever they did, she would do the opposite. Because they were dead now. She would play a part, like Cordelia. Strong and fearless. *Be Cordelia.*

His eyes were roaming all over her, like a ferret. A hungry ferret. She thought he could take a bite out of her with the teeth hidden behind the red mask. "I'm Katrina Simone Lamb. That's my name. Did you know that?"

But he didn't appear to hear her as he came closer. He gestured at the bag.

Katrina shivered. Keep him talking. When he's talking he's not killing you. "You can take your mask off," she said. As he stood over her, her eyes drifted down to the crimson spots on his boot.

Katrina didn't want to think about how they got there.

"I don't do that," Hangman said slowly. "I don't take things off. You put things *on.*" He reached over and grabbed the bag.

She turned her head violently away, but out of the corner of her eye, she saw him slowly pull the zipper back and reach into the bag. He began to lift something slowly out.

It wasn't the missing girl's head. It was another mask—like a hockey mask but with something taped over the front. It was the picture of a woman's face, cut into pieces and taped together, pieces of different pictures, mismatched eyebrows over the eyeholes. It was just horrible.

Her breathing stopped.

The mask dangled in his right hand.

"Isn't it beautiful?" he said, holding it out to her, and the terrifying thing was that she saw in his eyes that he was serious, that he expected her to say, *Oh, isn't it?*

Katrina backed up, the stone jutting into her back.

Hangman's eyes were smiling now. "This is what you'll be wearing," he said, "when it's time."

43

Abbie found him on the porch of her house, sitting in one of the lean-back wooden chairs that they'd bought at a yard sale over in Williamsville. The light was on, sending a cone of light onto the dark porch. They'd spent their spare hours this summer in the two olive green chairs, drinking Abbie's homemade mojitos and watching the neighborhood parade go by, the young mothers with their strollers, the jean-jacketed hipsters, the elderly couple, Mae and Frank, from around the corner.

Mills was cleaning his hunting rifle. It was disassembled in pieces around him, along with a bottle of Elite Gun Oil and several different-colored cloths.

"You shouldn't do that here," Abbie said, folding her arms, leaning against a post.

Mills looked up at her, smiling. "I've done this a thousand times, Abbie."

She nodded. She knew that. "I have to tell you something."

He looked up, worry in his eyes.

"Not about us," she said, giving him a quick smile that flexed back into a frown. "Well, kind of about us."

"Okay," he said, laying the gun barrel down on a piece of chamois spread across the footstool. "Shoot."

"I'm thinking of accepting McGonagle's offer."

"You're not," he said flatly. "Why would you even consider it?"

Abbie felt him look at her anew. *I'm not going to be the good girl anymore.* But it hurt, his look.

"Because of a woman. A mother I should say, whose last sight on earth was the man who was going to kidnap and kill her daughter. Hangman. The last thing she thought was, Hangman is going to kill my child."

Mills's eyes brushed over her, then settled on his hands. He was studying his left palm. "We all deal with victims' families, Abbie. It's the worst thing in the world."

"No, not being able to save your daughter is the worst thing in the world."

"What exactly are you thinking of doing?" Mills said.

Abbie lifted off the porch column and looked away. "Having McGonagle talk to some people."

Mills shook his head. "You know that'll just be the beginning," he said. "What are they going to ask for in return, Abbie? These things are never, ever free. What don't you understand?"

Abbie sucked in a breath. She wanted to bring the barrel of his rifle down on his stubborn, uncompromising head but she also knew Mills was right. Every cop who crossed the line had a monologue running in her head, some clause that proved she was an exception to the rule. *Just this one time, so I can pay off my tab with the Italians . . . because the judge will never give the murdering bastard what he deserves . . . because Hangman is unique and I'm special and Katrina is young and I promise I will never, ever do it again . . .*

"I'm not looking for a conviction," she said quietly. "I don't need this to hold up in court. I'm trying to catch a homicidal rampage killer. It's *different*."

"Like hell it is," Mills said, louder than she'd ever heard him. "I talk to mothers who've lost their kids and I don't make deals with skels to catch the killer. You do this once, you'll never get clean."

Abbie felt her cheeks go hot. "Buffalo isn't like everywhere else,

Mills. There are areas closed off to me that I need to get into. Just look—"

"Listen to yourself! Do not do this," Mills said. He reached down and took up the bottle of gun oil and carefully squeezed out a few drops onto a piece of cheesecloth. Then he picked up the gun barrel in his left hand, slid his hand along it to the base, and began to gently work the oil onto the dark steel.

"Mills?"

He shook his head once, his lips pressed tight. She watched the gleam of the gun barrel as he slid the cloth up and then back. She watched for a good thirty seconds.

Abbie turned away and clomped up the stairs. She usually couldn't sleep when she was angry, but as she hit the top of the stairs, she felt drained. She walked into the bedroom, peeled off her clothes, locked her gun in the gun safe, and went to bed.

The next morning, he was gone. The rifle, too. A note said, "Went to NW."

Northwestern Ontario, she thought. Moose hunting. Was it even moose season?

No return date specified.

She felt empty, and light. She hadn't planned on risking Mills to get Hangman; she didn't know she was capable of doing such a thing. But now she'd done it.

Abbie sat in her empty kitchen, echoing with the sounds of cars passing on Elmwood Avenue, and stared at the chair across from her. She felt like an old butterfly cocoon rattling back and forth in the wind. Something warm had left her.

She wiped away a tear, made toast and tea, dressed in an olive green suit and her Tory Burch flats, and drove to Del Sasser's bar on Seneca. What she had to say to McGonagle she needed to say in person. It was 10:15 when she got there.

She found him on the same stool. He looked thinner somehow. There were two phones on the bar and he was staring at them when she walked in the place.

"McGonagle?"

"Yeah?"

A man sitting next to him looked up at Abbie. She stared at him stone-faced until he muttered something to McGonagle and slid away toward the pool table, which had an Africa-shaped stain on the green felt cloth.

Abbie slipped onto the stool.

"Are you aware," she said, trying to keep the emotion out of her voice, "that I was going to arrest my own brother? And put him away for the rest of his life? And that I would have killed him if it had come down to that?"

"That's . . . widely understood," said the old detective.

"Good. So can you imagine what I'd do to you if you fuck me on this."

He grunted. "On what?"

"I'll use your boys to catch Hangman. But if you do me wrong, I will bury you while you're still breathing. Do you understand?"

A tiny ruffle of breath. A laugh or a sigh? Was he disappointed that there wasn't one cop in the entire city of Buffalo that could resist the temptation?

"Done."

"Good. Frank Riesen doesn't want to talk to me."

McGonagle considered that. "Well, that's rude of him, ain't it?"

"Follow him. Find out where he's going, who he's meeting. See if you can get someone on his bank accounts, see if he's been making any large payments with regularity. I need dates, amounts, recipients."

"Why aren't you doing this official?"

Abbie frowned. "Think it through. Can you imagine me going to Perelli and saying I want the father of the last victim to be followed? What if word leaks, or Riesen suspects something and goes to the press? 'Father of Victim Suspected of Collusion in Hangman Murders'? I'd be off the case in three seconds."

"So you want me and the boys to be the fall guys?" McGonagle asked.

"Do you mind?" she answered.

"Not fucking especially. Anything else?"

Abbie looked toward the bar's dingy front window, a BUD LIGHT neon sign reflecting back from the glass. "Follow Hangman's friends, anyone remaining in the area. High school and college."

McGonagle whistled. "How much manpower you think I have?"

"All you need," said Abbie.

"All right, they'll be covered by tonight at the latest. But you're wasting your fucking time. Riesen is not the second man. The others aren't, either."

Abbie shook her head. What is the most dangerous Daddy figure possible, she thought.

Yourself. If *you* try to become John Kearney, you will need psychiatrists from here to eternity.

I'm not trying to become my father, she told herself. I've mourned him and I miss him terribly, but I'm not becoming him, I'm becoming the best possible cop for this case. And that means using every resource I can get my hands on.

She closed her eyes.

Oh God, Abbie. Really?

44

Hangman had left. Katrina was alone again.

He didn't even tell me to stop screaming. What does that mean? Wherever I am, no one can hear me? Or would the screams be his excuse for coming down here and killing me?

She was afraid to scream now. Save it. There's time yet.

The bowling bag sat on the floor. The mask was hung above it on a nail driven into the cement between the stones. The mask's broken face was to the wall, the black silk straps hanging down. It looked like a crazy man's idea of a human face.

If Hangman puts that on me, I'll gag, she thought. I'll pass out for real. What if he does? Will it smell like the other girls?

If he puts the mask on me, I am as good as dead, Katrina thought.

Should she scream now? Was it her last chance? She'd wait until she heard voices, or footsteps. But she didn't know where she was. She could be in someone's basement or in a hole in the ground lined with rocks. She could be in Cleveland, for all she knew.

She heard a rattling coming from the left, far down the dark corridor she'd glimpsed when Hangman opened the wooden door. Katrina thought of the leg in the trunk. Someone was with me then. Maybe that person is locked in another room nearby. She pushed her back up against the wall, grimacing as the rough stones scratched her skin through the thin blouse, then rushed to the door. She leaned, listened again, then tapped on it gently.

"Hello?" she whispered.

A faint sound, again.

It wasn't Hangman's deep voice, but a lighter one, male or female she couldn't tell. Katrina's eyes went wide. For a moment, she thought it might even be her mother.

"HELLO! CAN YOU HEAR ME?"

She heard her voice echo out into the big room to the right. *Hearme-hearmehear.* She closed her eyes and put her ear to one of the cracks that split the thick wooden door.

From the left, Katrina could hear the sound of someone crying. She pounded on the door. "Oh please, who *are* you? Can you hear me?"

What if it's Mom, she thought. Is it male or female, older or younger? Only the high notes were reaching her, and the sound was being refracted by the stone rooms and the corridor.

There. Again.

Katrina caught her breath, and lowered her voice. Be soothing. "Let's help each other," she cooed into the passageway. "Tell me who you are. Let's help each other, please?"

Nothing. Silence now.

Abbie turned up the walkway toward the house of her neighbors Charles and Ron. If there was anyone who knew what an obscure Buffalo reference meant, it was Charles. After leading tours of the city's most dusty corners for years, he'd absorbed as much minutiae as was humanly possible, making him a bore at dinner parties but invaluable in other ways. He collected things like pamphlets explaining who the Madeleines were, among other things. Maybe he could tell her something about the "kings abide" lead.

She tried to ignore the clock ticking in her head. Hangman was working fast. He'd barely been with Martha Stoltz for an hour before killing her. If Katrina Lamb was even alive, today would probably be her last day on earth. Tomorrow would be the latest, Abbie just felt it.

She ran up the Tudor's flagstone pathway. Just as she reached the doorbell, she saw movement upstairs at the bedroom window—a curtain let fall and swinging for a moment before coming to rest.

Sounds of feet pounding down wooden stairs. The door opened. Charles. He was in his mid-forties, deep brown eyes, waxy skin, chiseled features, his hairline receding over a forehead that itself seemed muscled, a gym bunny turned English professor.

"Hi Charles."

Charles nodded. "Abbie. Nice to see you."

"I don't want to disturb you, but I need your help with some Buffalo history."

Charles blinked. "The Madeleines? Ron told me . . ."

"Actually, it's something else."

"Of course," Charles said, a little stiffly. "Come in?"

"I don't have time," she said, a little out of breath. "I'm trying to track down a reference, just one line. It goes: 'I live where the kings abide.' I believe it refers to somewhere in Buffalo."

Charles stared at her, but his eyes were far away, his mind already flitting through dusty papers in some enormous file room at the back of his mind. "What era are we talking about?" he asked.

"Era?" Abbie said. "Fairly recent, I would guess. Don't rule anything out, but let's say the last fifty, sixty years."

"No kings have ever visited Buffalo in that span," said Charles, "except for the opening of the Peace Bridge. Edward VIII, the Prince of Wales at the time, was there, as well as an array of dignitaries."

"But he wasn't king yet?" she asked.

"No. It was ten years, give or take, before he ascended to the throne. And then, of course, he abdicated for that slut Wallis Simpson, so he was king for less than a year."

It felt odd, talking about English royalty in pursuit of a serial killer in her own backyard. "Doesn't sound right. No one lives on the Peace Bridge."

Charles screwed up his face, as if he were in pain. "You said it was 'kings.' Plural?"

"Yes."

Charles's face seemed to grow a tinge redder. Abbie thought the failure to come up with an answer might induce a stroke. "The mil-lionaires who lived along Delaware Avenue. They were sometimes called the 'kings of Buffalo' by newsmen of the day. They were fabu-lously rich, like Turkish pashas. But we're talking a hundred years ago."

Delaware Avenue was the North personified. If that was it, the clue did little for her. There were a hundred and fifty houses strung along the avenue, she guessed. "Any home in particular?"

Charles shook his head. "It was a general term. I'm sorry, I . . ."

"Listen, call me if you think of anything. And please don't tell any-one that I asked you."

Charles scoffed. "Who would I tell? Ron? He couldn't care less about these kinds of things."

Abbie heard in the distance the dispatcher's voice on her handheld radio notch up a decibel. She couldn't make out the words, but she turned quickly and began running.

"Thank you, Charles," she cried out and dashed for the Saab.

45

"—repeat. All units in the North. Corner of Elmwood and Summer. Man in red hood running."

Abbie spun into the driver's seat. Her eyes went wide and she reached for the key, jammed it forward. The Saab's engine roared to life.

"I repeat, red hood or mask. Spotted in the backyard of 242 Summer Avenue. Heading west toward Bryant."

Abbie whipped the wheel left and the Saab's rear end swung in a lazy arc before the tires caught on the wet pavement and it shot off west on Delaware.

"Male, black jacket, black pants," the dispatcher said tersely. "Approximately six feet, thin build."

That was on-target for Marcus Flynn. Abbie called McGonagle. If you're gonna use the Network, might as well get all you can. The phone rang twice before McGonagle barked a hello.

"You listening to this?" she said.

"Yeah."

She heard McGonagle typing. The sound of the turbo whining and the parked cars on both sides merged into a continuous stream of colors and chrome. The needle hit 65 and kept climbing, Abbie's eyes straight ahead, hitting the horn as cars braked and then fell away to the side of the road.

"Where are you?" he said.

"Elmwood and Bryant."

"Head east," McGonagle barked.

"Dispatcher said—"

"Fuck the dispatcher."

She slid into the next intersection and whipped the wheel right. The car shuddered, the engine whining, but she barely made the turn without slamming into the curb.

"Left on Remsen."

There were people on the streets, more than she'd seen in three days. Men running, tilted forward, calling to each other. Were these undercovers, or search team members, or was the whole city coming to watch Hangman go down? She hit Remsen and slammed a left. A whiff of burnt rubber came through the vents.

A shot rang out. Close by. Abbie felt her heart skip a beat.

"Get there," McGonagle said.

Shouts from ahead of her, a vague commotion of bodies near the corner.

"I don't see him!" she cried.

She saw flashing lights ahead and the hood of the car leapt as she hit the gas.

"Where is he?" Abbie shouted into the phone.

"Hold on."

She heard a text-buzz on McGonagle's end. "Left on Delaware."

She swung the car and it drifted onto Delaware, nearly hitting a parked SUV. The sound of another shot, and yelling from over the rooftops growing louder.

A man came tearing out of an alleyway forty feet from the Saab, running breakaway toward Abbie. Abbie saw his eyes, impossibly big beneath a red hood. He ran past the streetlight and broke to the right, between two parked cars, the crimson hood bobbing in the darkness.

Abbie felt something spring up inside her at the sight: a visceral desire to kill this thing running amok, to stop its motion. She slammed on the brakes, jammed the car into Park and was out of the door and running. There were screams from up ahead, then two more shots. Their concussion reverberated through her chest like a depth charge. Big rounds, .45s.

Abbie cut a corner and hopped a short hedge that loomed up out of the night. There, twenty yards away, the man lay facedown on the road, the red hood pulled tight around his face. A pale blue Impala was stopped fifteen feet away, its driver door hanging open. A male police officer with a gun held in both hands was approaching the hooded figure, crouched as if he was ready to spring on top of him. A group of men from the neighboring houses was approaching the body from the other side.

"Back off!" the armed cop called out. He was pointing the gun not at the body but at the group of men.

It was like when they caught the Night Stalker in L.A., Abbie thought. He'd been recognized and the neighborhood came after him like a mad dog, beating him senseless. The cops hadn't caught him— they'd saved him from the people. Abbie felt a wildness in the air, a fire ready to ignite.

The figure was still as Abbie raced toward him.

"Buffalo PD!" she yelled to the gun-holding cop. He nodded without looking her way, then dropped to his knees by the red-hooded man laid out on the ground. He pulled at the hood, then twisted away. The cop began to talk furiously into a handheld radio.

As she came closer, she saw the body splayed, arms out. The jacket was denim, black, matching the pants.

Something was wrong. The body was taller than six foot, maybe six-four. Too tall. The hand that lay palm-down on the tarmac was smooth and the color of caramel.

Latino, Abbie thought. What the hell.

Breathing hard, she came up to the man.

The cop gave her a look of disgust, a look she knew, a cop look that meant *I hate this world and everything in it.*

"A fucking kid," he whispered hoarsely. "I nearly blew his head off."

Abbie knelt beside the figure in the black jacket, and bent down to his face. It was a boy, not more than eighteen, curly, close-cropped hair and a high forehead, eyes bugged open, the flesh under the eyes purplish. He wore a red sweatshirt under the black jacket. The cop pulled back the jacket. No bullet holes were visible.

Abbie bent her head down in relief.

"They dared me to wear it!" the boy cried.

"Who did?" Abbie hissed.

"My boys," he said, breathing hard. "It was a dare. All it was, I swear."

The red hood was attached to a St. Francis sweatshirt—a local Catholic high school. Abbie thought: how many downtown Latino kids made it to St. Frannie's? Here lying on Elmwood Avenue was some kind of star, the class valedictorian, the neighborhood's brightest. Inches from a bullet.

It wasn't Hangman, just a stupid innocent kid in a red sweatshirt. Abbie felt the desire to turn, walk away, and never return.

46

The voice had gone silent hours ago. Katrina had crawled back to the corner of the stone room and was sitting, knees up, her taped hands folded across her knees.

From the other direction, footsteps. The hairs on Katrina's arm rose and her heart went ice-cold as she heard someone walking in the room beyond.

The footsteps stopped. There was a distinct metal click, and a light buzzed on. Slivers of its hard white glow reached through the crack at the bottom of the door.

The footsteps resumed and got closer.

The door rattled in its hinges and a shadow moved through the slits between the boards. He was fiddling with the lock, grunting, trying to get the key to work.

The door screeched open and Katrina stifled a scream.

Hangman. A key was hanging down, clutched in his hand. "Out," he said.

Katrina crouched down and stumbled toward the light. It was to her right, throwing shadows onto the wall near Hangman as he stood in the dank corridor waiting for her. She sniffed stale water and a mossy smell. Gross.

She passed by the mask. She wouldn't put it on. When I put that on, I'll be ready to die, she thought, and I'll never be ready to die.

"I want you to see something," he said.

Katrina glanced at him, and she couldn't disguise the hatred. "Katrina," she hissed at him. "My name is Katrina Lamb."

He reached down and grabbed the tape stretched between her hands and pulled up. Katrina rose unsteadily, nearly tipping over, before she stumbled forward and followed him. As she was pulled out of the stone room, Katrina turned and glanced back at the inky corridor to the left. But it was swathed in blackness. She could hear and see nothing. No cell doors, no one slumped in the shadows. It was as dark as a well.

Hangman shoved her past him with a grunt. The corridor led to a series of steps going up. They were covered with green slime, water trickling down the cement and running over the vines or moss or whatever the hell it was.

"Up," he ordered.

She put her foot on the first step, her nose wrinkling, and started climbing. There was no door at the top, just an empty doorway into some kind of high-ceilinged hall. Chunks of the wall were missing, with riblike pieces of wood behind it. A light burned brightly. She reached the top and turned into the room, stirring up clouds of fine dust with her feet as she shuffled forward. Katrina choked as it was sucked into her lungs. She stopped and bent over, coughing, her throat on fire.

Gloom, darkness to her left. It was nighttime. To her right, a bright spotlight turned upward, sending a beam of intense light to the high ceiling twelve feet above. Trash, wrecked things thrown around. She spotted an old-fashioned wheelchair—the wooden kind that looked like a dining chair on wheels—and an old bedpan, its metal surface turned green.

Two windows covered with rough planks of wood nailed over them from outside, a roof open to the sky in the far corner, stars visible through the holes. The only illumination came from the spotlight. In the gloom it threw into the rest of the room, Katrina saw old wooden boxes with faded writing on the side amid piles of broken plaster.

"Where am I?" she said to Hangman as he came up behind her.

I'm doing what the other girls did, she thought, and he's going to kill me. Think, Katrina, think, you stupid little girl.

What did the other girls say, Katrina asked, panicked. I have to say something different. Maybe there's a word, a sentence, that will get me out of here.

But all she could say was "Where am I?" She repeated it again, her mind whirring.

He turned. The mask, it rippled when he turned, the material bunching at the neck.

Katrina wriggled her hands. "I'm scared, really I am. Please tell me. Am I still in Buffalo?" She felt danger with every word.

"This is where they kept her," he said.

"Kept who?" she managed to ask.

He pushed her again and she stumbled toward the right-hand boarded-up window. A piece of one of the boards, gray with age, had been hacked away at the bottom right corner. She saw a faint gleam of moonlight illuminating something out there.

He wants me to scream, Katrina thought. *I won't I won't I won't.*

The room was filled with junk, untouched for years. There was nothing in here, no knives, no guns she could see that would help her get away. And clearly no one except Hangman came to visit. They were alone.

She was going to die.

Pretend he's someone else. Pretend he's a boy having problems with his girlfriend, some geek like Harry Jacobson next door. Harry with the bad posture and addiction to *World of Warcraft*, which he talked about constantly. You became his friend. You knew how to talk to him. Do the same thing here.

"What did she do to you, the girl they kept here?" she said, as she walked slowly forward.

He coughed out a dry laugh. "Why do you think she did something to me?"

"Because . . . because you killed all those girls. Someone must have done something to you to want to hurt us."

He pushed her, a painful shove in the small of the back. "She didn't do anything to me. People did things to *her.*"

Katrina nodded, turning toward the red mask. The eyes darted at hers, then away.

"Your name's Marcus, right? Can I call you that?"

He stopped. The broken plaster and dust under her feet crunched as she stopped, too. He shoved again, a little more gently this time, and her foot slid into the base of the black wood. They were at the window.

"Look," he said.

Katrina hesitated.

"Look!" he cried, and the violence in his voice made her legs tremble. She bent and peeked outside.

Trees. A grove of dark-limbed trees.

"I don't see anything."

The rain had stopped. The moon was behind the trees and their branches were lit up, snarled and black as charcoal.

He pushed her head roughly to the left, but there was nothing there, only twisted branches and black sky.

"Where?" she cried.

Then she saw it. It was the only thing moving out there. A rope, hanging from a thick tree. At the end of it hung a noose in the shape of a teardrop.

Katrina's head jerked violently back. She was breathing fast.

"Do you remember my name?" she said between breaths. "It's Katrina."

He put his hand on her neck and squeezed. Katrina gasped and struggled to get away. She didn't want to look again. But he forced her head down to the hole. She saw the rope swaying slightly, a ripple of movement sliding up its neck as the noose jerked back and forth in the wind.

"You're a smart girl, Katrina. Too bad for you."

He stopped, and Katrina looked up, meeting his gaze. His eyes looked like he was balanced up high and he was afraid of heights. His eyes were full of fear.

"What was the girl's name?" Katrina said. "The one they did stuff to."

He mumbled something, but she couldn't understand. It was dangerous, but it was the only way. She heard him breathe. He could lunge forward and choke her in ten seconds. She felt if she said the wrong word, he'd explode.

"What . . . did . . . they do to her?"

He studied the floor, then looked up. Some kind of magic trick. The fear was gone—or else he'd been faking it—and now he looked at her, confident, smiling. Predator eyes. "Thank you, Katrina. That was very good. We're going back now."

Katrina nodded. Be on his side. She turned, her heart beating like crazy.

"I want to understand. Please. You're doing this to get back at . . . who?"

He pushed her again, not so roughly this time. She didn't want to go back in the hole. Up here, there was the chance of escape. Downstairs was a tomb.

"When I kill you, you won't be you. You'll be their children, all of them. They think I'm crazy but I'm not."

Whose children? But something told her not to ask. "Of course you're not," she said. "You're just angry. Really angry. I know what that's like."

He laughed.

"I have an idea," she said, quickly. He grabbed her taped hands and pushed her forward.

I will be brave now, she thought, and then I won't have to be brave for a very long time.

The voice from behind the mask was snide. "Oh, I can't wait to hear it. Rich girls always have ideas."

Rich? Was she even rich? Her mother was always complaining about the dry cleaning bills and last year they'd never even gone on vacation. She stood there, confused.

It doesn't matter, she thought. Don't worry about him, worry about you. "We go after the people who did this to the girl," Katrina said, and she was proud of her voice, how steady it was. "We find them and . . . and punish them. I can help you with that."

He stiffened. "You can?"

She nodded, looking down at the swirls of dust on her shoes. They were halfway across the room. She couldn't hear traffic or airplanes or anything. Where in God's name was she?

Hangman stopped, and Katrina stood there, waiting. He leaned toward her. "Would you really do that?" She couldn't tell if he was mocking her.

Katrina looked down. Hangman was looking up at her, but the spotlight threw crazy shadows across the mask and it looked like he had no eyes at all.

"Yes. I really would," she said. And then she added, "I swear."

Hangman nodded, the mask wrinkling as his head bent up and then down. Then he reached up and grabbed her hair, pulling her toward him. Katrina closed her eyes, feeling his breath on her lips.

"I have a better idea," he whispered. "*You die.*"

47

Abbie was parked in front of City Hall. Night had fallen on Lake Erie, and the yellow lights that lit up the old Depression-era building glowed softly on the old stone.

She didn't want to go home. She had NPR on low in the background, letting her thoughts float with the news and the small bits of music. She was trying not to think about Katrina, to let something float in, like a bottle on a tide. Something she didn't expect.

A car rolled up to her left. Abbie shifted away, her hand dropping to the Glock in the holster. A door slammed and she saw McGonagle walking around the front of the car. He waved to the driver and the car moved off a few lengths ahead and parked, engine still running.

"How'd you know I was here?" Abbie said.

He got in, collapsing into the passenger seat. McGonagle ignored the question and she didn't press. Her eyelids were heavy. She felt her body wanting to sleep.

"I got to Riesen. He'll talk to you."

She sat straight up, her jacket squealing on the Saab's worn leather. "God bless you," she said. "Who's your contact?"

McGonagle chuckled. "No, you don't get that. Someone he trusts, okay?"

Abbie frowned. The Network moved in its own mysterious ways.

"He won't deal with Buffalo PD, not officially," said McGonagle. "Still has a bad taste in his mouth from '07, the arrogant fuck. I told him you're different, that you could act on your own if necessary. And I told him you had new theories on the case that might interest him."

"That's dangerous," she said.

"It's what got him to agree. No promises. He wants to meet you face-to-face, and hear what you have to say. But it has to be somewhere out of sight."

"Wait," Abbie said. "Does Riesen think Hangman is *watching* him?"

"I have no idea. He's skittish. He feels he's under surveillance by somebody, that's what I got from him."

Or he's involved in the murders. Abbie thought of the signet ring. How had he gotten it?

Abbie's eyes swept Niagara Square. There were a few college students, two guys and a girl, wandering over from the direction of Chippewa Street, the nightlife strip where bars stood shoulder to shoulder. The students swayed, laughing. They were too old for Hangman. Like immune people during a plague, tipsy and free.

"How do we do that?" she said.

"Fucked if I know."

Abbie chewed on her bottom lip. "Parking garage?"

"There's none that you can drive in and drive out without the attendant seeing. I checked. No automatic ones in Buffalo that aren't on main drags. And why would he be going into a parking garage and then coming out a few minutes later?"

The girl, in a colorful knit hat, balanced on the edge of the fountain in the middle of the square and tried to walk the edge. Drunk, without a care in the world. Abbie felt like she was observing another species.

"How about under a bridge?" she suggested.

McGonagle breathed out. "Yeah, that could work."

"Something in Black Rock," she said. "You know Austin Street?"

It was an old railroad trestle in the industrial part of town, with little traffic or street life. It was in darkness all night, no fluorescents on the struts underneath. Perpetual shadows. The BPD had tried to have the Streets Department install lights underneath it for years, to scare away the vagrants and the drug dealers that sometimes hunkered there, but budgets were tight.

"What time does he want to do it?" asked Abbie.

"Ten o'clock."

She checked her watch.

"Forty minutes. Fine. I'll park nearby and walk in. He pulls under the bridge with a driver. If anyone's tailing him, he stays in the car. Even if he thinks someone is watching from a ways off, he can get out and we talk without anyone spotting him, unless they're close. The car can head off for a few minutes and circle back."

"Done. I'll text you if there's a snag."

48

Abbie stood in the darkness underneath the Black Rock bridge. The iron struts above her were painted black and seemed to suck in the weak haze of the streetlights, allowing only a tiny glow along the rivets, which humped off the metal like black ladybugs. Ten feet from the street, there was solid darkness. It smelled faintly of urine and the Niagara River, which was only a stone's throw away. No vagrants or crack-slingers in sight.

Abbie pulled her black wool coat tight around her shoulders. She smelled the churning river, the wind-whipped spray as fine as perfume.

She closed her eyes and heard something rumbling far off. The ground beneath her feet shook. The sound seemed to crackle around her.

The air around her pulsed with compression waves and the bridge above her moaned and shook. Abbie ducked. A train slammed over the rails on top of the bridge and Abbie felt the iron flex down as if it would tumble onto her head.

Twenty seconds later, the train had passed. Abbie stood and looked left. There was a pool of streetlight there, and gray moonlight to her right. Cars moving. It felt like a sleepy old New England fishing town. A bell rang crisply from a ship passing on the river.

She thought of Raymond. He was out there pursuing the leads she'd put him on, and she was here, behind his back, setting up meetings he knew nothing about. The devious mentor. She hoped he'd understand, if he ever found out.

Headlights swept in from a side street. A white Roadmaster paused and then nosed left, toward her.

Abbie stepped back off the sidewalk up the cement slope that rose behind it. She crept back under the overpass, ducking her head. If it wasn't Riesen, she didn't want anyone to see her. The car pulled up and stopped with barely a sound. The beams of the headlights were two cones of light. A figure stepped out of the backseat, turned and quietly closed the door.

Nicely done.

Frank Riesen walked toward her. Abbie inched down the slant of the underpass wall until she was standing in front of him.

"You have something to tell me?" he said.

Abbie tried to read his eyes. Impossible in this murk. "I want to talk to you about Hangman," she said.

He glanced at his watch. "The car comes back in four minutes."

"I want to find him," Abbie began, "and I want to find out what happened to your daughter. I don't care who gets him, whether they wear a badge or not, or who gets credit."

He stood, listening, emitting no vibration, perfectly controlled. "I've heard that many times before."

A boat horn sounded from the river.

"But you're not cooperating," Abbie said. "You're holding something back, Mr. Riesen. That's a problem. Because Hangman leaves few clues, he has few friends. It's hard for me to get a fix on him. I need to know what you know."

He shook his head. "No."

"You're refusing to cooperate."

"Yes."

There was no embarrassment. Did the man know she was aware of the abuse report? Had this man really beat Sandy with a whip? Was he involved in his own daughter's death?

"Three minutes," he said.

She had to reach him now. "I believe that Hangman has an associate who's helping him."

Riesen's face froze.

"Someone was paying a guard at the facility to be in contact with Hangman," she went on. "The psychologist at the prison was also approached. Were you offering to pay those people for information about your daughter?"

It was hard to make out his expression. She felt a tiny waver in his control, a leap of excitement.

"So there was someone helping him, someone who could have kept Sandy all these years?"

Abbie caught her breath. Oh, God. She shook her head. "That's not what I'm saying. Someone's been monitoring Hangman's recovery from his gunshot wound, tracking his memory. Did you make an offer to these two men?"

"At the prison? Never."

There was no offense taken, no theatrics. Riesen didn't care about her suspicions. The knowledge that there was a second man had only done one thing: given him new hope for his daughter.

"You had no contact at all with either of those people, Joe Carlson or Dr. Andrew Lipschitz?"

"I just told you. No."

Abbie stepped closer. Her breath lit up the space between them with curling gray steam. "But you're in touch with Hangman now."

Riesen held his hand in front of him. In the darkness, she never saw it leave his pocket.

"Quick," he said.

She looked down. In his hand was a hairband.

"Sandy's?"

"Yes. From the day of her kidnapping."

"When did you receive this? Yesterday? At Hoyt Lake?"

Riesen shook his head. "That doesn't matter."

"He gave you the signet ring as well."

That stopped him. He stared at Abbie, then nodded.

"Do you have the envelope?" she asked.

"I do." He reached and took the hairband back, gently, and placed it in his coat pocket.

"I'd like to see it. We can—"

"Test it for Marcus Flynn's DNA?"

Frank Riesen was no slouch. "Yes."

"It was him," Riesen said. "I had my own people look at it."

Abbie decided to let it go.

"Is this the only communication?" she asked.

"I was promised another one."

"What exactly did—"

"That you don't get. Two minutes, Detective."

"What does he want from you?" Besides your pain, Abbie thought.

"Money."

"Are you going to give it to him?"

"Yes."

Abbie paused. Riesen's exchange could give her a chance to catch Hangman or his accomplice. But at the price of what? Sandy was dead.

"Your nephew is toying with you, Mr. Riesen. He's a sadist. He enjoys watching people in pain and you're a new level, like on a video game. It fascinates and excites him. He's just getting revenge, making up for lost time."

What she didn't want to say was, he wants to torture you because Sandy is now dead and he can't hurt her anymore. He will hurt you now and he'll enjoy it almost as much as he did when inflicting pain on your daughter.

Riesen smiled. "You don't have children, Detective?"

"No."

"Then I understand what you're saying, but you're ignorant of this. Any chance I have of seeing Sandy again, even of touching something she wore, I would pay any amount of money for it. There's nothing else left in life for me now."

There were other things to discuss, and time was short. "What did he promise?"

"He said that if I wanted Sandy's emerald ring, the one she was wearing when she was taken, to bring the money and not to call the cops for any reason. The ring belonged to my mother, and her mother before that. It's a family piece, and I've wanted it back. But he said there might be a surprise, a big surprise, with it. I think he meant that he would show me evidence my daughter's alive."

Abbie stared. "I want to see the letter."

"No."

This link between Hangman and his uncle was unnerving. Who knew what they were saying to each other? "Where is the exchange going to take place?" she asked.

Riesen frowned, as if he were dealing with a child. "I'm not telling you that. This is all you get."

Abbie heard a car engine purring. She looked up. The white car was approaching from the same side street it had come from. "Why won't you let me—"

"Because he said if he spots one suspicious person, he will break it off. There is no discussion."

"Mr. Riesen—"

The car pulled up and Riesen turned toward it.

"I want to be there," Abbie said.

Riesen stopped and turned.

"Why should I let you get near this?"

"Because I've caught killers like Hangman before. No one else in this city has. Don't go in there blind. Just take me and a couple of men."

He turned to the car, eager to get away now, to finalize the arrangements, probably. Because he now believed Sandy was alive and the thought that she was out there, in pain, imprisoned, was unbearable to him.

"I can't risk it," he said.

"He'll never see me."

Riesen walked to the car, pulled open the back door. He looked around, scanning the low industrial buildings and the roads leading to the river. Then he looked at her.

"When I have Sandy back, I'll tell you everything I know. I'll give you the envelopes he sent me. But even meeting you here . . ." She saw something flash across his face. Fear. The thought that Hangman was watching them, that he'd blown Sandy's last chance.

"No one is watching us," she said quickly. "Mr. Riesen, if it was my own daughter, I'd give this a chance. I swear to you."

"McGonagle will call you," Riesen said, stepping into the car and pulling the door shut softly. The car purred away. The struts of the underpass glowed red in the light from the taillights.

49

Walking back to her car, Abbie's footsteps echoed along the narrow streets. She passed a tackle shop and then a bar, both closed.

She took out her phone and called McGonagle.

"Yeah."

"You know mailmen?" she asked.

"You mean, in a social sense?"

"Cut it out. Riesen is communicating with Hangman. He's already gotten one package from him and he's expecting another. I want to see his mail before he does."

There was a murmur, a man's voice in the background. "Let me make a call," McGonagle said. "See who's on the route. I can't reach everyone, you know."

"Sure you can."

He cackled and was gone.

It was close to midnight by the time she got home. She climbed the stairs to her bedroom, the wood creaking, and took a stinging hot shower. After, she nibbled on a few homemade cookies from Mae and Frank, her friends from around the corner. Oatmeal raisin. Her favorites. While she was drinking a full glass of ice-cold milk, the phone rang.

"It's set for tomorrow," McGonagle said. "Riesen's house is in the last part of the guy's route. It usually takes him four hours to complete the whole run, about three and a half to reach Riesen's place. He gets his stack of mail for the day around 8:15 from the distribution center at 1200 William. He'll go through it and hand off anything suspicious to us as soon as he leaves the main post office. We can have it for three hours, with thirty minutes extra for travel time."

Abbie tapped her fingernail on the kitchen table. "Why not hold it for a day?"

"Because the guy's six months from retirement and he won't risk it. Letters are stamped when they're routed through the distribution center, so they know when the carriers get them. He doesn't want this getting traced back to them."

"McGonagle!" she cried. "You can't twist his arm?"

"Listen, you," he said in a low snarl. "The mailman's old and stubborn and I've already got my neck out for you. Three hours it is."

"I'll be waiting to hear from you," she said.

"You're worse than a fucking wife."

50

Abbie woke at 6 a.m., watched the trees outside her window as the morning sun burned around them. Dead still. No wind.

She couldn't get back to sleep, so she dressed in a knit J. Crew jacket and gray slacks, and headed downtown. Pulling into the Police HQ parking lot, she saw that Raymond's car wasn't there yet. She breathed a sigh of relief. She felt somehow she was deceiving him by using the Network behind his back. Every detective has informers, she said to herself. Mine are just ex-cops.

At 8:20 a.m., a text from McGonagle.

"Handwritten letter to Riesen, no return address."

Abbie's hand shook as she typed back. "Bring to BPD, meet out back."

Hangman's DNA picture, the splotchy, parallel bands that gave his genetic profile, was in the files. She'd seen it when looking through the boxes—a stiff white card issued by the FBI's CODIS program, for Combined DNA Index System. If he licked the envelope, all the lab had to do was swab it and generate a DNA profile. That could take a couple of days.

"Done," McGonagle wrote back.

The DNA was just insurance. What mattered was what the letter said.

McGonagle was waiting in the driver seat of his old two-tone Ford Explorer. A man with a porkpie hat and a thick overcoat sat in the back and watched through the dirty side window as Abbie walked up. The passenger side of the Explorer was sprayed with a single thick arc of drying mud. Opening the door, Abbie smelled Genesee Cream Ale and chewing tobacco.

She slipped into the back of the car. The man in the porkpie hat had a pale, priestlike face and a shock of dark hair over sleepy eyes. He grinned at her.

"You are?" she said.

"No names, thank you," McGonagle said, turning in the front seat. The dark-haired man smiled wistfully. In his hand was a large Ziploc bag holding a letter. Abbie took the bag, which crinkled as she handled it, and stared at the white, standard business envelope. It was the security version, with swirls of blue patterns printed on the inside to prevent anyone but the intended recipient reading the contents.

"What do you think of the handwriting?" Abbie said to McGonagle.

"It's him, or a damn good imitation," he said. "We steamed it open already. She's all yours."

Abbie looked at the envelope.

"You swab the glue where he might have licked it before closing?"

McGonagle looked at the dark-haired man.

"It's a self-closing envelope," he said. The man had a strangely high, girlish voice. "You pull away a strip and then seal it. No chance for saliva there."

Abbie looked at McGonagle. "You didn't look inside?"

McGonagle's face was a mask. "It's your investigation," he said. "Don't insult me."

Abbie pulled out her thin leather gloves and slipped the right one on. She didn't have any surgical gloves on her—they were sitting on the Saab's passenger seat so this would have to do. She slid her hand into the bag, caught the corner of the envelope and pulled it out. As she did this, the flap caught the lip of the bag and pulled away from the envelope. Inside was a folded sheet of white paper, unlined.

As the dark-haired man watched her intently, Abbie pulled out the paper and read it. Script, not block letters. "Allegany. The Old Stone Tower, 8 tonight. Leave the money on the top of the tower. One cop and you never hear from me again."

Abbie slumped back against the seat, which gave up a puff of chewing tobacco scent. Abbie could smell the mint in it.

She showed the letter to McGonagle. The dark-haired man bent over and peered at it as well, his face somber.

"Good place to meet," she said. "I have to tell Perelli."

McGonagle looked out the window, then turned to her. "Yeah, you do."

Abbie sighed. "Though I'd rather not."

51

When Abbie was a girl, Allegany State Park had been the forest primeval. Acre after acre of thick-trunked trees with spreading roots that looked like dinosaur feet, an impenetrable curtain of green above, paths curling away into the distance, the sound of running water, and voices emerging from the tree cover. Happy voices. Children calling out, parents telling ghost stories over campfires. Peaceful summer nights.

The park had once been called "The Playground of Western New York," but there was nothing exotic or fancy about it. It was old forest, run-down in places, an affordable place for Buffalo families to get away from their lives for a week or two, working people with no real camping skills who could rent a cabin and build campfires and play Frisbee while the teenagers eyed the other families driving by. The cabins were humble, unheated.

She'd arrived at 1 p.m., believing that Hangman wouldn't arrive before dusk for the 8 p.m. meeting. The extra hours allowed her and Raymond to scout two positions and to watch the tower, to see who came and went. She needn't have worried about that part. The park was nearly deserted. No one had been throwing Frisbees or making campfires as she'd hiked in that morning from the parking lot. The high season for the park was over, the families gone home. Allegany had a few bird-watchers strolling its pathways, but that was about it. She'd heard nothing all day except the tentative steps of deer rooting in the brush and one family of raccoons that had found her hiding spot and had come to investigate, their eyes black hollow discs in a circle of white.

The conference with Perelli at his office had gone . . . well, it had gone. His color had been one shade lighter, and she guessed he hadn't emerged into the sun since Hangman had escaped. She'd told him that information had come to her indicating that Hangman would be meeting with Frank Riesen and she wanted herself and Raymond to cover it, along with a nearby backup team. Maybe ten more.

Perelli looked at her like she was offering him a reprieve of some sort. "Tell me everything," he said.

"He chose Allegany Park because there's no one up there right now. You can't have guys with mikes in their ears pretending to be out for a morning stroll or selling pretzels from a cart. It's deserted. Every extra body is a risk."

Perelli had looked beaten down. She'd expected more resistance. He asked how she'd gotten the information but she looked at him and shook her head. She wouldn't lie about it, but she wasn't going to draw him a map, either.

In the end, they'd agreed on six extra state troopers at the entrances to the park, where all vehicles came in or left. The troopers could plausibly be said to be on normal park duty and could check for anyone unusual entering or exiting by car. A mile from the Stone Tower, they put three SWAT members on the shoreline of Red House Lake, pretending to be buddies camping out after fishing all day for northern pike. They had long guns in their tents and night-vision goggles in their backpacks. The four state forest rangers for that part of Allegany, the rangers who rode lazily around the winding roads inside the park and were a well-known feature of the place, had been replaced by Buffalo cops. They had their own guns and they would be patrolling in the area of the tower, although Kearney had given them a minimum distance of three hundred yards until they heard from her.

So, thirteen men would be listening to their radios. They could get to the Stone Tower within two to ten minutes, as well as watching the approaches to the monument. The best they could do. But up close, it would be just her and Raymond, with radios on Band 5.

Perelli's eyes were lined with red veins. "This is it," he'd said. "We have to get him."

"I know," she'd answered softly.

There were no cabins in the immediate vicinity of the Stone Tower—which she could see clearly now in the last of the evening sun—and she'd seen no tents as she'd walked in that morning. She'd borrowed camouflage gear and binoculars from Perelli, who was a deer hunter. The Remington 700 sniper rifle with the Leupold Tactical Scope that was laid carefully next to her right knee belonged to the SWAT team. Pinned to the ground around her was something else Perelli had suggested: a mirrored blind, made of metalized polyester, that reflected the leaves and undergrowth around her. She'd never known such things existed; her father and she had been city campers, roasting hot dogs and tramping the local trails looking for deer, her father a few belts into a pint bottle of Scotch. The only special equipment he'd bought was a metal contraption for making toasted sandwiches over a campfire.

For a moment, she missed her father so much that she thought she would cry out. She cupped a hand to her mouth and closed her eyes.

Too many hours out here alone, she thought. Too much time to think. Someday I'm going to put six months aside and grieve for him properly.

Abbie raised the camo-covered binoculars above the edge of the blind and found the Stone Tower. It was an octagon of rough granite blocks, maybe twenty feet high, with a small balustrade on top. There were three open rectangular doorways letting visitors inside the damp structure, which had smelled faintly of stale beer when she'd inspected it that morning. The inside of the tower had been empty, featureless except for spray-painted graffiti—DANE—on one wall. There was a series of steps leading up to the platform above, which was paved with stones, bordered by a low wooden fence, and was open to the air. It, too, had been empty, the floor slick from intermittent rain. The platform gave a view of the rolling hills that ran to the horizon in all directions.

She pulled up the microphone dangling on the earphone wire. She, Raymond, and thirteen other men all wore the same headsets. It allowed them to talk in low tones and still be heard in the earpiece.

"Raymond," Abbie whispered. "Anything?"

The bud earphone in her ear hissed slightly. Then Raymond came on. "I got a damn coyote or something crawling around the bush. That's it. How long till Riesen's scheduled to show up?"

Abbie pulled back the sleeve on her camo jacket. "Fifteen minutes."

Abbie guessed that Riesen would park in the Red House parking lot half a mile away. The path bringing him to the tower cut between two meadows, skirted several groves of birch, and over one rickety wooden bridge. The killer would easily be able to see that he was traveling alone.

Raymond's voice came over the earpiece. "You ever hear this thing was haunted?"

Abbie scanned the scrub with her glasses. The sun sent beams of golden light shooting through the tree branches; it was setting, almost level with her across the tops of the hills to the west. The colors of the leaves were merging together, deep reds becoming browns and the browns now shaded with black.

"What?" she asked.

"The tower."

"No, I never heard that."

"Supposed to be. Indians sacrificed white people on the site."

"And that bothers you, Raymond?"

Raymond laughed softly. "Oh, I didn't say I had a *problem* with it. The white man is always poking his nose somewhere it's not wanted. Speaking of which, if this coyote doesn't stop messing around, I'm going to shoot it."

Damn, thought Abbie. I have the choice of the Buffalo PD, which is filled with hunters and fishermen, and I end up with a black cop afraid of coyotes.

"Quiet," Abbie hissed.

She'd seen something move thirty feet left of Raymond's position. A pine tree shook and she'd heard the distant snap of a branch, a solitary hard crack. Abbie scanned the trees with her glasses. There was a slight wind and the tops of the pines were bending with it, but this thing had shaken the entirety of the tree.

"I got a, what the fuck do you call 'em, *possum* climbing down a tree," said Raymond.

Silence now. Abbie watched. "The pine thirty feet to your west?"

"Yeah. Got a baby with her. Go on, Mama, get out of here."

Abbie looked out over the greenery.

"Hey, Kearney."

"Yes, Raymond?"

"You ever come to my side of town?"

Abbie was turned away from the tower, scanning the pines fifteen feet behind her. Nothing, but the light was starting to get tricky. She put down the glasses. "You asking me out on a date?"

"I'm just asking if you come to my side of town, ever."

"Yeah, he's asking you out on a date," said a chesty voice. It sounded like Thompkins, who was leading the SWAT team.

"Only Raymond and me talking on this channel, please," Abbie said. "Everyone else listening unless it's urgent."

"Yes, ma'am."

Abbie's eyes raked the tower again. Nothing.

"Sure I get to the East Side, Raymond," Abbie continued. "Usually for drug shootings, but once in a while there's a gang war, or a—"

"Ha. That's the Genesee Street Boys. Don't mess with them, now."

She thought of Mills. She'd called his cell phone twice, though she knew it was shut off. She'd wanted to hear his calm, steady, Canadian voice.

"If you do come over," said Raymond, "I'll take you to this new jazz spot on Bryant. They have a guitarist will make you find Jesus."

"I have a boyfriend, th—"

Raymond cut in. "What's that, on your eight."

Abbie turned quickly, bringing up the glasses and peering through the undergrowth. "How far?" she whispered.

"Ten feet."

Abbie's heart froze. She hadn't heard a thing.

She rose up on her knees. There was a shifting black shape drifting across the binoculars' viewfinder. "Forget it," she said, exhaling loudly. "Some old garbage bag blowing from tree to tree." She settled back in.

"You two thinking of moving in together, I hear," Raymond said.

Abbie rolled her eyes. The BPD gossip machine was ridiculous. "Is that your business, Raymond?"

"All those Canadian boys are good for is waxing you down with otter grease or some such."

Abbie holstered her Glock and laid the Remington rifle lengthwise. The valleys between the smooth hilltops were settling into gloom. The only sound was the breeze in the trees and birds chattering before darkness came.

Is Hangman here? Has he swept up this hill toward the tower, ghost that he is?

"Mind your manners," she said, and picked up the glasses again.

The temperature must be hovering around 20 degrees. She checked her watch: 7:54. Riesen would be on his way in from the parking lot.

She heard Raymond breathing in her earpiece. He was scanning the landscape, too, head on a swivel. After a while you could sense what the other person was doing from listening to them breathe, the rustle of the mike, the background scrim of noise.

Abbie heard something, a sound that had been there for a while but had grown just loud enough to emerge from the background shirr of wind. It was a chunking sound, the sound of feet on gravel. But it was distant. She swung her glasses over to the path, which now glowed a light tan in the deepening dusk.

It was Riesen, wearing the same trench coat and dark slacks he'd been wearing the day before. He carried a plastic bag in his left hand, and she heard the sound of his feet clearly on the stony trail.

"Riesen," she whispered to Raymond.

"I hear something else," he whispered back.

"Where?"

"Twenty, thirty yards to my left."

Abbie needed Raymond's eyes on the tower.

"Stay where you are. Thompkins, come up with one additional to Raymond's left."

"Roger that. Moving."

Riesen was approaching the tower, his head raised in the air like a pointer sniffing. He was eager. Abbie turned the glasses quickly, but she couldn't see anything to Raymond's left.

"How long, Thompkins?" Abbie asked.

Sound of movement in her earpiece, scraping branches.

"Two minutes," Thompkins said quietly.

"Red," Raymond said, his voice higher. "Red through the bushes."

"Leave it," Abbie ordered. "Thompkins is backstopping you. I need—"

"Too long, I got this."

"Raymond, stay where—"

She heard Raymond breathing hard in her earpiece and she saw a flash of camo from his position.

Damn his overeager— Her eyes flitted from the movement in the dry bush to Riesen.

"Stand down," she said urgently on the mike.

No answer. Maybe a branch had ripped Raymond's mike away. She felt the situation begin to tilt out of control.

Without Raymond, one of the three entrances to the tower was hidden to them. She saw Riesen, thirty feet away, hurrying toward the south entrance, the bag swinging in his hand.

"Thompkins, where are you?" Abbie whispered, realizing Riesen might have been lured here in order for Hangman to kill him.

Breath, panting.

"Coming up . . . just left of Raymond's position."

Right where he should be to catch anyone running downhill from the tower. But where was Raymond?

She brought the mike to her lips and whispered his name urgently. All she heard was scraping and the sound of breathing. Raymond cleared his throat. He began to breathe hard and then she heard a commotion in the earpiece.

Abbie looked toward Raymond's blind. Forty yards to its left, something moved in the bushes. Raymond or Hangman?

"You have a visual, Thompkins?"

"Negative."

She shot a glance at the path, and caught Riesen disappearing into the gloomy interior of the tower.

Ten seconds later, a shape emerged at the top and was framed against the last rays of the sun.

A scream burst through the earpiece. Abbie barked into the microphone. "Raymond? Is that you?"

She dashed out of her blind, her feet clearing the vines that surrounded it and hitting the hard pate of a path. Abbie sped down it, heading up toward Raymond's position, her Glock pointing left where she'd seen the trees shaking.

She stopped. She heard breathing in her earpiece now, slow breathing. It was different.

"Raymond?"

The voice was low, deep.

"*Hangman, Hangman,*" it said, and the back of Abbie's neck went cold, "*what do you see?*"

It was Marcus Flynn, the voice from the trial clip she'd watched in the crowded bar the day before. Slow, deep, and perfectly calm.

Abbie's heart seized up. She hurried toward the trees. There was no movement now.

"*Four little girls.*"

"Flynn, listen to me," she said.

"*Cute as can be.*"

Abbie cat-footed toward the black hillside that faced her. She brought her gun up with her right hand and pulled the earpiece away, listening for the man in the open air.

The earpiece dropped to her chest. She could still hear the voice.

"*Hangman, Hangman, where do they go?*"

Her eyes scanned the dark branches.

"*Down on the ground, where the daffodils grow.*"

The earpiece went dead.

Abbie ran into the brush just below the spot where Raymond had disappeared, thrashing at strong thin branches with her gun. Vines grabbed at her legs and branches whipped her throat. She smelled the deep musty tang of decaying leaves and she shouted Raymond's name again.

Something large and fast burst from the scrub on her right. Abbie whipped her gun up but saw orange and immediately pulled it down.

Thompkins's face was red as he hustled to her, another burly man just behind him. The SWAT leader was breathing hard.

"You see anything?" Abbie asked.

He shook his head. "Must have gone west. Nothing came by us."

Abbie nodded, pointed right and the two men shot by, headed for a small trail barely visible between two raggedy pines.

Ahead and to her left, she thought she saw something red moving along the trail, hidden by thick leaves. She brought the gun up, but held fire. It could be Raymond. She pushed her way into the vines and broke through, her feet finding a small animal path on the other side.

"Raymond!" she called.

Ten steps later, she found him. He was sprawled out on the trail, his service gun in his right hand. The back of his scalp was crisscrossed with blood.

Abbie felt her heart thumping hard. Dark trees lined the little path, left and right, leaves silvery in the moonlight. She couldn't see between them. If Hangman was lurking there, he could be on her before she could point her gun.

Abbie bent down, the tip of her Glock shaking ever so slightly.

"Raymond, stay still."

Her hand slid along the back of his neck, over the turtleneck. She felt for the jugular and found it, beating.

And then she heard a noise from behind her, like a dog baying in pain.

She turned, her eyes wide with fear.

It wasn't a dog. It was Frank Riesen, screaming.

52

She didn't want to leave Raymond. He was out cold, in the open. Hangman could watch her leave and then come back and cut his throat.

"Thompkins," she called into the mike. "Come back to where we met and proceed northeast from there thirty yards. Under a big oak. It's Raymond."

A curse. "Roger that."

Riesen screamed again, some words Abbie couldn't make out, but the sound communicated a prehuman anguish.

Abbie began to move. She brought out her radio from the camo's hip pocket and called in her position.

"Go ahead," called the dispatcher.

"Need a Medevac for Raymond. Unconscious, lacerations to the head. Bring other personnel to the Stone Tower now. Thompkins will be with him."

"Where is Hangman?" said the dispatcher.

"Last seen moving northeast toward the Red House lot. Bring the copter in and spotlight the trails between here and there."

"Roger that," the dispatcher said.

She had to get to Riesen. Abbie jumped onto the narrow path out of the stand of trees, then hooked left. The tower was forty yards away and as she dashed toward it, gun pointed down, Riesen went silent. The light from the moon edged the parapet in gray, but she couldn't see a human form anywhere.

"Riesen," she yelled. "Stay where you are."

Abbie came down the hills and sprinted toward one of the doorways. She reached the structure and threw her back against it, then swung through, bringing the Glock through the entire arc. She raced for the stairs, her feet splashing in unseen puddles.

The stairs were bathed in a weird glow. She pointed the Glock up and dashed to the platform on top.

The moon lit up the stone. Riesen was hunched against the parapet across from her. He was as still as a gargoyle.

"Mr. Riesen, are you all right?"

Abbie approached slowly. Riesen began to rock back and forth and now she heard him mumbling. But his voice was baby talk, interrupted by groans.

She pointed the Glock at the stone floor and crept over to him.

"Mr. Riesen?"

As she came closer she saw over his shoulder and there was something placed on the stone floor. It was laid out on a dirty gray cloth.

At Riesen's side, she placed her hand on his shoulder. His shoulder muscle seemed to ripple underneath his coat, in revulsion or fear.

Abbie saw what was lying on the cloth in the moonlight. A severed hand. On the third finger was Sandy's emerald ring.

53

Abbie drove home alone in the Saab, her face drained of color in the light of a half-moon. The radio was off. Riesen was in an ambulance somewhere up ahead of her, suffering from shock. Raymond was at Erie County Medical Center after being airlifted out of the park. As for Hangman, there was no sign. He'd gotten to Riesen, grabbed the money, and left his daughter's hand in exchange.

This is why cops never talk to their wives, Abbie thought. Holding it all inside, they grow distant and sleepwalk into divorce. I thought I understood why, in Miami, but maybe that was just me. It's not PTSD or that other crap. It's—how to put this—solidarity.

Cops think to themselves, Why should I have comfort when the parent or the loved one I just left behind gets none? Is it fair that I get in my car and on the way home I'm somehow forgiven for not finding the killer and by the time I walk through my front door I can tell my boyfriend or husband, "You'll never guess what just happened"?

"Bad day?" he says, setting the wineglass next to the plate of pasta.

"Honey, you wouldn't believe . . ."

No. There must be some kind of alliance with the victim or you're a piece of stone.

She looked at her phone. But she shouldn't call Mills, not yet. She hadn't earned it, that relief.

Hangman is a sadist. Every time you feel pain, he wins. Special bonus for pain caused to families and random cops. She'd been ready for that.

Frank Riesen hadn't.

And so if you're not a complete monster, you can't let the parents suffer alone. You have to take a little of their pain and tuck it away inside yourself. It's not stress, or whatever the hell the psychiatrists say it is. It's not the same as a soldier who's seen his buddies blown up. It's just the minimum purchase price for the job.

For the split second after she'd seen those pale fingers, and Riesen moaning like he'd been speared in the gut—oh, that sound, couldn't it go away just for a minute—she thought, It's not her hand. That clever bastard cut off some other girl's hand and put the ring on it, just to be playful. Sandy is still alive.

Hangman was capable of that.

But the hand, when Abbie examined it, had clearly been severed postmortem, the cut mark showed no fresh blood at all, just a clean line of desiccated flesh. The finger around the ring was swollen, and the skin underneath was discolored and slightly indented from long use. The ring had been on Sandy's finger for years. It was her. The lab would confirm it, she was sure. One of the techs had asked Riesen. And he'd nodded. That was after he'd vomited over the edge of the parapet, splashing the gravel below with the acid in his stomach. Which was, in itself, another kind of confirmation.

Hangman had just turned Riesen inside out like a gutted deer. He must be pleased. Was he listening to Riesen moan up there on top of the tower?

She feared Hangman now, the way you did an animal sniffing outside your tent. She'd become one of the people who'd seen his work up close.

Forget capturing him to learn about Hangman's brain. Forget studying his methodology. She'd be just fine with killing him.

* * *

Her phone, buzzing in her bag. Abbie glowered at the yellow line disappearing under the Saab, then finally picked it up. The screen read "Perelli."

"We had him," he said simply.

Abbie closed her eyes briefly. "How's Raymond?"

"Stable condition. Only thing permanently damaged is his reputation."

Abbie frowned. "Chief, I missed Hangman, too."

"But you didn't get knocked out by him, did you? Raymond got close."

She had nothing to say to that.

"Listen. We're doing a status meeting at 9 a.m. tomorrow. Everyone who's done anything on the case since the fucking beginning of time is going to be in that room, except for the guys running the search teams. I want you there."

54

The next morning, Hangman drove through the back alley parallel to Delaware, hearing water drip, the remains of a storm that had just blown through. The alley was narrow, and the old Cadillac barely made it through, the twin side mirrors only a couple of inches from the yellow brick of the buildings on the left and the raggedy chain link fence on the right. But he knew from long experience that the car would fit.

The building was up on the left another two blocks. As he passed a vacant lot on his left, the perspective allowed him to glance up and see the domed concrete roof. It had been a Masonic lodge back in the days when powerful men lived in the North. Powerful men still lived in the North, but the city itself was no longer powerful.

He told himself that an ordinary man, an ordinary killer, would be going to his mother's grave at this time, with his latest quarry locked up and ready to be taken. Even among killers, there were clichés, but he didn't avoid the grave because it was a cliché. No, it was just that his particular formula didn't have death on both sides of the equals sign. He was going to kill the girl, but he didn't want to remember his mother in death as he did so. No, he wanted to remember what they stole from her, and him. Life. And this was where his mother had felt most alive.

He pulled up to the lodge, the broad span of the Cadillac's hood nearly touching the brick on the left. If he pulled all the way up, there'd be no room to open the door. So he stopped short and, low-slung in the car's plush, old leather seats, he studied the windows of the two-story frame houses over the fences and small backyards to his right. No one there. He could risk it. Two minutes for his tradition.

He came here every time before the kill. Except for Martha Stoltz. No time then.

Hangman got out, his wide lapels pulled up over his chin. If the coat had been patent leather, licorice black or caramel-colored, it would have gone with the Cadillac, he supposed. The whiff of pimp-wear. But it was wool, a little outrageous but not enough to cause stares. Better to be a little outrageous than to be seen attempting to blend in. That wouldn't do. And besides, this alleyway was always deserted. Business had fled to the suburbs, leaving the half-empty city for him to hunt in.

He touched the brick corner, the color of pale mustard. He ran his hand along the brick and smiled. He'd been inside only once. His mother had taken him to a dance here. It must have been 1973 or '74, when he was seven or eight. She'd dressed up in her green "mermaid" dress, all sleek spangles that mimicked the skin of a she-fish, and taken him along, awkward, dressed in plaid Sears Husky polyester slacks and a white shirt. He wore the vintage jacket in remembrance—'70s fashion.

Oh, but those were good times. His mother's pale face, framed by the curls darker than the darkest black, and a vivid slash of lipstick.

The dance had been fun. A black DJ with a modified fro, cheap drinks set out on a plywood table. She said she'd brought him because he always seemed so quiet, so withdrawn. "Let's have some fun, just the two of us." But he knew that they were too poor to afford a babysitter, and she didn't trust him to the neighbors. And he would have thrown a fit if she'd tried to leave him with anyone. He didn't want to be with anyone but her.

So the dance at an old Masonic temple fallen on hard times. A mixed crowd, black, white, students from Buff State. The music had been good. "Bad, Bad Leroy Brown." "Crocodile Rock."

He whispered the words to the latter song as he ran his hands along the brick. There was a back stairway, three steps up with a metal rail, painted brown once, now the metal shining through here and there. This is where they'd come out. He climbed up slowly.

He'd danced one song with her. "Love Train." People had laughed and a couple had clapped. *The kid's got some moves.* Not really. He'd felt awkward and soon retired to the wooden chairs set up along the wall and sipped his fruit punch while his mother danced with men.

Hangman danced a step as he went up the stairs. He laughed. He thought of Katrina and a shiver went through him. The one before her, Martha Stoltz, he'd been far too impatient with. He'd put her up in the tree in a burst of exuberance, just wanting to feel what it was like again to see one of them dance on the end of a rope. But Katrina he was doing right. Taking his time. Observing the ritual.

Were the girls vengeance for what had been taken from him? Or had the killings slowly transformed into something else? The simple joy of taking a young girl's life?

"No," he said, and it came out as a gasp. He'd been through this before. It could be both things; one didn't necessarily cancel out the other. What did it matter if he enjoyed getting back at the vultures for what they'd done to his mother? It didn't invalidate the act. It didn't mean . . .

He wrenched his thoughts away from it.

Hangman went to the door. It was steel, painted dark brown like the railing, set flush into the brick. There was a small rectangular window with old security glass in it, the kind with triangles of wire set into the glass. He brought his eyes down and stared into the interior.

Milky gloom. No light. But his eyes were remembering; he didn't want to see what it looked like now.

What if . . .

Hangman gritted his teeth. He took a deep breath. He thought he'd gotten beyond this. The girl was waiting. The North was panicked. Everything was just as it should be.

Then his mother's voice, deep and fragile in his ears. *What if you're doing this not for me, only for yourself?*

Hangman stared through the little pane of glass.

I'm doing it for both of us, he thought.

He stood there a long time, looking.

55

The conference room was big and airy. It was where they swore in the rookies after they'd graduated from the academy, and where they gave out commendations for cops who'd dove into the Niagara River to rescue fishermen or boaters who'd toppled into the water. But there was no media here today. Reporters had bayed at the cops as they'd entered the building, shouting "Katrina" and "latest" and "dead"—those words jumbled into a hoarse cry as she ducked into the entrance.

An enormous map was pinned to the wall behind the podium, a pointer next to it, like Abbie remembered from high school geography lessons. The room hadn't been fitted out with AV equipment and there was no computer in sight.

At the lectern, Perelli looked shrunken in his white shirt and abstract pattern tie, all reds and blacks. He looked out over the crowd. "Let's begin with yesterday."

No pep talk, no introductions. Perelli was sick that the madman was still at large and his attitude toward the cops spread out before him verged on the reproachful. We haven't caught him yet, so let's dispense with the niceties.

The men and women in the room leaned forward, their faces lined with exhaustion.

"For those of you who've been out in the field, Hangman has been in contact with the father of Sandy Riesen. Hangman offered to give Mr. Riesen back a memento from his daughter for $50,000. The meet was arranged for 8 p.m. last night at the Stone Tower in Allegany State Park. We were able to introduce only two cops to the immediate scene, due to the danger of alerting Hangman to our presence. But we thought we had a chance at catching him." He looked for Kearney, his eyes darting beneath his brow. When he found her, he frowned sourly and went back to his notes. "As you know, that didn't happen. Detective Raymond was attacked and struck with a heavy object. A branch with his blood was found thirty yards from the attack scene. Apparently, Hangman was able to spot our team ahead of time. Sandy Riesen's amputated hand was found on top of the Stone Tower, apparently left by the killer. Unmarked bills brought by Frank Riesen were taken. Any questions so far?"

"How's Raymond?" someone called.

"Recovering," Perelli said.

He's pissed, Abbie thought. Well, the hell with him.

"Did the techs get anything from . . . ?"

"Sandy Riesen's hand? No. There was grit under the fingernails but nothing else. The DNA check will take a couple of days."

A sheriff raised his hand. "Time of death?" he drawled out.

"Can only be guessed at," Perelli barked. "The aging of the . . . dead matter can depend on where it was buried and how the environment accelerated or decelerated the decomposition. But it appears that it's consistent with her dying shortly after she was kidnapped."

Abbie raised her hand and was met by Perelli's stern glare.

"Kearney," he said.

Abbie leaned forward.

"What kind of dirt was underneath the fingernails?"

Perelli blinked twice. "What do you mean what *kind* of dirt?"

"Did we get an analysis of the type of dirt that was found and compare them with local . . ." For a moment, the word escaped her. "With local samples? Different areas might have different kinds of soil. I'd imagine that ground closer to the lake is different than ground near the mountain. If we found out where she was buried, that might—"

Perelli did not attempt to hide his disdain. "We're not trying to solve a crime, Kearney. It really doesn't matter where Hangman buried Sandy Riesen. He's somewhere in North Buffalo."

"We think."

Perelli's eyes closed to slits. "To go and collect soil samples from all over Buffalo and then to compare them to the dirt from the corpse would take weeks. We don't have weeks, or days. And the Buffalo Police Department doesn't maintain a library of soil samples."

Abbie hesitated. It would be better to discuss this in private, but Perelli had chosen the forum. "The FBI has a mineralogy unit at Quantico. We used them in Miami."

She saw his neck muscles bulge.

"Fine. Go," he ordered, and she was off.

56

The Medical Examiner's Office was northwest of the city's downtown, near the university's medical school, and Abbie made it there in her Saab in fifteen minutes, calling ahead to let the ME know she was coming. She pulled up in front of the low-slung brick building, hidden behind a boxwood hedge, and hurried up the walk. She rang the bell and, after a minute or two, a pretty middle-aged black woman in a pristine lab coat came to the door. "Detective Kearney?"

"Yes."

"Great. I'm back here."

The woman held the door for Abbie, then strode purposefully ahead, the wings of her lab coat flapping back to reveal a gray-green patterned dress and fashionable black leather heels. Abbie followed. The receptionist nodded and they made a quick left turn toward a pair of steel-faced elevators. The woman, Dr. Braintree, Abbie noticed from her nametag, hit the button and then turned and smiled.

Abbie reached to take her jacket off—the building was stuffy—and Dr. Braintree shook her head.

"You might want to keep that on. We keep the examination room at a steady 62."

Abbie nodded, shrugging back into the jacket. The doors pinged open and they stepped in.

"You spoke to my assistant," Braintree said, eyeing her. "You wanted to know about the soil under Sandy Riesen's fingernails?"

"That's right."

"Compare them to the FBI's forensic geology database?"

Abbie nodded.

"We can do a basic comparison online now," Braintree said. "If you want something more definitive—" The doors opened and a rush of cold air swept into the car as they stepped out and began walking down a hallway tiled in aqua green.

"—we'll have to send them to Quantico."

"I know," Abbie said, struggling to keep up with Braintree. "I've dealt with them before. All I want now is to see if there's something distinctive about the samples under the girl's fingernails. A quick hit."

Braintree pushed through a pair of swinging doors and two minutes later they were in the examination room: modern, white-tiled, smelling of formaldehyde and a strong disinfectant that burned the lining of Abbie's nostrils. There were four stainless steel examination tables lined up in a row at the center. On top of the second one was a white cloth that looked like a dinner napkin. Braintree went to the table and swept the cloth off, laid it next to the metal tray underneath.

Sandy's hand was shrunken and gray under the bright fluorescent light. The fingernail on the ring finger had been removed, and the flesh under it was dry and fissured, like old wax.

"The dirt was found underneath the nail of the fourth finger," Braintree said. "I believe the hand had been cleaned before . . ." Braintree looked up, at a loss for words.

"Before the exchange," Abbie said, nodding. "Go on."

"But these grains were further down, between the nail itself and the nail bed, almost halfway to what we call the matrix, which is here."

Braintree pointed to the base of the nail, near the cuticle.

"Even a thorough scrubbing might have missed them."

Abbie looked at the hand. At the base, where it had been separated from the arm just below the wrist, a yellowing bone sat at the center of the darkened skin.

"This was done recently?" Abbie said, pointing.

"Yes," Braintree said. "The amputation was done with a very sharp knife, most likely. No saw or anything with serrated teeth."

"Have you looked at the soil samples?" Abbie asked.

"No. I can do that right now, if you like."

"Please."

Braintree covered the hand and Abbie found herself staring at the white square as Braintree walked toward the rear wall.

"Detective?"

Abbie stepped forward and lifted the cloth. She bent down and studied the hand, moving left. The nails were done in a pale green color, almost a pistachio. Abbie reached out and touched the nail on the index finger. It was cool to the touch, glossy.

"Nail polish survives pretty well, doesn't it?" she said when Braintree returned.

"Yes. It's similar to the paint on a car. Resins and polymers, basically. Tough stuff." Braintree smiled wanly and brought her French-manicured hand up. "If we're ever murdered and our bodies are found years later, at least our nails will still look hot."

Abbie smiled. She and Braintree were both well dressed, their shoes expensive and their nails done. She looked at her own, painted just three days ago in Big Apple Red. "Morgue humor, Doctor?"

Braintree shrugged. "We take it where we can find it."

Abbie's brow creased. "Were you here when Sandy was killed?" she said. "In Buffalo, I mean."

The smile disappeared from Braintree's face, and was replaced with a look of mild shock. "If you're saying I'm being insensitive—"

Abbie reached up a hand and waved it. "Nothing like that. I'm just trying to . . . It probably doesn't matter." Abbie rubbed her forehead. "Can I have the fingernail you removed?"

Braintree pursed her lips. "Really?"

Abbie looked at her. "Is that a problem?"

"No. It's just . . . I thought only killers kept mementos."

"It's just a hunch. I'd like to have it."

Braintree went to a drawer and pulled it open. Out came a small Ziploc bag with a pistachio-painted nail inside.

"Thanks," Abbie said.

"Should we continue?"

Braintree went to the long steel counter that lined the near wall and flicked a power button on a large microscope bulging with buttons and knobs. She leaned over the eyepiece. Her black Dell laptop was open on the counter next to the scope, and Abbie saw she was logged on to the FBI secure forensics website.

"I don't know how much I'm going to be able to tell you," Braintree said. "I did a course in soil forensics in postgrad, but that was about ten years ago. We don't get much call for it here."

Abbie nodded.

Braintree reached up and turned a small dial on the base of the microscope. "God, I hope it's not granite. There are literally thousands of kinds of granite and we'll be here all day trying to find the right variety. What that will tell you"—Braintree glanced up at Abbie—"I have no idea." She pushed a glass rectangle onto the lighted pad at the base of the microscope and hovered over the eyepiece. "Let me start with low power, see what kind of sucker we got here."

The hum of the fluorescents droned in Abbie's ears as she watched Braintree.

"This is strange," the examiner said after a minute. She turned a dial on the right side of the microscope. She straightened up and reached for the laptop. She began navigating the FBI site, a frown on her face. She clicked through several pages, shaking her head briefly at each.

"Sand, pollen, diatomaceous earth . . ." Braintree's brow creased as she flicked through more images on the site. Abbie saw ghostly gray-and-white shapes that looked like amoebas or tiny boulders. "What the hell is this? Looks a little like black basalt but not really." She went back to the microscope. Two thin gold bracelets jangled on her right wrist as she adjusted the knob slightly.

"It's an oh-point-oh-five."

"Huh?" said Abbie.

"The size," Braintree said. "It's small."

"Small compared to what?"

"The FBI gives a basic identification chart for podunks like me, ME's with limited experience in this stuff. If you want something for a court trial or for a subpoena, you have to send them the physical samples. But"—she was back at the microscope, talking as she looked—"there are about two hundred minerals on the basic chart. And damned if I haven't ruled out about 190." She clucked her tongue. Braintree straightened up, turned, and gave Abbie a questioning, squinty look. She clicked the laptop keypad once and turned it to face the detective. "You're sure Sandy was buried around here?" she said. "And not, say, West Virginia?"

"I'm not sure of anything. Why?"

Braintree pointed to the laptop screen. "Because this here is what was under Sandy's fingernails."

Abbie stared at the screen. There was a jumble of tiny jagged pebbles in red, topaz, tan, and deep black. Her eyes flicked up and read the header. "*Coal?*"

"Coal dust," Braintree said. "Six of the seven particles found under Sandy's nail. The other one looks like a granite. These are black coal dust, not from anthracite, which is really clean, but the softer, messier stuff."

Abbie peered at the image on the screen. "What the hell," she said softly. "Where did he bury her?"

"That I can't tell you."

They stood there, the only noise the sound of people passing in the hallway and the hum of a refrigerator. Abbie had trouble focusing. The sound of the fridge intruded. What was the machine keeping cold? She imagined its contents, lit by a bright bulb as you opened the door. Ruby red bottles of blood. Pale fluids in test tubes. The effluvia of the human body, neatly stored.

Braintree hit a button on the keypad and a printer whirred to life in another part of the room. She walked toward the sound, heels clicking, and came back with a sheet of paper, which she handed to Abbie.

She studied the printout of the coal. "Coal dust, you're saying. Not coal *soot.*"

Braintree smiled. "Well, aren't you the A student? I hadn't thought of that. I don't know if the heat of the fire would change the composition of the particles. I'm going to have to call Quantico on that."

"Would you?" Abbie said, already moving toward the door. "I left my card. And, Doctor . . ."

"Yes, I know. There's a girl missing. I'll get right on it."

Abbie pushed through the steel doors and headed for the exit.

57

The Assessment Office of the City of Buffalo is located in Room 101 of City Hall, across the blank expanse of Niagara Square from Police Headquarters. The door was old wood with gold lettering, "Assessments" painted right onto the varnish. Abbie knocked.

The door cracked open. A pale young man stood there, dressed in an orange dress shirt, khakis, and a striped bow tie, along with fashionable glasses that he wore without any confidence. Eyes magnified slightly by the lenses looked at her.

"Are you McGonagle's friend?" he asked.

Abbie nodded. The door swung open. The room smelled of decaying paper and ink.

"I'd like to see some blueprints," she said.

"You've come to the right place. I'm—"

"You don't have to tell me your name," Abbie said. "I'm not sure if this is an official visit yet. It's easier this way."

The young man smiled uncertainly, then led her to one of the broad, polished tables.

"I'm looking for homes with coal bins," she said, taking her jacket off. "I'm most interested in ones near the Delaware Park area, but show me everything."

The man frowned. "I thought . . ."

"Yes?"

"I thought I was just letting you in."

Abbie smiled. "McGonagle can be a little slippery. I'm going to need your help."

The boy—she thought of him as a boy, something she suspected he would reluctantly agree with—licked his lips. "Coal bins," he said.

McGonagle had chosen well, Abbie had to admit. The kid was surprisingly knowledgeable about the city, and he carried on a mini-lecture as he hurriedly brought her blueprints from behind the counter, where they were stacked on caramel-colored wooden shelves with the varnish beginning to flake off. The blueprints were bound between heavy blue-gray covers, the material worn and fraying at the edges, and they slapped down with a soft *thwap*.

As she opened the books she listened to the kid's lecture. The gist of it was that little of the city's Civil War–era housing stock had survived. Most of the oldest buildings still standing dated from the late nineteenth century, when Buffalo, as the western terminus of the Erie Canal, was churning out hairpins, automobiles, and steel braces. That's when the new millionaires who owned the factories built their stone mansions along Delaware Avenue. Most of those mansions burned coal. With the city being so close to Niagara Falls, hydroelectric power in the form of electricity soon made its way over wires to Buffalo, which got the first electric streetlights in the country in 1881.

Abbie whipped through the plans of what looked like a church. "So I should be looking for stone houses?" she said.

"Yup," the clerk said. "I've never seen a coal bin in a frame house. The city changed over to electricity and then oil and then gas. The only houses that I've seen where the coal bin wasn't switched over to something else are the big mansions. They had so much room that sometimes they didn't need to do anything with the bins, which were dirty and out of the way to begin with. I've given you four books," the clerk said, pointing to the one she was flipping through. "This is the Delaware area from Niagara Square to Amherst Street."

Her eyes were struggling to trace the blue lines along the faded yellowing pages.

"Look at each address and start with the first page," he said. "Those will most often be the ground floor. Usually they'll say 'Coal Bin' or 'CB' for short. They'll be out back, and the way you can tell is that there will be a window marked at the top of the room."

"Why a window?"

"Originally it would have been an opening for the chute to come in and dump all the coal into the bin. When they stopped using them, the owners usually changed the opening over to a window."

Abbie nodded. "How many houses total are we talking about?"

The clerk got up, walked toward the counter and then turned quickly and leaned against it. "Two hundred, maybe two fifty. Only a small fraction will still have the bins, but if you want a complete picture, you're going to have to check them all."

Abbie let out a small moan. "Buddy, I don't know your name and I don't want to know. But please grab a book and start looking."

He jumped up from the counter and sat across from her.

Her phone buzzed. "Yep," Abbie answered.

"Spoke with Quantico," said the voice. Dr. Braintree.

"Shoot."

"Well, it's good and bad," said the medical examiner. "Coal dust, the stuff we found under Sandy's nails, is different than coal soot, which is produced when the stuff has been burned at high temperatures. What the FBI is telling me is that the heat changes the shape of the residue molecules. Got that?"

"So this means what was under the girl's nails was—"

"There's an eighty percent chance that what we're looking at is dust from coal that hadn't been burned. Stored coal."

Abbie thought about that. "Eighty percent? I like that number."

"So do I."

"Dr. Braintree, do you see what this means?" Abbie said quickly.

"Not really."

"Sandy Riesen was kept in a place that used to store coal, long enough to get particles deep under the skin. You think this was premortem?"

. "To be that deep under the nail, I would think so." Braintree thought about it for a moment. "How would that happen when the poor girl was alive?"

Abbie pictured it in her head. "Only one way," she said. "She was trapped somewhere, and was trying to scratch her way out."

58

Perelli was waiting for her in his office. She swept in and closed the door against the hum of ringing phones and frustrated male voices.

"I need search warrants," Abbie said, pulling out the folder stamped "Assessment Office." The first Xerox was a blueprint shrunk down to fit an 8½ x 11 sheet, and was marked "34 Summer Street" in old-fashioned script in the upper right-hand corner. The copy didn't reproduce the original's faint blue pen lines but it was clear what they were looking at were house plans.

"Where's this?" Perelli said.

"In the North, Summer Street. I went searching for every structure in the area that has an existing coal bin and these twenty-four buildings are the only hits."

"Coal?" Perelli said, and Abbie explained about the coal dust found under Sandy Riesen's fingernail.

Perelli looked at her like she had two heads. Lack of sleep seemed to magnify the confusion in his eyes. He narrowed his eyes and repeated, "Coal?"

"I need search warrants for twenty-four buildings."

"Explain, Kearney."

Abbie tried to keep her temper. "Six out of the seven grains of dirt are coal dust," she said. "That's a very high percentage. It indicates"— she almost said *preponderance* but she was trying to keep it simple for Perelli's exhausted brain—"a lot of coal where she was kept. I believe that's consistent with an old coal bin."

"You know what it's also consistent with? The fucking ground. A hundred years ago, Buffalo was probably covered in coal dust up to the curbstones."

"The odds are this is premortem. The FBI lab says there's a good chance—"

"Are you a mineralogist all of a sudden? I thought we had a break here."

He waved his hand and walked slowly back to his desk chair, dropping into it with a *thunk*, then leaned back and closed his eyes.

"Chief."

"This is all you've got?"

"No. I've been wondering how Hangman kept the girls without their screams being heard. If they were in one of these stone rooms, in an old house with thick walls, that would answer the question."

"You finished?"

In response, Abbie only glared at him.

"That body was buried five years ago," Perelli said. "The coal dust could be from anywhere. And on this basis you want to target homes in the North? Not going to happen."

"Who cares if it's the North?" Abbie yelled. She could feel a vein at her right temple begin to throb ominously. "There's a connection to Hangman. Because these homes are owned by CEOs and such, we can't take a look?"

Perelli slammed both palms onto his desk and leaned toward her, his face going a darker shade of red. "It's not because they're rich! It's because this so-called connection is weak as hell. The particles could be from anywhere."

Abbie's vision shook. She took a deep breath, then opened her eyes and stared at Perelli, who held her gaze. Her hand trembled a bit as she reached toward the folder and placed her hand over it. "Trust me on this, Chief. If I'm wrong, I'll fall on my sword. I will write a letter of apology to every rich bastard—"

Perelli held out his hand. "Give me something stronger, Kearney. Something connected to Katrina Lamb, not a five-year-old case and *not* some fucking dirt from under a dead girl's fingernails. Do that and I'll blow down doors all over town with dynamite." He pounded the Assessment Office folder with an extended index finger. "But not on this."

Abbie slid the blueprint back in the folder and left without another word.

59

An hour later, Abbie parked by the underpass where she'd met Riesen. McGonagle's Explorer was idling in the half-darkness. She got out of the Saab and walked toward it.

I feel like I'm in a damn mob movie, Abbie thought. A sense of un-reality swept over her. "You look like absolute shit," McGonagle said as she got in.

"I'm not in the mood."

McGonagle snorted. "So what brings you out?"

"I need one more thing."

She heard him breathing in the dim light.

"Go on."

"Let me say first that, if we agree on this, no one can know it's related to Hangman. No one. I don't know how it came to be that I'm trusting you on this, but I have no choice. Can you tell me that I'm making the right decision?"

McGonagle smiled. "Trust is about status, Kearney. If you trust me with some information, and I'm presented with a choice between you and someone else, someone I like more than you, I might rat you out. Their status is higher, so they get the nod."

"You realize that doesn't make me feel better?"

McGonagle hmmphed. "It should. I told you before, Hangman is my number one concern. He's a blot of fucking acid on my career, eating away at it and at me. I can't rest until he's caught or dead. Most of my friends feel the same way. That means you get the nod every time, because of who you're chasing."

"So what you're telling me in this annoyingly roundabout way is that I can trust you?"

"Right now? Yeah."

Abbie watched him. McGonagle was corrupt in any number of ways, but she believed he wanted Hangman as much, if not more, than her.

Abbie reached into her pocket and pulled out the Assessment Office folder and handed it to McGonagle. His face didn't move an inch, but he grimaced and looked down in that cop way of receiving a payoff.

"What's this?"

"Inside you'll find twenty-four pieces of paper. I've taken six of the commercial buildings and will cover those myself. You have the private homes. Each paper is the blueprint of a building. You're looking for the coal bin. I don't have time to explain the history to you, but only a small percentage of the houses in Buffalo still have a coal bin shown on their blueprints. The only homes that kept the coal bins without converting them tend to be in the North. The addresses are on there."

McGonagle stared at the street for a moment, absorbing this. "Where?"

"It will be in the basement. It will be a small, unfinished room with a window—that's where the coal man would put his chute and let the stuff down into the bin. But some of them have been boarded up or cemented over. The bin could be used as a storage room, or it could be empty. I want someone to get into the houses and take a look at each one."

McGonagle's forehead crinkled, high ridges of dry red flesh. "Why didn't you go to Perelli with this?"

Abbie gave a small laugh. "I did. He, uh, declined."

McGonagle whistled. "What you're telling me," he said, "is that you're looking for Hangman in the richest fucking homes in the city?"

"Yeah. One of which, by the way, belongs to Walter Myeong, the father of the third girl, Maggie."

McGonagle frowned. "I remember him. Slippery little fuck."

"Put him near the top of your list."

McGonagle gave her a fish eye. "Lovely. And how, d'ya mind telling me, am I supposed to get some people in and out without being seen?"

Abbie dropped her head and gave McGonagle a stare. "I expected more."

McGonagle's face flushed red. "I told you we have nobody on the north side."

"You did," said Abbie. "But I know rich people. I went to school with them, I lived with them. And they don't wash their own clothes, they don't clean their own homes. You do know some maids who work in the North, don't you?"

McGonagle looked over at her slowly, his mouth open slightly, then back. "Yeah."

"And the guys who deliver the oil? And the washer-dryer repairman?"

McGonagle closed his eyes. "I get you now." He barked with laughter. "No wonder you didn't tell Perelli."

"He wouldn't have gone for it," Abbie said. "This is the only way."

McGonagle looked over. "Why would some rich fuck from the north side want to help Hangman kill girls? Is there that many torturers in the city?"

Abbie paused. There was a spark of bright doubt in her eyes—like she was on the verge of saying something. "I don't think he wants to help," she said finally.

McGonagle's eyes widened. "You think Hangman's got some power over him?"

"Something like that."

McGonagle's eyes swiveled to the icy road. "I thought I'd heard everything," he said.

Abbie checked her watch. "We need to get—"

"What am I looking for?"

"Anything that shouldn't be there. Clothing. Food. Anything out of the ordinary."

"What else?" said McGonagle.

Abbie said nothing. The air in the car, the sound of a car's tire on the road.

"Kearney?"

"Look for anything unusual and report back to me."

"Is Katrina Lamb down in one of these coal pits?"

"I don't know."

McGonagle turned away. He slapped the envelope on the steering wheel. Then he opened the clasp and took a look at the first page.

"It'll take time," he said.

"We don't have any." Abbie shook her head. "Maids can change their schedules. Security alarms need to be checked. Boiler manufacturers can issue recalls for parts. Use your imagination, McGonagle. It has to be invisible, but more than that it has to be quick."

"You *do* think she's down there."

Abbie reached for the door handle.

"Where are you off to now?" he asked.

Abbie studied him. "If I refused to tell you, you'd probably find out anyway."

He nodded, seeing nothing amusing in this.

"I'm going to the Galleria."

McGonagle goggled at her. "The fucking mall?"

She drove to the Galleria, whipping the Saab along the highway at 90 mph and squealing to a stop in front of the back entrance. Abbie pulled the Buffalo PD placard from the glove compartment and placed it faceup on her dashboard so she wouldn't get towed. Then she opened the door and ran into the main entrance, disappearing into the roiling mass of afternoon shoppers.

60

Forty minutes later, Abbie was driving along Delaware
Avenue. The afternoon light was the color of old pots in a dark cup-
board, pewter shining occasionally through the dimness, as she sped
past the commercial district, then slowed as the houses got bigger and
grander. The kid at the Assessment Office had plotted out all the
houses on a map of the North that he printed on the back side of some
letterhead. Clusters of stone houses and a few commercial and state
buildings. He'd even placed numbers over the houses with existing
coal bins reported on their architectural drawings, then at the bottom
matched the number to the address for that house.

Abbie passed by the first one, 42 Delaware. The sign out front said
it was the Western New York headquarters of the St. Vincent de Paul
charity. She parked in the lot, then hustled up the walkway, tapping her
police issue flashlight against her thigh.

Her phone buzzed in her coat pocket. She picked it up.

It was a text from McGonagle.

"128 Elmwood. Clear. Storage room, cleaning supplies." Abbie
pulled out the list and crossed the address off the list. One down,
twenty-three to go.

This is not the one you want to check, she said to herself. You want

to be looking at Walter Myeong's house. But McGonagle was still trying to find a way in there.

Somewhere within a radius of two miles, more or less, there might
be a girl in a room where the darkness seems to come off the walls onto
her hands and blacken her skin. How horrifying it must be for Katrina,
the first time she holds her hands up and they, too, have disappeared
in the blackness. She won't know what it is at first. She will feel she's
losing her mind.

The door opened. "Kearney, Buffalo PD," she said. "There's a gas
leak in the area and I'm helping out Nat Fuel. May I check your basement, please?"

The coal bin at the St. Vincent de Paul building was now a janitor's
room, filled with mop buckets and floor cleaners. Abbie tried the Red
Cross next, four doors down, using the same gas leak excuse. The receptionist, a heavyset woman with a unibrow, made a face, then led her
down to the basement. Abbie first found the boiler room and shone
her flashlight at the pipes coming out of the wall.

"Looks good," she said to the woman. "I'm going to look around a
little, see if there are any other connections. I'll meet you upstairs?"

The woman nodded, eager to get back to her work.

Abbie pulled out the sheet for this building. The old coal bin was
catty-corner from the boiler room, all the way across the basement.
Abbie shut the door to the boiler room, walked down the hallway, listening as she walked.

If they heard a scream down here, wouldn't they have called 911?
Wouldn't they have done it for Sandy Riesen?

Another text from McGonagle. "12 Bryant, 34 Summer, clean."

Abbie felt a wave of fatigue drift through her body. She reached the
end of the hallway. There was a door on her left and another on her
right. The bin would be on the left.

She turned the old brass knob and pushed open the door.

Boxes and boxes, stacked from the floor nearly to the roof. The walls
were clean, any hint of coal dust gone long ago. Abbie tore open one of
the boxes. Fund-raising pamphlets for a post-hurricane drive.

She was looking in the wrong places. Who leaves a room coated with coal dust for decades? Not a place like the Red Cross, with janitors and inspectors and a need for every inch of space.

Maybe a man who lives alone in a mansion.

Hurry, McGonagle.

She shut the door angrily and headed quickly up to the first floor.

Abbie dodged a car as she ran for her car, pulling her phone out of a coat pocket.

She hit "recents" and dialed the last number.

"Yeah," McGonagle said.

"What do you have planned for Myeong?" she said.

"He's a fucking hermit. He has no regular house cleaner, calls Merry Maid when the place gets too bad. I spoke to his meter reader from Nat Fuel, but he says Myeong follows him down to the basement every time he goes by there."

"Follows him to the basement?" Abbie said.

"Yeah."

"Why would he do that?"

"Because he's annoying."

"Then a meter reader's not going to work," Abbie said. "And we only get one shot without Myeong getting suspicious. If we send a boiler repairman and then someone from the water company, talking about a main break or something like that, he's going to know something's up."

McGonagle grunted.

"So what do you have in mind?"

Abbie put the Saab in gear.

"I don't know. I want to see the back of the house first."

61

Abbie passed in front of the mournful facade of Myeong's corner house. She made the turn onto the side street, and parked in back of a silver Volvo, got out of the car and crossed the street. The houses along Summer weren't as grand as the ones on Delaware, mostly old Tudors or Colonials, some of them in need of a good coat of paint. Abbie walked past the Myeong house and glanced into the backyard, which was separated from the sidewalk by an old chain link fence. There was a gate near the corner, where the property ended, but it was locked with a hefty-looking chain.

From the back the house looked abandoned. There were weeds that had grown most of the way up the fence and the old trees—were they chestnut?—that she could see through the shade from the tangled branches were gnarled and uncared for. The yard itself was long but shallow, and butted up against the new vinyl fence of Myeong's neighbor to his rear, a yellow Victorian with white trim.

Abbie's phone buzzed.

"234 Bryant, clear."

Abbie fumbled for the list of houses and found it, then pulled out a pencil. She crossed off the address. Nineteen to go.

She found McGonagle's number and called. "Can you get someone to his front door in ten minutes? They can be taking a survey or selling insurance, whatever. When I know he's occupied at the front of the house, I'll take a quick look at the coal bin myself through the back."

McGonagle hmmed. "How about a chimney cleaning service?"

Abbie glanced toward the house. On the right of the house, toward the rear, was a brick chimney spire, in the same yellow brick as the rest of the house.

"Fine," she said.

"I'll text you when he's walking up."

The wind was tossing the limbs of the tall chestnut tree in the corner of the yard. The ground was covered with fallen chestnuts, and she heard one or two thump when they hit the packed earth. Did kids collect chestnuts anymore? When she was growing up in the County, the local boys tossed heavy sticks at them up in the trees, gathered them in paper shopping bags, and then had chestnut wars for weeks afterward. She'd been hit by more than a few. But here she could see the dark nuts gleaming through their split green skins.

Abbie waited until the impatience got to be too much, then put the toe of her boot in the chain link and climbed to the top bar, holding on to the top of the vertical pole for balance. She brought her left knee up to the bar, careful not to snag her wool pants, then paused and jumped. She landed on the sun-dappled ground and walked quickly toward the tree. She stepped on a chestnut and nearly rolled her ankle, but hopped up to recover before the bone twisted. Cursing under her breath, she limped to the tree and rested her back against its thick trunk, which shielded her from anyone looking out the back windows of the house. Abbie crouched down, rubbing the ankle and whistling softly.

The pain began to pass. More chestnuts struck the ground as the wind picked up.

A taxi went by on Summer. Abbie checked her watch. It had been thirteen minutes.

"Damn it, McGonagle," she hissed. "Come *on*."

Her phone was silent in her hand.

Abbie peeked around the tree trunk and looked at the back of the house. It was yellow brick with a cement base and the windows were depthless black, like you'd see in a museum. She pulled out the blueprint of the house; the wind caught it and tried to tear it from her hands. She put the paper against the tree trunk, then turned it right way up. She was standing closest to the northeast corner of the house. The little room marked "C. bin" was at the opposite end.

She tapped her phone impatiently against her thigh. It immediately vibrated. Abbie looked at the screen. "He's ringing the doorbell."

Abbie crouched down and scooted diagonally across the yard toward the far corner of the house. She heard the noise of traffic passing in front of it, but the brick was too thick to hear the bell. Myeong would be moving toward the front door as the fake chimney cleaner waited for him.

She reached the corner of the house. The base of the brick was hidden by a foot-high fringe of grass that swayed back and forth in the wind. The man never cuts his grass, Abbie thought. He doesn't call a lawn service to cut it, or have a regular maid, and he doesn't let kids come in the backyard and get the chestnuts.

Reaching down, she felt along the stone, her hand skimming just behind the grass. The surface was cool, rougher than the cement above it. She bent over and walked forward slowly.

After a few feet, she stopped. The window should be here, she thought. I can't be that far off. But under her palm she felt only cement. She moved her hand back. There was a ridge where the material rose slightly and then dipped again.

The coal window was right here, but someone had patched it over. Years ago.

She walked slowly, her hand still on the house, crouching as she crept along. There was an earth smell back here, and her hand touched only concrete. Abbie counted out another eight feet, then ten, before she came across a thick black pipe that turned on an elbow joint and went into the cement.

"Damn it," she muttered, then pushed ahead. Five feet later, her hand dropped onto the cool surface of glass.

Abbie dropped to her knees. It was an old, leaded glass window set deep in the base of the house. The glass was dark and greenish and looking through it was like staring into a deep pond where the bottom wasn't visible. If the diagram was right, she was at least fifteen feet from the coal bin. Abbie took out her flashlight. At least she'd get a look into the basement.

She flicked the flashlight on and turned it toward the green window. A bright cone of light lit up the surface. She moved it down and dropped to her knees.

I hope McGonagle chose a talker. Tell Myeong a story, comment on his chimney, scare him into getting an estimate.

The cone of light spread itself into an egg shape as it shone on the basement's dusty floor. It was like looking at objects at the bottom of a well. She could only make out shapes.

Her phone buzzed.

"Done?" the text read.

"Not even close," she muttered and stuffed the phone back in her pocket.

There was a box, maybe wood, maybe not, with some writing on the side. Abbie pressed her face to the glass, the light skimmed over something flat, something familiar. She moved it back.

It was a desk. She recognized it from her days at Mount Mercy High School. A school desk with an attached seat, held together by a gray metal tube.

Basement clutter, she said to herself.

The phone buzzed again. She didn't look at it. Instead, she moved the flashlight to the right. Something glowed in the light and disappeared. The back of her neck went ice-cold. Abbie moved the beam back.

A human hand, pale in the dark cellar.

62

Abbie gasped and pulled the flashlight back. She couldn't see past the wrist, there was something large—a dresser?—in front of the arm blocking her view. Abbie sat back, a surge of terror inching up her throat.

She couldn't make out any details, beyond that the arm looked thin and wasn't moving. Abbie rubbed the heavy glass of the window with her sleeve, then shone her light back on it. The arm hung there. A young girl's arm.

Abbie banged the flashlight on the window. "Katrina," she called.

No movement.

Something buzzed on her thigh, and she jumped back. The phone again.

She looked down at it. "Myeong antsy. Be ready to move."

Abbie reached for the window and began to push it with both hands splayed against the glass. The frame groaned, but refused to give. She turned her head and pushed harder. Either the window was painted shut or it was locked from the inside.

"Katrina," she cried out.

Abbie moved along the base, feeling through the thick grass. Five feet down was another window inset into the concrete. She pushed on it and it gave a half-inch before springing back. Breathing hard now, Abbie turned and sat on the cold ground, putting her riding boots against the frame. She took a breath, held it and pushed, her hands gripping the dirt underneath them.

The frame gave way with a horrendous shriek and dropped inward on a rusted hinge. A smell of dampness came rushing up into Abbie's nostrils. She coughed and turned away.

The buzzing from the phone again. Abbie ignored it. She was going in.

The interior of the room was dark as a shroud. Abbie pushed her head and shoulders through the gap and felt for something in the semidarkness. Her hand dropped down until it touched steel, round and cold. She pushed against it and it held. Abbie braced herself against the pipe as she pulled the rest of her body in and lowered down face-first toward the floor. Oh, God, she thought, don't let it be a torture rack.

She held the bar and swung her feet to the floor. Abbie stood, grasping for her flashlight. The basement was quiet, the silence enveloping her.

Then she heard footsteps from above.

Abbie clicked on the light and dust rose from the floor. She'd disturbed the tiny particles, but through the veil of motes she could see objects: a low dresser, and something turned against the wall, tall and rectangular with something silvery at the center. A mirror, Abbie thought.

Another noise from above. A door closing? She no longer heard footsteps.

The phone buzzed. She snapped it out of her pocket.

Text from McGonagle: "Run."

Abbie shoved the phone into her pocket and moved the flashlight to her right hand. As she did so, the shaking light revealed paintings stacked against a concrete wall. Abbie pulled the Glock from the holster, its raised grip cold and damp, then turned toward the steel thing she'd felt when climbing in.

An old bed frame, painted with that black old enamel that gleams.

On it hung something small and square. Abbie walked up to it and reached for it in the darkness.

A baby's building block, worn, with some of the edges chipped. The letter A, painted in blue, the background in white. Abbie stared at it, then twirled the block slowly in her hand.

A baby block.

Her eyes were wide with adrenaline and she felt her hand shaking. Easy, Abbie. You're close now. Get to the girl and get out.

Abbie flashed the light ahead and approached the door. She took two steps, more dust billowing up, golden in the light. She touched the knob. The room's mustiness nearly choked her.

She opened the door a crack. Air came rushing in through the dark gap and Abbie listened into the room ahead. Silence.

Why didn't the hand move when I tapped the glass? She had a vision of Katrina Lamb hung from a rafter, hand dangling down, like Martha Stoltz up in the tree. The stillness of death.

Abbie pushed open the door and put the flashlight through first, turned it slowly to the right, followed by the Glock. Shoulders squeezed together, she pushed through the doorway.

A low-ceilinged hallway led to steps twenty feet away. Seven of them, she counted. And a door in the wall to her right. She moved toward it quickly.

Steps again, closer now, definitely on the floor just above her. The floor seemed to creak under someone's weight. Abbie took a shaky breath and flexed her palm over the Glock's grip.

Should I text McGonagle, tell him to get some cops down here? No time, she thought. What if Katrina is still alive?

Abbie dashed toward the room with the body and pulled on the knob. The door pulled back but the top corner was jammed in the frame and the door torqued back without releasing. Abbie set her feet and pulled away. The corner stuck fast. She closed her eyes and tried again, the veins in her neck beginning to stand with the effort. The door creaked, then all of a sudden it shuddered open. Abbie fell back against the far wall. Crouched against the cold, jagged stones, she shone a light into the doorway.

A dresser, oak. A nice one. Newer than the stuff in the next room. Abbie got up quickly and stepped toward the room. She listened almost subconsciously for the creaking of a rope, a rope with something heavy on it. She slid in, an icy tremor sweeping across her face as she entered.

There was a body straight ahead of her, turned away, motionless. Abbie felt her skin tingle with horror.

Abbie pulled the Glock up and was about to draw on its chest when she noticed the outline of the head. It was odd, misshapen.

She brought the flashlight up and saw a head with no eyes or ears.

"A mannequin," Abbie whispered. It wore a tartan skirt and a crisp white blouse. She was momentarily confused, until she recognized the uniform from her school debating days. Sacred Heart Academy. Maggie Myeong had gone to Sacred Heart.

Abbie moved closer.

Another mannequin to her left. This one wearing a flowing green dress, one-shouldered. Abbie stared at it in horror, not understanding.

"Can I help you, Detective?" she heard behind her.

She swung around, her hand shaking.

"Mr. Myeong," she whispered. His eyes were covered by shadow, which cut across his chin.

"What are you doing in my house?"

Abbie breathed, her heart pounding furiously. Was Katrina Lamb nearby?

"What are these mannequins, Mr. Myeong?"

He stepped closer. Myeong was pale, his face tight with anger or surprise. The eyes were agitated and red-rimmed. His hand came up, pale as a ghost in the moted light, and he seemed to cover his eyes. "When you lose a girl," Myeong said, and came toward her into the room. "You want to keep as much of her as you can."

She saw his eyes now, and they were angry, but they wandered past her and focused on the mannequin just over her right shoulder, the one wearing the school uniform.

Abbie's eyes took in the things behind him. A bedroom set. Canisters leaning against the wall, the kind you'd put art, or posters in. A padded jewelry case sitting on a chair.

"You moved Maggie's room down here?" she said.

Myeong looked around, then nodded.

"I couldn't walk by her room every day. It's just down the hall from my bedroom. Even if the door was closed, which is how I always kept it . . ."

He paused. Abbie released a breath and dropped the Glock to her side.

"Their clothes keep their smell the longest. Especially a girl who liked perfume." He wasn't crying, he was far past crying. He was numb.

Abbie felt her body droop. The room was a shrine to his daughter. Hangman wasn't here, Katrina either.

His eyes were on her, dead black eyes. "Why are you here, Detective?"

"I'm looking for Katrina."

His eyes seemed to dilate inward. "And you thought she might be here?"

"We're searching the area. I saw this"—she pointed to the mannequin, its fingers elegantly curved.

Myeong nodded. "Do you think I'm insane?"

"No. I don't."

"Because only an insane man would take a girl when his own had been killed." Then he said something low. She thought it was, "I loved her very much," but she couldn't be sure.

Abbie stepped toward Mr. Myeong. She couldn't go without knowing.

"In the other room, there's a baby's building block. The letter A looks just like the one carved in Maggie's hand."

He nodded and seemed about to speak, but he turned and walked out into the corridor. Abbie followed him, terror at the thought of being locked in this room blooming in her chest. By the door was a jewelry chest, covered in dust. Abbie instinctively reached over and brushed some of the grit off the dust. When she turned back, Myeong was watching her.

"This way," he said.

63

"The symbol on her hand was a threat," Myeong said, sitting in the front room with the grand piano gleaming under a picture window. Abbie perched on the edge of the piano seat, while the diminutive man was sunk into the folds of an enormous leather couch. She smelled the Pine-Sol that had been used on the piano, which looked like the only thing in the house that Myeong cared for.

Abbie didn't take out her notebook. They were way past all that.

"Something that happened in Arizona?"

Myeong shook his head. "Before." His eyes were far away, fixed on something out the window. He sat slumped forward, his feet spread apart.

"Mr. Myeong?"

"You were right, the A was a baby block. I knew it right away."

Abbie took a deep breath.

"But she was your child, you have no doubt?"

He nodded quickly.

"You see, the year before she died, Maggie had a child. Secretly. She wanted it that way, and we agreed. Afterward, when it was all over, I'd find her in her room. She . . ." He hung his head and his eyelids pressed close. Myeong's ribs strained against his shirt as he cried. He was breathing fast.

"It was a boy. She thought she would call it Alexander." He came up, took a ragged breath, then wiped his eyes with the sleeve of his shirt.

"*If* she'd kept it?"

Myeong stared at her, shaking his head, his lips pursed to speak but no sounds coming out.

Abbie closed her eyes.

"Maggie gave the baby away?"

He nodded violently.

"Yes. She did. I never knew she was pregnant until the end. I thought she was putting on weight, that's all. It was partly my fault, we never talked about personal things and she was terrified of disappointing me. I think my wife knew this."

"And you took her to Arizona . . ."

"There's a psychiatric facility in Tempe that deals with young mothers. She felt guilty about the whole thing. So we brought her there."

"But why would Hangman carve that into her hand?" Abbie asked.

"It was a message, a warning. Hangman had time with those girls; he talked to them. What else could it be? A message to me that she'd told Hangman about Alexander. I thought he was threatening to reveal it to the world. A final humiliation."

"Is that why you went on TV?" Abbie said.

"Of course. He wrote me, threatened to send a letter to the newspapers. I paid him $40,000 not to reveal Maggie's secret. It was the least I could do."

Abbie stood up. Her feet rang out on the cold hardwood floor as she walked to the window. The trees lined in the front yards of the nearby homes were filled with leaves, just beginning to change color. A fall day heading into the depths of winter.

She turned. Myeong's head was down, bobbing just above his knees. It looked like he was shaking off a punch.

It felt like there was a magnet in Abbie's head, with ideas flying toward it: images, snatches of conversation that before had nothing to do with each other. They were forming themselves into a pattern. She closed her eyes.

"You're right," she said. "The letter A was a message to you. But not from Hangman."

64

Abbie sat in her car after finishing with Myeong and watched the leaves fall, swaying and dipping, from the trees that lined Summer. The dark gray asphalt was covered with them near the gutters, and she watched two swoop and fall to the top of the yellow pile.

The magnet was still pulling things from her memory. Something Myeong said had triggered it.

"Do you think I'm insane?"

Walter Myeong wasn't insane. He was just grieving, and would be for the rest of his life.

So what was it?

Her nerves were jangling, her body felt twitchy. She was close. The case's dark matter was acquiring a shape. What is it? What am I missing?

Walter Myeong wasn't insane, but he'd brought Maggie to a psychiatric facility in Arizona.

Abbie got out of the car and went to the trunk. She popped it open and there was the case file. She hadn't given it back to HQ.

She brought it back to the driver's seat, and closed the door. Abbie opened the file and began flipping through the pages.

There. Maggie Myeong. She hadn't been seen by a psychiatrist in

Buffalo, not according to the file, but she'd wanted to become one. "For her school project junior year, she'd done after-school work at a psychiatric facility," Abbie read. Her junior year. She was killed in 2007, and she'd been a senior at Sacred Heart. She'd volunteered to work with psychiatric patients in 2006.

Abbie flipped forward in the file to the Marcus Flynn profile. She flicked through his bio. But there was nothing there.

Whatever was niggling at her brain wasn't from the file. It was from something else.

An interview?

Let it come, Abbie. You know it's there.

McGonagle. The EDP episodes. Marcus Flynn had been brought in twice for public disturbances, both along Chippewa, in the year before the murders began. Which was 2006. Evaluated as an emotionally disturbed person and released, McGonagle had said. But evaluated where?

She snapped up her phone.

"Perelli."

"It's Kearney."

"Where the fuck have you been?"

"Just tell me one thing. If an emotionally disturbed suspect was arrested in North Buffalo, on Chippewa, where would he be taken?"

"Wh-aat?" Perelli sounded brain-dead.

"Where would he be taken?"

"The Psych Center."

Abbie closed her eyes. The old Buffalo State Asylum for the Insane over on Elmwood Avenue, a huge complex of brown brick buildings inside its own neglected acreage. Most of the old wards—in a separate part of the grounds, built God knows how many years ago and hidden behind acres of forest—were abandoned, with only a few modern buildings grafted onto the old structures, which were visible behind a black-spiked iron fence. In front were two looming towers, capped in green metal, their windows staring balefully out at passersby on Elmwood.

No kings and queens lived in Buffalo, Abbie thought. But Abbie would bet there were patients at the Buffalo State Asylum who believed themselves to be Napoleon, or the kings of England, or Louis XIV. *I live where the kings abide.*

Something an inmate would say.

The buildings were old, late nineteenth century at least. At some point in their history, they would have been heated by coal. She grabbed the folder and paged furiously through the blueprints.

The second to last was marked "The Buffalo State Asylum for the Insane." Abbie stared at the thin, spidery lines that traced the walls of the old wards.

She turned the key on the Saab and revved the engine high, swinging out onto Delaware Avenue. "Still there?"

"Yeah."

"Send SWAT to the Psych Center, the abandoned part in the back of the grounds. I think Hangman's there—and Katrina. I'll explain why after we check it."

Maggie Myeong was an intern there in the fall of 2006. Marcus Flynn was detained for being emotionally disturbed in that time span, which means he must have gone to the Center. They had brushed across each other's paths. It had coal bins.

Three minutes away. Hold on, Katrina.

"Kearney, you feel good about this? I can pull guys off the third search team to go in there with you."

"Do it."

"Listen, that place is like a fucking series of dungeons. Half the buildings are abandoned, the roofs falling in, the whole facility's locked up, and everything's connected to everything else by corridors."

"I know. But I want to be first."

"Give me fifteen minutes," Perelli said. "We're going to need bolt cutters and all that shit. And bodies."

65

She approached the Psych Center from the public side. The front part of the old asylum grounds, the acreage fronting on Elmwood Avenue, had been taken over by Buffalo State University. Best to come in through the campus. No one would notice her that way.

She whipped the Saab along Grant Street, the turbo whining, and made a right into the college entrance. The early evening sky was clear, the sun dropped somewhere behind the soaring trees to the west. Abbie dropped her speed down as she drove the campus roads, passing an imposing building with six stone pillars in front. She came to a crosswalk and a trio of overweight female students stared at her as she nearly plowed through them.

Come on, girls, for God's sake. It took an eternity for them to cross.

Abbie grimaced and stepped on the accelerator. She passed large, newish dorms in bright tan brick and rolled by the baseball field. She went slowly, so as not to attract attention. She hadn't told Perelli everything, of course, but enough to get what she wanted.

A large round brick smokestack loomed up on her right. The college power plant. She drove past it and over a large avenue and the character of the landscape changed. The modern buildings and the dorms fell away and were replaced by a range of peaked roofs ahead of her, casting sharp shadows, like a piece of sooty old London transported to the middle of a bucolic campus. She was driving west, so the setting sun was behind the wards, filling their windows with darkness. The ones to the left looked abandoned.

The old asylum.

Abbie parked by a large playing field where young women were practicing lacrosse. Their sudden shouts and calls carried over the grass cleanly and came to her. Abbie pretended to watch for a moment, walked along the line of cars parked on the access road, then turned and strode quickly for a grove of black-trunked trees that shaded a path to her right. She hurried down the path away from the college and the fields, the sounds of lacrosse slipping behind her.

She passed the modern part of the asylum as she raced ahead. Through panes of clear glass, she saw patients moving through the corridors, a security guard standing with hands on his gun belt through the front door. The buildings were the rehabbed wings of the old facility, and they looked like brownstones in a nice part of Brooklyn. This is where they took Marcus Flynn when he was acting crazy. Before the murders started. Abbie hurried on.

The grounds grew more overgrown and tangled the further she went. On her left she spotted the remains of a rusting wire fence that had once crossed over the path, now choked with vines. To her right was an old metal swing that had provided entertainment for the inmates on summer days, but the top bar had rusted through and the wrought iron seat had crashed to the ground. She moved quickly, listening. There were forest sounds: birds chirping in the sunlight and branches of trees thwacking against each other.

She came to a new galvanized steel fence that ran across the path and continued both right and left. A white metal sign had been screwed to the horizontal fence posts, with bright red lettering. CONDEMNED BUILDINGS, it read. PROPERTY OF THE STATE OF NEW YORK. KEEP OUT. Abbie glanced around before putting her boot on the lowest rung and beginning to climb. In ten seconds, she was over, landing in a patch of dry grass.

The old asylum wards were ahead to her left. Dark rectangular windows, many jagged with broken glass, stared back at her. It seemed impossible that Katrina could be in there, so close to the idyllic scenes of college life. Obscene. How could Hangman keep her down there? But these buildings were long forgotten, shut away, full of bad memories the city wanted to forget. No one came back here.

The line of trees on either side of the meadow that fronted the wards seemed to funnel wind down their center. Abbie pulled the collar of her coat tight around her neck. She leaned against the last elm, watching the sun dip below the horizon. Shadows were her friends now. She was a shadow herself, hoping to blend into the tree line. She checked her watch.

6:53. If Perelli was right, she'd have backup in about ten minutes.

She waited. The sound of bells came over the elms, all the way from the red-roofed bell tower of Lafayette Presbyterian, she guessed. Abbie slid the magazine out of her Glock, glanced at it quickly, and then jammed it back. A nervous habit.

Then she heard it. A clear ringing scream, rising quickly from the sound of birdsong, then cut off in mid-shriek. A cry of pure arcing horror.

Abbie stared at the line of jagged-roofed buildings. Had it come from them, or had the wind carried it from the main psychiatric facility a quarter-mile behind her? Her eyes raked the dilapidated structures, but the shabby redbrick buildings showed no movement. Abbie moved out of the line of trees and headed straight for the door of the middle ward.

The second scream was louder. A guttural moan twisted into a screech of pain. Abbie ran. Her vision shook as she raced over the uneven ground, her feet bouncing off little hills of rock and earth, the facade of the buildings jarring and twisting as she sprinted over the lawn straight toward one of the darkened hallways. The sound rang in her ears. It was a girl's scream, not a woman's.

Bringing the Glock up in a locked-arm stance, she reached the porch and dashed up the steps to the wooden door. She threw her shoulder against the door, but it didn't budge. Abbie took a deep, shaking breath, and tried the handle. Locked. The place was silent as a tomb.

Abbie tried to wrench the door. These buildings had been abandoned for decades and the locks were probably rusted solid. She ducked to look in the tall, black-framed window next to the door frame; it was streaked with dirt and the rain had made a pattern on the grime. Inside, she saw a partially razed room, plaster torn from the yellowing walls, abandoned equipment. It sent a chill rattling down her backbone.

Turning back toward the playing fields, Abbie brought her elbow back and smashed it through the window. Tinkle of glass shards. She knocked away more glass with her Glock until there was a hole big enough to get through. It was too far from the door to reach around and unlock it from inside.

The building had swallowed up the screamer. Only a breath of stale air from the hole in the glass. Abbie holstered the Glock and stepped through the frame.

Sirens in the distance. Perelli was coming. Hurry, damn it.

Abbie ducked her head past the broken glass and found herself in a high-ceilinged room strewn with old bedpans, a broken bed frame, fallen plaster everywhere, a shattered mirror on the wall above a chipped mantelpiece.

Her pulse was jumping and her mouth went dry. She couldn't call out or Hangman might kill Katrina.

Had he heard the glass break?

Abbie dashed across the room toward a doorway set in the corner of the far wall. The passageway to the next ward. She put her hand on the cool enamel-coated knob, and slowly pulled open the door. Half-light. To the left was a short hallway into a dark, vaulted room. To the right were stairs descending into cryptlike darkness.

Abbie brought the Glock up and marched slowly ahead into the gloom.

Gleams of light showed puddles of oily black water on the floor. Flaking green paint on the walls showed patches of white primer underneath. Abbie's mind flashed on hordes of zombified people pushing along these walls, terrified of the staff, pushing themselves into the plaster and rubbing away the paint. Armies of the mad marching through here, gone now.

Where was Katrina?

She heard cranking, like a machine with a sprocket. Click, click, *click*. But it was faint. Abbie turned left.

It came from outside. Abbie found the first window, streaked with grime. Through it she saw a semicircle of dark, leafless trees. Abbie scanned right. *There.*

A girl in a blue sweater and dirty white pants with her neck in a noose, swinging.

Abbie reared back and kicked out the glass.

"Katrina!" Abbie cried, vaulting through the glass, curling her head over her knees as she tumbled forward. She landed on her back, and felt a shard of glass cutting through her coat into her flesh, but she was quickly up and running toward the grove of twisted trees.

She dashed for the girl. The body turned and she saw the girl wore a bizarre mask. She was wriggling, hands tied behind her back. Abbie raced up to the girl and grabbed her by the legs.

She tried to lift her but couldn't. The girl was making a noise in her throat. As if it was cut and the air bubbles were escaping out the sliced airway.

Abbie spotted the box the girl had been standing on, an old wooden one. She gasped and stepped up on it. Immediately, the box began rocking underneath her feet on the unsteady ground, threatening to tip over.

Abbie saw terrified eyes behind the mask. She grabbed Katrina around the waist with her left arm and lifted. With the right, she pulled out her Glock.

The rope looked thick and strong as iron. Abbie pointed the Glock a foot above the noose and pulled off four rounds, the sound exploding in the stillness.

Katrina didn't fall.

Oh, God, the shadows were going to reach out and put their fingers around her neck and then get the girl. Where was Hangman?

The echoes of the gunshots faded into the sky. The rope, snipped by the bullets, was still holding by a few cords. Katrina's fingers closed around Abbie's arm and the choking noise pitched higher. Cold as icicles.

Her brain is dying, Abbie, hurry. But her strength was failing just from the effort of lifting the girl a few inches. Her vision shook as Abbie raised the Glock again, the left arm screaming in pain. She took aim and pulled off another three shots.

Dizzy now. No change in the rope. The shots had gone wild. Abbie's legs began shaking from the strain.

She holstered the gun and grabbed Katrina around the waist.

"Hold on," she cried, and taking a jagged breath jumped off the box, clasping the girl to her body.

Katrina gasped painfully. A horrible moment of suspension, then the rope snapped with the sound of a pistol shot and the two of them spilled to the ground, the impact pushing the air from Abbie's lungs.

Abbie pulled her gun hand free and found the grip of the Glock, wrenched it out, her other arm still wrapped around a gasping Katrina. She ejected the magazine, pulled a fresh one from her pocket and slammed it in, her eyes scanning the shadows cast by the eaves of the old asylum.

Abbie got her finger under the noose. It was wrapped around the girl's throat, biting deep into the skin. Abbie pushed two more fingers inside the noose, pulling desperately at the rope. She grunted with the effort, and heard the grunt echo out into the grove.

Slowly, Abbie worked the coil until with a cry of effort she lifted the noose and pulled it over the girl's hair. The mask came off with it.

Katrina Lamb, a red-ball gag around her mouth, stared at her in oxygen-deprived shock. Abbie grabbed her and rolled toward the base of the tree.

As she did, an impression flashed across her mind: something had just moved in the darkness underneath the old ward's windowsill, second to the left. A shift in the bunched shadows.

She pulled off Katrina's gag and the girl gasped. Abbie brought her mouth to her ear and whispered.

"Where is he?"

Katrina was panicking, taking huge gulps of air as if she were drowning.

"Rrrrrr—"

"Where, Katrina?"

"Rrrrrright behind you."

Abbie's eyes went wide. She whipped around.

Emerging from the gloom of the trees to her right was Marcus Flynn. He wore a dark boiler suit and his hands were down by his side. In his right was a black .45. His eyes open nightmare-wide, mouth gaping, staring at her like she was a ghost escaped from his own nightmare.

"Marcus," she cried, raising the gun.

He came, shuffle-stepped, the .45 bouncing by his side.

"Put the gun down!" Abbie shouted, her voice shaking.

He kept coming. Abbie pointed at Flynn's chest.

"Marcus," she said. "Stop right there."

Fifteen feet. Twelve. His face was strange, a half-smile on his lips.

Abbie caught his gaze. "I know you didn't kill those girls, Marcus."

The shuffling stopped.

A gunshot. Abbie twisted away as Flynn jerked to the ground. Abbie dashed back and pulled Katrina away and they huddled behind the gnarled trunk.

Katrina was shrieking. Abbie cooed to her softly. "It's almost over. Almost."

Marcus Flynn was bleating like a stuck animal. The sound filled the little grove of trees. Abbie peeked around the trunk.

BAM. Another gunshot. Marcus Flynn's body jumped, and he let out a long groan, then lay still, twisted over on his right side.

A voice called out. "*You* were supposed to shoot him, not me."

Katrina's body twitched violently and she clung to Abbie, her nails biting into Abbie's arm. The two of them were barely covered by the tree and its roots. Abbie smelled pine needles and dirt. The voice came from her left, at the corner of the old ward. To escape, she'd have to either turn and run into the forest or dash for the far corner of the wards, away from the man with the gun. But both would expose her to moonlight and bullets.

Katrina's hand was clamped on Abbie's gun arm. Abbie slowly peeled the fingers off. She turned toward the corner where the shots had come from.

"Why would I shoot an innocent man, Doctor?" she called out.

Andrew Lipschitz's rippling laughter echoed through the grove. The branches above Abbie's head whispered as a breeze moved through them. "How did you know?" he asked. The voice seemed to be moving in the gloom.

She couldn't see anything there; it was in deep shadow from the roof above. Was he hiding behind the corner of the ward or coming toward her, covered by the inky blackness?

Abbie took a deep breath. She knew the endgame here. To kill Katrina and bury her with Marcus Flynn where they would never be found. And leave her, Abbie, dead in this grove.

Abbie leveled her gun, but she could hear skittering. Lipschitz had the advantage. He didn't mind killing all of them. With Fatty Joe Carlson's gun. It would make for a perfect ending to the story.

"Because you don't know women," Abbie called out. "You kill them, but you don't know them."

She felt him listening. He was too curious for his own good.

"When you gave Mr. Riesen Sandy's hand, you forgot to take off the polish from her nails."

"And?" said Lipschitz.

"Did you know that the makeup companies change the colors all the time? It's called fashion. Bad mistake."

"Is that right?"

The voice had shifted a few feet right. Abbie pulled Katrina away, keeping the tree between them and the gunman.

"The one on her nails was China Glaze Groovy Green—I checked at the mall. Which means you must have bought it yourself, because it didn't come out until June 2008. Marcus Flynn was in prison in June of 2008, Doctor. So I knew he hadn't killed Sandy. You did. You killed all the girls. But you kept Sandy alive for a while, didn't you?"

The wind chinked the dry branches overhead. No answer from the doctor.

Just give me a shot and I'll take him out. How long until SWAT arrived? If it was more than a few minutes, she'd be dead, most likely.

Lipschitz's voice came floating out of the gloom. "If that was my last mistake, what was my first?" The laughter was gone out of his voice.

"Maggie, of course," Abbie said. "She was an intern at the Psychiatric Center. You worked here. You saw her here. And you chose her."

"Yes. I did."

Abbie heard the sirens, closer now. They were coming up the path she'd walked, taking no chances. Two minutes and it was over.

"It was a bad move, Doctor. If they traced back where she'd been working, who she knew, they would have eventually come here and started talking to the staff. And then she carved that A in her hand, so that her father would know that Hangman knew about her baby. Because you talked to her about it, didn't you? She wanted to talk to someone, she was in bad shape. And she told you about baby Alexander and the rest of it."

Laughter. "All true, Detective. But I had to have Maggie. I don't regret it. Our time was short, but it was sweet."

"Drop the gun, Doctor."

A bark of scoffing laughter. "Do you think I'm going to Auburn, with those Mongoloids? It was hard enough working with them, I'm not about to join them."

Abbie put her hand on Katrina's shaking shoulder and slowly circled behind her. She checked the angle from the right. No better.

"So you looked around for someone to be Hangman, to take the rap for you. You found Marcus Flynn. He was your patient here?"

"I was on duty when they brought him in. Marcus had problems. It wasn't much of a loss to society, was it?" His voice was neutral, but she knew he was waiting for her to make a mistake. Lipschitz was crafty as hell.

"You sent the letter to Child Welfare about Sandy being abused," she said. "And you told Marcus about it?"

"Yes."

"Who was the girl who died here, Doctor, the one who started you killing?"

She heard geese shoot overhead, honking, then quiet settled onto the little grove.

"I thought you already knew. My mother."

Abbie closed her eyes. She flashed on the photo of the dark-haired young girl on Lipschitz's desk at Auburn. Of course. Hiding in plain sight.

She peeked around the tree again and the bark exploded just above her right eye. Abbie snapped her head back.

"Let's gooooooooo," Katrina moaned.

"Quiet or we die," Abbie hissed back.

He still had time to kill them both and get away. No one knew his identity, except her.

"She was a maid in the North, just sixteen, when it happened," Lipschitz said in a voice filled with acid. "That's where she was raped. After that, they fired her, left her to rot and she never forgot it. Years later, she ended up in this hellhole. That was when they still believed in plunge baths and indiscriminate beatings to cure the patients. She hung herself from a tree not ten feet from where you are."

Abbie glanced at Marcus Flynn in the paleness of the moon's light. A smear of a face. Blood beneath his flung-out right arm. But his chest was rising and falling.

"I came here to see if I could find out who the family was," Lipschitz said. "But the records were gone. I only had the diary they gave me years later."

The diary he made the girls read. *The evil-doers are not punished.*

Lipschitz was punishing them.

"One man from North Buffalo raped your mother. Not all the families you targeted were guilty."

"They're all the same to me."

A nickel-plated barrel emerged from the darkness at the corner of the ward. Then it was gone.

She heard the click of a gun being cocked. He was crouched down, waiting for the right moment. He was going to rush her.

Abbie's heart jumped. Wait here for his charge or take a shot at him? Abbie's mind froze. He would come around the tree to her left, firing at her and Katrina. Blitzing them.

Katrina was shouting something unintelligible and shaking her head violently. Abbie grabbed her sweater. "Don't run," she whispered. "*Do not run.* He'll shoot you."

"They treated her like garbage, Kearney," Lipschitz's voice called. "And I can still—"

Katrina screamed. Abbie saw what was going to happen before it did. The girl wrenched away from Abbie's hand and flung herself away from the tree cover, running for the corner of the old building.

Lipschitz emerged out of the shadows, his face, shock-white, staring at the fleeing figure as he rotated the gun barrel toward her, the nickel sparking bright.

Abbie snapped the Glock toward the pale smear of his face and pulled off four fast shots, deafening her. The grove rang with echoes as Lipschitz twisted and tumbled backward.

Still screaming incoherently, Katrina Lamb sprinted toward the building and disappeared around the corner. No one back there but SWAT. Let her run.

Abbie got up, the point of the Glock shaking, and ran over to Lipschitz, his khaki pants and dark black shoes etched in the gleams of moonlight, the rest of him in shadow. He was groaning and trying to get up, his right hand lifting gently before falling back to the ground. The gun was a foot away, the barrel faced back toward him now. Abbie kicked it away and stood three feet from the doctor.

She heard blood gurgling in his throat. It also soaked his white cotton shirt red from a point just above the left pocket, like a dark, poisonous flower.

From behind her, she heard Marcus Flynn. At first Abbie didn't understand, but then she heard his words clearly: "Please don't hurt him."

Lipschitz died in the half-gloom.

66

Statement by Marcus Flynn. Buffalo Police Headquarters. 74 Franklin Street. September 26, 2012. 10:45 p.m. In attendance: Detective William Raymond, Detective Absalom Kearney, Mr. Albert Hernandez (attorney for Mr. Flynn).

I have to tell you the truth. My heart is going a thousand miles an hour. Do I sound normal? I feel like it's hard to breathe and that the walls of this room have moved a couple of inches inward since I sat down.

I know, I know. I'm just here to give an account of the Hangman case. But it's not that simple. I really didn't want to come here today; I almost turned my car around two times. Walking in that door . . . I felt like if I walked inside Police Headquarters, it would trigger the nightmare all over again. I'd be sitting across from you and we'd all be smiling, like we are now, and then you'd say, "Marcus, you have the right to remain silent."

May I have some water? Thank you.

When it happens to you once, you never quite believe it won't come true again. I'm not being charged with any crimes? Please say it for the record. OK. That's better. I believe you. I'll take a deep breath now.

I first met Dr. Andy Lipschitz when I was brought to the Buffalo Psy-

chiatric Center on September 4, 2006, after drinking too much in the Eagle Tavern on Chippewa Street and getting into a fight with the bartender. Dr. Lipschitz was the psychiatrist on call that night and I remember speaking to him for over an hour about my life and the reasons for my outburst. I was unhappy. Nothing in my life had worked out the way I'd planned, and I didn't know why. I was probably a little suicidal, to tell you the truth. Maybe a little part of me wished one of those cops had taken me out while I was screaming and running around on Chippewa. It would have been easier that way.

Dr. Lipschitz saved me. Ironic, I know. He . . . he didn't look at his clipboard and rattle off questions to me. He leaned forward and listened when I talked, really listened. I don't think anyone had listened to me like that for ten years. I liked him. When I was brought in again three weeks later, I asked for Dr. Lipschitz by name and he came in to talk to me, although he'd been off-duty that night.

He didn't cure me or anything. My problems—with women, with work, with trusting people—went pretty deep. I guess you could say now I was paranoid, but that's not how I saw it at the time. I saw people working against me: people at work, people in my family especially. I'd never had good relations with them, especially my father, who's a psychopath in a three-piece suit, and I'd lost my mother when I was a teenager. The same thing had happened to Dr. Lipschitz. When he told me that, I was like, he could be my brother. Or, he's the person I should have become. His life had been crap at the start and, look at him, he was a doctor, helping people. It inspired me. I wanted to change.

We kept in touch after that by phone and would occasionally meet for informal sessions at his offices on Elmwood Avenue. He didn't charge me anything, although I offered. He seemed offended by that and I never offered again. It was more like a friendship, you could say. I spent the day before we met going over the things I'd talk about, but when I got to his office, it all happened so naturally. Dr. Lipschitz helped me trust people more. Maybe I should say he helped me trust him more.

Toward the end of that year, I can't remember the date, I learned from my Aunt Flora that an investigation had been opened by Child Welfare Services on my cousin, Sandy Riesen. I flipped out. I'd always felt protective of the women in my life, and I thought, "Here's another person being ruined by my evil goddamned family." I cared about Sandy. We joked that we were twins under the skin: she was a rebellious teenager and I was a rebellious adult. So I was very, very upset. I didn't like my Uncle Frank, never had really, found him to be a cold, calculating individual, which runs in my family. On my next session with Dr. Lipschitz, I told him about Sandy. I was afraid that Uncle Frank would be able to sweep any allegations about him under the rug because of his wealth. You have to understand, I'd seen things like this happen before. My family is very good at twisting things so that the victims become the bad guys.

Can I have more water, please? Thank you. I don't want to talk about my family anymore, if it's all the same to you.

So, Dr. Lipschitz. He volunteered then to talk to Sandy, to get at what was really happening with her. I thought, thank God this man is on my side. I felt grateful to the universe for sending him to me. We set up a meeting with Sandy.

My cousin was always complaining about how strict her father was. I told Sandy that I'd take her for a ride some Saturday—I always talk best when I'm driving a car, don't ask me why—and we'd solve all her problems in one little trip. She said she thought that would be fun; she wanted to go rowing on Hoyt Lake. I didn't make any promises but I said that was a possibility, depending on the weather. Dr. Lipschitz wanted to meet at a motel, a neutral site. It was raining that day, so I told Sandy we were going to drive into the country and hang out in this hick town I knew with a friend of mine. She laughed about that. I was the crazy cousin, you see. She expected nothing less.

I thought I was rescuing Sandy from a horrible situation. I felt good about it. I was an idiot, of course.

When I got to the motel with Sandy, Dr. Lipschitz hadn't arrived yet. Sandy and I talked about fun things, like summer trips to the theme park Fantasy Island, classes at her school. When Dr. Lipschitz arrived, I introduced him and said this was the friend I'd told her about, and that he was a psychiatrist. He asked to speak to Sandy alone and took her out to my car. She was comfortable with him. He was so good with people; it's hard to explain, but she didn't tense up for a moment. I waited inside, watching some TV while relaxing on the bed. When Dr. Lipschitz returned, he came through the door alone. He was smiling. That is the last *thing I remember about that day. Lipschitz shot me, I believe, and placed the gun in my hand. But I don't remember it. I certainly didn't shoot myself.*

I was numb inside and out those first four years after the shooting. Even if I felt my mind get clearer, I'd try to coax it back into numbness, into not feeling or thinking. Because what was there to think of besides what a sick, demented person I was. I believed I was Hangman, of course I did. Everyone else told me I was; it was just the reality I woke up to. My memories were very disjointed, never fitting together. I remember bits and pieces of my time in the hospital. There was one fat-necked nurse, Dennison, that was awful to me, letting me piss myself in my bed without coming to help. The trial? It was like watching a show on a black-and-white TV with bad reception, a trial in which you wanted the defendant to burn. Except I was the defendant.

It was only last year that I felt my head getting clearer. I didn't remember Dr. Lipschitz from before the shooting. I only knew he was my psychiatrist, and he became important to me again. The same warmth, the same real attention to my life, the same feeling of closeness. We talked about the murders. I was consumed with guilt, even though I couldn't remember the actual details. The papers and the authorities and the other inmates said I did it, so I assumed I did. I questioned every other thing in my life, but for some reason I thought that the justice system would never convict the wrong man in such a big case. I trusted people like you, Detective Kearney.

But about seven or eight months ago, Sandy's face started coming back to me clearer and clearer. At first, I would just pound my head against the wall in my cell, trying to get that image out of my head. I didn't deserve to remember her; I didn't want to see her face, with her eyes trusting me, the way I'd left her. I couldn't stop them, though. I started to remember the times we'd spent together when she was young. I drew her face; I enjoyed it, it helped me remember Sandy the eight-year-old, Sandy the carefree troublemaker. But the day at the Warsaw Motel, that was still a blank to me.

The other inmates used to give me advice on killing myself, how to do it. Some of them even offered to donate their sheets to the cause. I didn't

blame them. How could I hate them when the same thoughts were run-
ning through my own head? But Carlson. Him I hated.

Every night, I'd hear his footsteps as he came up to my cell. I'd close
my eyes and he'd start whispering, "Why'd you kill those girls? Where's
Sandy?" The funny thing is, I wanted to answer him, more than you can
believe. I'd rack my brains trying to remember, where is Sandy. A few
times I screamed back, "I don't fucking know!" But that never stopped
him. He was relentless. Don't believe that bullshit you read in the
papers. He enjoyed what he was doing. He'd just keep whispering, and
then when he saw me in the hallways, he'd give me this little smirk. I
dreamed of catching him alone in a prison hallway, some night, without
my cuffs on.

The day of the escape I remember clearly. Carlson and the other CO
were talking back and forth about something they'd planned and Carl-
son was being a dick, as usual. He let the white CO out at an AutoZone.
I was thinking the whole time about Sandy, remembering driving some of
these same roads with her. Carlson brought me to the hill and he tried to
degrade me even more, treating me like I was some kind of a dog. Then,
a miracle. Dr. Lipschitz came out walking from the tree line with a gun.
He was smiling, and I knew he was going to take care of the guard and
free me. He was my friend, you see? I believed that. And so I leaned over
and told Carlson that he was going to get his answer. He was finally
going to find out what happened to the girls, after all his torturing of me.
Because he was going to join them! Don't ask me to feel guilty about
that, because I don't.

After he shot the guard, Lipschitz said to me, "Marcus, do you remem-
ber this?" It was a brochure from Hoyt Lake, the rowboats there. He was
testing me to see how much had come back to me, if I remembered telling
Sandy we'd go rowing there. But I didn't remember anything. Maybe he
would have killed me if I had remembered.

The rest of the escape, I can't tell you much. I felt like a vegetable.
Lipschitz said to me, "I have to give you a little medicine." I trusted him,
I thought he was trying to help me get away from that horrific cell in the
prison, so I let him inject me. From then until the police took me away
from him, I was walking through a cold fog. I remember a small room and

being in the trunk of a car, but I can't tell you which day was which or if it was day or night. Dr. Lipschitz asked me to write some things, like letters, and I was happy to help. I was the perfect unwitting accomplice. It makes me sick to think about it.

When he shot me at the asylum, it was a terrible shock. It ripped away the fog in my brain and I thought the pain itself would kill me. But you know what? I thought it was you, Detective Kearney, who'd fired the gun. It's true. Why would my friend do something like that? It couldn't be. So even in the depths of my drug-induced state, I was defending Dr. Lipschitz.

That's all gone. I know now that Lipschitz was the killer and that he was probably insane, in some very strange way. But it's hard to get those years out of my system. For a few days after I was freed, I'd wake up in the middle of the night and think I'm back in that cell at Auburn, and my drawings of Sandy are looking down at me from the wall where I'd taped them, and Carlson is whispering outside and I will never, ever get out of there.

I've gotten a different therapist now. The dreams have stopped. I have to learn to forgive myself for being a messed-up human being who was used by a far more messed-up human being. And I'm learning to do that. Lipschitz stole so much time from me, I won't let him take another day.

After this interview, I'm going to see my daughter, Nicole. My beautiful, athletic daughter, who plays volleyball at Stanford, did you know that? She believes in all the things I never did, like family. In a sick sort of way, this whole ordeal has reunited me with her. I don't even feel the need to punch people in the face who talk about silver linings, because it's true, it really is. My suffering does have a reward.

OK? That's all I remember. I can't add anything that would help you understand Lipschitz, if that understanding is even possible. If I do remember something, I'll send you an email, Detective Kearney, or I'll write you a nice long letter. Because this part of my life is over and I am never, ever coming back here again.

67

Mills slabbed some sauce on the meat sizzling on the grill in Abbie's backyard and a puff of smoke erupted from the grill. Abbie studied the lines of his back as he worked, the broad shoulders, the curlicue at the base of his hairline that she liked to play with. She took a sip of her Chardonnay, holding it in her mouth, savoring the taste of late summer in its tartness.

Ron sat across from her, dressed in a sharp cotton windbreaker, a white polo shirt, and jeans. He took a sip of his wine and eyed Mills nervously. "Abbie?"

"Mm-hmmm?"

Ron leaned toward her. "It's not *really* moose," he whispered.

Abbie shrugged. "So he says. I hear it's delicious. If you bite down on a bullet, just ignore it."

Ron made a face. "Honey, thank you very much, but I'm not eating that. I don't care how much wine you pour into me."

Mills clicked the top of the grill shut and more smoke came leaking out the side vents. He walked to the table, sat next to Abbie, and took a swig of his Molson Golden. He smiled pleasantly at Ron.

He'd come back the night before, the moose meat packed in ice in the cooler. Forty-six-inch antlers, he'd said. And that was about all he'd said.

"How long?" Abbie said.

"Ten minutes." He didn't look at her. His voice was neutral, even cold.

Ron raised his eyebrows and smiled at Abbie. "Great. I, uh, better get Charles."

"And the salad," Abbie said.

Charles was next door, finishing up grading some papers for his class at UB. Ron got up and sauntered toward the front of the house. "I have a yen for salad today," he said, looking back at Abbie.

She pulled the collar of Mills's heavy fisherman's sweater close to her cheeks. Mills looked at her. In his eyes, so many things. Anger, yes. Love, maybe. Definitely exasperation.

Mills wasn't the only one exasperated with her. She was suspended from the Buffalo Police Department while her conduct in the Hangman investigation was reviewed by a disciplinary board. Rumors were flying around Buffalo about unauthorized checks of certain basements in the North. Perelli had told her that the fact she'd caught the real Hangman, and saved Katrina Lamb, was the only thing that had saved her job, that and the fact that she was John Kearney's daughter. She hadn't talked to McGonagle, but she wondered if someone in the old boys' network had released the fact that she'd used the Network. Maybe they wanted her gone. Or maybe they wanted to punish the Network for cooperating with someone like Abbie.

In any case, her job was hanging by a thread. She hadn't slept more than three hours each night since the shooting of Dr. Lipschitz. To lose her father's badge . . . it would be a humiliation. A disgrace she didn't want to think about.

"Our last cookout of the year," she said to Mills.

"Probably."

Leaves scrabbled across the little concrete deck that the lawn set rested on. Abbie took a pita chip from the bowl that Ron had brought over and dipped it in the hummus. Delicious.

"Another beer?" she said.

Mills shook his head.

"Are you going to talk to me?" she said. "Like, ever?"

Mills said nothing.

"Mills . . ."

"How'd you do it?" he said flatly.

It had been nine days since she'd shot and killed Dr. Andrew Lipschitz. Sandy Riesen's body had been found buried in a grave twenty feet from where Lipschitz had died. Marcus Flynn had been discharged from Erie County Medical Center already, the wounds less serious than they appeared at the time. He was moving to California to be near his daughter, a junior at Stanford. Of all the people who'd emerged from the Hangman case, he—ironically—seemed the happiest.

Katrina Lamb was with relatives in the suburbs. Abbie had met with her a few days before at a Tim Horton's donut shop—unofficially, because she wasn't supposed to be in touch with anyone connected with Hangman. Katrina had apologized about freaking out and running off at the asylum. "Honey, if you don't freak out when a serial killer's trying to recapture you," Abbie told her, "you probably aren't normal." They'd sipped hot chocolates and quickly moved on to other subjects—Katrina didn't want to talk about what happened. Abbie listened as the girl gushed about her upcoming performance as Cordelia in *King Lear*. Her eyes were bright, the words tripping as they came out. Abbie saw a tiny bit of desperation in the gushing report, a desperation to be normal again, but that was to be expected. She told Katrina she'd be at the opening night performance, and made a mental note to check in on the girl regularly after the play had run its course.

Abbie had spent the last few days leafing through the diary of Mona Lipschitz, Andy Lipschitz's mother, composed while at the asylum, 1979–82. Abbie had painstakingly matched descriptions of the many homes where Mona had worked as a maid. She'd been an immigrant from Belorussia, abandoned by her husband, hoping for a new start in Buffalo with her young son. It hadn't worked out that way. She'd committed suicide at twenty-nine in the asylum's third ward. Her diary was filled with memories of her rape in one of those houses years before as a teenager. But she never named the attacker.

The names of the first two victims did match up with the family names in the diary, Breen and Kent. Those families had hired Mona

Lipschitz in the late 1970s. But after that, Abbie's hunt had turned up nothing. There was no evidence that Mona had ever worked for Maggie's family, or Sandy's, or Katrina's. Blinded by the vision of his mother hanging by a rope in that shabby asylum ward, her son had gone after every family in the North who had a young girl in the house. He'd simply been killing a class of people, the evil-doers. There was a kill list, it turned out: every brunette teenager in the North.

Abbie shivered, stuffed her hands in the pockets of the nubby sweater.

"Well?" Mills said, taking a pull on his Molson.

Abbie squinched up her eyes. "Patterns. Everyone seemed to have some connection to psychiatry. I got to thinking about psychiatrists, about asylums, about people who believed they were kings."

Mills nodded.

"Marcus Flynn had been taken to the Psych Center," she continued. "Lipschitz worked there part-time. It was on the list of buildings with coal bins. Simple, really."

Lipschitz had been the dark matter warping things. Calling her to claim he'd been offered money for the Hangman transcripts, so that she would think there was a second man out there. Telling Flynn that Sandy Riesen was being abused. Volunteering to talk to Sandy about the alleged abuse if Marcus would bring him the girl. Then he took Sandy and shot Flynn. Then, years later, roaming the city, Lipschitz snatched new victims, while everyone was looking for his escaped patient. Cocky.

Flynn was even in the trunk of Hangman's '77 Cadillac when he'd put Katrina in there. Lipschitz had even played part of his recordings of Flynn's prison interviews to her over the radio at the Stone Tower so she would think he was the killer.

"Hangman, Hangman, what do you see?" Abbie said.

Mills eyed her. "Like hell it was simple."

Abbie tilted her head back and regarded him. "Are you mad at me or proud?"

Mills ignored that, squinted into the afternoon light. He crossed one leg over the other and looked back at Abbie. "So because Hangman was on the loose, Lipschitz had nothing to worry about," Mills said finally. "He kept him in one of those cells in the basement of the old asylum—I don't even want to imagine why they put the inmates in there years ago—and he was going to kill Flynn and the girl and bury them where no one would find them."

He looked over at her.

"That's about right," Abbie said.

Mills watched smoke pour through the vents of the grill and disappear into the evening air.

"You stopped a lot of killings," he said, raising his beer. "Congratulations, Ab."

Abbie drank. "But you don't like how I saved them, do you?"

"No, I don't."

Abbie crossed over to him, pushed his leg off its perch, and scooched onto his lap. "Mills?"

"Kearney?" His eyes, up close, were startlingly green and none too friendly.

"I had to do it. Show me another way I could get there before he kills Katrina."

Mills's eyes were cool. "You go down that alley you never walk back out, Abbie. Like I told you."

"*I've seen it a thousand times,*" she said in a husky voice, imitating him.

Mills eyed her dangerously. "You wanna play?"

"No," Abbie said, sinking into him until she was laid out against his chest. "I want to have a nice peaceful life. For the first time in my life, that's what I want. Maybe even with you."

She didn't feel as lighthearted as she sounded. Sometimes she believed that each case left a bit of sediment behind, traced along the lining of her heart. Accumulating. Like black lung disease. An occupational hazard.

But the sun was out and Mills was here and Buffalo was her city now.

"Maybe you weren't cut out for a nice life," Mills was saying.

Abbie made a face. "That remains to be seen."

"If I see that guy McGonagle around, by the way, I'm going to bury him in the backyard."

"He'd poison the roses," she said.

"Abbie."

She put her fingers to his lips.

"It's over," she said. "I know what I'm doing. You just have to believe in me."

She was going to a public memorial service for Wendy Lamb, Katrina's mother, the next day. Her clothes were all picked out, the black dress with the thin leather belt and the new heels. She would go with a full heart. But she'd held up her end. She was at peace with Wendy Lamb.

And what about Mills, she thought. What about yourself? That would take a little longer.

About the Author

STEPHAN TALTY is the author of the crime novel *Black Irish* and six widely acclaimed books of narrative nonfiction. He's contributed to *The New York Times Magazine, Playboy, GQ,* and many other publications.

stephantalty.com
@stephantalty

About the Type

This book was set in Caledonia, a typeface designed in 1939 by W. A. Dwiggins (1880–1956) for the Merganthaler Linotype Company. Its name is the ancient Roman term for Scotland, because the face was intended to have a Scottish-Roman flavor. Caledonia is considered to be a well-proportioned, businesslike face with little contrast between its thick and thin lines.